Contents

Napoleon's Guard	...ii
Chapter 1	1
Chapter 2	11
Chapter 3	19
Chapter 4	31
Chapter 5	42
Chapter 6	55
Chapter 7	68
Chapter 8	78
Chapter 9	91
Chapter 10	101
Chapter 11	113
Chapter 12	124
Chapter 13	136
Chapter 14	148
Chapter 15	161
Chapter 16	173
Chapter 17	181
Chapter 18	192
Chapter 19	201
Epilogue	213
The End	214
Glossary	215
Maps	216
Historical note	218
Other books by Griff Hosker	220

Napoleon's Guard

Book 2 in the Napoleonic Horseman Series

By

Griff Hosker

Napoleon's Guard

Published by Sword Books Ltd 2013
Copyright © Griff Hosker First Edition

The author has asserted their moral right under the Copyright, Designs and Patents Act, 1988, to be identified as the author of this work.
All Rights reserved. No part of this publication may be reproduced, copied, stored in a retrieval system, or transmitted, in any form or by any means, without the prior written consent of the copyright holder, nor be otherwise circulated in any form of binding or cover other than that in which it is published and without a similar condition being imposed on the subsequent purchaser.

A CIP catalogue record for this title is available from the British Library.

Chapter 1

I had no time to mourn for my friend Michael. He had been beheaded by Barbary pirates even as we were edging close to Egypt. General Bonaparte had sent five chasseurs and a company of grenadiers to secure the harbour of Alexandria. Our mission was to make the port safe for the invasion fleet of the charismatic French general. Now we would have to do it with just three chasseurs and a company of grenadiers who had been sorely depleted in a pirate attack by three xebecs. We had beaten them off but it had cost us dearly. I am Captain Robert Macgregor of the 17th Chasseurs à Cheval. I had campaigned through Italy with the general and, with Major Jean Bartiaux, my friend and mentor we had acted as spies and scouts many times. This last occasion was the first in which we had lost men. Michael was dead and Sous lieutenant Pierre Boucher was seriously wounded.

"Robbie! Snap out of it!" Jean's voice brought me out of my reverie. I looked around and saw that we had just passed the entrance of Alexandria harbour and soon we would be landing. "Get rid of the hat and the jacket."

"Sorry, sir. You are right."

"Sergeant Major, go and get the spare pistols from Pierre and Michael they may come in handy." I did as ordered and he came closer to speak with me privately, "I know you are upset but Michael would not wish you to lose your life too would he?"

He was right and we all knew how parlous our existence was. A blade could come from nowhere, as it had for Michael or a volley of musket balls; both would be fatal to the unwary. This was a war which took no pity on those involved and made no allowances for sentiment and friendship.

The captain of the sloop edged us to a small beach some two miles from the port. We had seen the Ottoman flags, the Janissary guards and the guns, but the Maltese flag meant that we sailed by unmolested. We took our swords and a brace of pistols each. We had to find where the cannons were located so that, when we landed, after dark, Major Lefevre and his grenadiers could disable the guns and hold the entrance until the fleet arrived.

Francois, the captain of the sloop came down to see us. "I will sail out to sea and be back here in four hours. I will not be able to hang around."

Jean smiled, "We know, and we have done this before."

"These are not the Maltese so be careful. To these people, you are the infidel. They trade with the Maltese but if you step ashore then you become fair game. They still put prisoners into their galleys to row them."

We descended into the small skiff. The last time we had done this there had been five of us but on this occasion, it was not so crowded. I wished it was. We leapt ashore and raced across the soft white sand towards the line of palm trees. It was not much cover but it was better than standing on the beach. When we turned around the two sailors were pulling as hard as they could to reach the safety of the sloop.

We knew in which direction in which to travel and we also knew that we were conspicuous. We had white faces and there were not many of those. We did not speak the language and, if we had to run, then our means of escape was four hours away. The prospects did not look good. It was close to noon and unbearably hot. As Jean had said that gave us our only chance for most people would be indoors sheltering from the unrelenting sun. Who would be foolish enough to walk when the day was at its hottest? We began to pass small mud huts. The only creatures stirring were the cats and the dogs and they were just seeking shade. We had travelled a mile when we saw our first gun. There was a small stone wall and behind it was one old cannon. We had not seen it from the sea and it surprised us. Jean took out his crude map and drew an x where it was. The gun crew were nowhere to be seen. We moved in whatever shelter there was to hand.

There were more houses now and we moved more carefully. None of us had watches but we could use the sun to estimate time. We had been travelling for about an hour. We would have to turn back in half an hour. We could see the tower at the entrance to the harbour now. It was about three-quarters of a mile away. We also saw uniforms. We would now have to become invisible; not easy when you were as white as we were.

Suddenly Tiny stopped us and pointed. There was some washing on a line blowing in the sea breeze. It looked to be the long white cloaks worn by the locals and the headdress they used. We later found they were called the Thobe and the Keffiyeh but when we stole them we had no idea what they were called. The tunic was easy to wear but we just wrapped the cloth around our heads anyway we could. It didn't look perfect but it disguised us. When we had been in the country longer we learned to wear them as the locals did. We now headed towards the guns more confidently. We avoided closing with them; all we need to do was to locate them and then to have them marked on Jean's map. Instead, we headed for the harbour side of the sea wall. On the city side of the harbour, we could see what looked like a barracks. There was an Ottoman flag flying and sentries patrolling. As we closed with the end of the harbour wall we could now see the guns and cannons varying from ancient pieces to a couple of new twelve pounders. They looked like they could easily damage a ship; especially a slow transport loaded with men. Altogether there were twenty guns. Although we only counted thirty men, it was obvious from the buildings close to the gun emplacements, that there had to be many more who were now resting indoors.

Jean pointed east and murmured, "Let's head back we have seen enough." More people had come out of their homes as we wandered back down to the rendezvous point. They stared at us but said nothing. I suspected that our presence would be reported but, hopefully, we would have been taken off by then.

We reached the beach and there was no sign of the sloop. Jean took the opportunity of adding to his sketch map. "I think they will need eight or ten men for each gun. That is two hundred men altogether."

Tiny whistled, "Can we handle that number?" None of us knew the quality of the Ottoman soldiers. We knew Austrians, British and Dutch but this was a new enemy.

Jean shrugged, "We have to. The fleet is arriving tomorrow and our general expects the harbour entrance to be secured."

Just then two things happened. We saw the masts of the sloop to the north as it headed back and we saw to the west, a crowd of people approaching. Some waved ancient muskets. "It looks like we have been spotted."

The crowd was about half a mile away and they were gathered around the first gun we had seen. "Tiny, keep watching the ship; tell us when they are close. Robbie, let's check these pistols."

I took out the two pistols from my belt and made sure that they were primed and loaded. It was unnecessary but it gave us something to do. We watched as ten soldiers formed a column and began to march down towards us. I could see their muskets slung over their shoulders.

"The sloop is about a mile offshore and closing fast."

"Wave that scarf thing so they know it is us." He did so and I hoped that the red cloth of the headdress stood out against the white buildings. The soldiers were marching resolutely followed by a gaggle of onlookers. They reminded me of the crowds at the Place de la Revolution eager to see someone suffer. It was the same the world over. People enjoyed the misery of others.

Tiny's voice drifted over to us. "They have lowered the rowing boat!"

"Right Sergeant Major, get over here." We now had six pistols. Tiny stood next to us. The soldiers were a hundred yards away. The officer waved his sword and the men went into a ragged line. They advanced towards us.

I glanced over my shoulder, "Any time you like sir, the boat is almost close enough for us to wade out to it."

"Ready? Fire!"

The six pistols boomed at the same time and a wall of smoke appeared before us. We just turned and ran. I heard a ragged ripple as the Ottoman soldiers fired. The musket balls zipped over our heads as we ran down the beach towards the azure blue sea. The boat with the two sailors was in the shallows and we waded out. As Tiny helped Jean on board, I turned and saw the soldiers running after us. Some of the Ottomans were trying to load as they ran. The crew of the rowing boat hauled me on board. Tiny and I grabbed the spare oars and rowed for all we were worth out to the waiting sloop.

One of the sailors said, "We weren't certain it was you until you waved your towel thing at us. That was certainly cutting it fine."

Tiny laughed, "That is the only way we know how to do things!"

Once we were aboard François, took the ship north. "Well done Major Bartiaux. I am sorry we were slightly late." He pointed to the masthead pennant. "These winds are so fickle. We will head north to confuse the soldiers and then head west. I will take us south when it is dark. You will need to tell me the best place to land."

Major Lefevre came over with a huge grin on his face. "Pistols against muskets?"

Jean laughed, "It was all we had but it was effective."

"Yes, I saw that you killed none but you made them fire their muskets."

"We did not need to kill them, merely slow them down." He took out his map. He pointed as he spoke. "There are guns here and here which could damage our fleet and they will outnumber your grenadiers. We will need the lieutenant to bring his ship close and use his guns to keep the enemy from reinforcing the harbour. The guns can be isolated as they are all at the end but we saw what looked like a barracks a mile from the guns."

"Do the guns have trenches around them?"

"No, but they are protected from the sea by small mud walls. There are some hidden guns." He pointed again at the map and the crosses he had used.

"So there are twenty guns." Major Lefevre glanced at his men lounging on the deck. "We do not have enough men now to split into twenty groups."

"Then do it in two groups. If we drop half of your men at the end of the harbour entrance then the captain can drop the other half close to here, where we saw the first gun." Jean pointed at the map. "That way we can advance towards each other. Both parties will outnumber each gun crew."

Francois had joined us. "The problem is that while I am sailing east I will be at the mercy of all of their guns."

"It will be at night and the grenadiers can line the deck and fire at any gun emplacement which has any activity close by."

Major Lefevre nodded, "I agree. That is the plan. I will lead the assault from the harbour and Captain Blanc can lead from the other end."

"We will accompany Captain Blanc. We know the layout of the guns and it might help."

"Thank you, Major, I appreciate the offer."

With a darkened ship and a moonless night to aid us, we ghosted towards the harbour of Alexandria. It was well lit and we had no difficulty in identifying the section the grenadiers needed to reach. There were guards at the end and they were huddled around a brazier smoking. They did not appear worried by the 'Carillon's' approach until we suddenly headed east towards them. They began shouting; I think they thought the helmsman was asleep, and then they raised their muskets. By then it was too late. Even as they fired they were cut down by the deck gun, filled with grapeshot. Two sailors bravely leapt ashore and wrapped two mooring ropes around the bollards. The fifty grenadiers quickly leapt on to the quay and began to bayonet and shoot the guards who were gathered around the two large guns at the end of the defences. As soon as the soldiers had landed the two sailors jumped back aboard with their ropes.

Francois wasted no time and the sails filled as the ship sped swiftly and silently away. By now the gun crews were fully awake and racing to their guns. By the time they reached them, we were gone like a will-o-the-wisp.

"Lower the mainsail! A point to the north if you please helmsman." The lieutenant was a good sailor and the 'Carillon' as responsive as my horse Killer. The ship came to a halt against the ancient harbour wall and the two sailors again jumped for the quayside. One missed and disappeared beneath the dark waters. His companion made the rope fast and we were pulled next to the quay. Captain Blanc was the first ashore but, as he landed on the quayside an Egyptian officer rammed his scimitar into his stomach. Jean shot him and then took command. "Grenadiers ashore and form two lines, muskets at the ready."

Tiny and I quickly reached the dead officer. I checked but he was dead. I drew my pistol. Already the guards were running towards the ancient gun. I shot one and Tiny a second. Without waiting for the grenadiers we both drew our swords and ran to the gun emplacement. There were six guards left and they turned to fight us. One used the ram from the cannon which he swung at Tiny. The huge sergeant major ducked and skewered the Egyptian. I sliced across the face of a second and then the hands of the others went up. They had surrendered.

"Major, we have captured this gun."

"Good. Swing it around to face the town." He looked for a corporal. "You, Brigadier, take five of your men and man this gun. Fill it with grapeshot and stop anyone from approaching. Sergeant, tie up these prisoners. The rest of you forward, at the double. The next gun will not be as easy as this one."

Even as we moved forward Tiny and I were reloading our guns. We could hear the sounds of battle from the far end of the harbour. The Ottoman gunners had a dilemma; which force should they attack? Then the 'Carillon' went into action. Her little guns blasted the gunners as they dithered over which force was the most dangerous.

I heard Jean's commanding voice, "Grenadiers! Charge!" The thirty grenadiers charged the gunners and the surviving Janissaries surrendered at the next three guns. They had had enough. The grapeshot had done its worst and the sight of the tall grenadiers running towards them had finally ended their resistance. Waking in the middle of the night to be assaulted by unknown soldiers must have been terrifying.

"Robbie you and Tiny go and find the major. Tell him we have secured this end of the harbour." He turned to the big sergeant next to him. "Secure these prisoners and put two men to guard them. Then join me down there." He pointed to the first gun we had captured. He saw I had not moved: I was stunned by the speed of our success. "Come on captain, move!"

"Sir!"

Tiny and I ran. Any of the remaining gun crews were busily attending to their wounded. I could see the 'Carillon' tacking around to sail down the harbour once more. I hoped that François would look before he fired. At the eastern end of the harbour defences, all resistance had ended. When I reached the first of Major Lefevre's grenadiers I could see that he too was mopping up the last few Janissaries.

"Sir, Major Bartiaux has captured the eastern end and is building a barricade there."

"Good. Sergeant Major Lajune, take a section and help the major." He grinned. "That went better than I had hoped."

"I think we caught them at a bad time. It all depends now how many men they have in the garrison." I suddenly saw their prisoners. "We took many prisoners too, sir. What do we do with them? If we are attacked we will need every man to defend what we hold."

"True; Captain, go to the quay and signal the ship. The lieutenant can guard them and take off our wounded."

Tiny and ran to the side of the sea wall. "How does he expect us to do that sir?"

"Grab a lantern and I will show you."

By the time Tiny had returned I had taken one of the jackets from a dead Janissary. I held the jacket over the light and then flashed three times before covering the light again. I counted to thirty and repeated it. "I am counting on the fact that the lieutenant knows three flashes means us." I was using the signal we had used in Malta.

After four sequences I was relieved to see the signal repeated. I threw the jacket to the ground. The first glimmer of light from the east heralded the appearance of the sloop. Tiny and I caught the mooring ropes and tied the ship off. Two sailors jumped ashore and grinned as one said, "Nice effort sir. This is how it is done properly." They retied the lines and François stepped ashore.

The major arrived. "We have prisoners and we need them secured. Take them aboard your ship."

"What will I do with them?"

The major shrugged as though it was not his problem. I looked at the empty main deck. "They are all tied lieutenant. If you sit them on the deck then you can use your two-deck guns to cover them."

"What if we have to sail?"

The major said, "In that case, we will have failed for it will mean the fleet have not arrived. I think General Bonaparte will make it."

"Tiny, go and fetch our prisoners and tell the major I will join him as soon as the prisoners are secured."

The prisoners all looked sorry for themselves. I noticed how ill-dressed they were. Most did not have shoes and their uniforms were barely even the semblance of a uniform. They were discoloured and ill-fitting rags. It was just their turbans which marked them as soldiers. As soon as they onboard I ran down the wall to find Jean. Daylight showed just how effective our attack had been. The guns were surrounded by small huddles of bodies. The closer we came to the east, the more bodies we discovered.

Jean had not been idle and there was an effective barricade at the end with the cannon at its centre. The whole was protected by a hedgehog of bayonets and muskets and grim-faced grenadiers. Jean pointed to the barracks. "It looks like they are awake. I heard a bugle and saw men lining up outside. I think we may have our first attack soon."

"The Major is coming too." I did a quick headcount and saw that we had about eighty men. These were grenadiers and the best infantrymen France had. If we could not hold this narrow road against these poor Janissaries then it did not bode well for the invasion. By the time the garrison had stirred itself and marched towards us, the sun was beginning to warm the walls. The men had eaten and had water. They were ready. The column of soldiers who marched towards us looked to be about two hundred strong. They marched in a column eight men wide.

Major Lefevre smiled, "This is almost too easy. Grenadiers, ready muskets. Front rank ready?"

The sergeant-major roared, "Ready!"

When they were eighty yards away the major yelled, "Fire!"

The smoke prevented us from seeing the results. "Second rank, fire!"

The crash of the weapons mingled with the screams of the Janissaries. As the smoke cleared we saw the remains of the column fleeing back to their barracks. Before us, lay forty dead and dying soldiers. Even as the men cheered we heard, "Sails! It is the fleet, General Bonaparte is here."

We went to the Ottoman soldiers and rescued as many of the wounded as we thought might live. Some of them were going to die and the kindest gesture would have been to slit their throats but Jean advised the major against it. "Let the locals look after them. They would see it as savagery in us. Remember major, we are in a foreign land with different cultures and our only way home is by the sea."

I looked out to sea. "And remember sir, if the Royal Navy wants it back then there is little we can do about it is there? Our fleet is not the greatest in the world at the moment."

The large battleships entered the harbour first and their open gun ports threatened the barracks. As the transports disgorged their troops the Turkish flag was lowered. The city had surrendered. We felt a little disappointed. I had expected more resistance. We were ignored on the sea wall. The prisoners still sat aboard the 'Carillon' and the grenadiers guarded the guns. The three of us returned aboard to see how Pierre had fared. As we stepped aboard François asked, "Can I disembark these prisoners now sir? The crew object to the smell because the deck is covered in piss and shit!"

I yelled over the side, "Sergeant, we are returning the prisoners to shore. Find some men to guard them." The grenadier sergeant shot me a filthy look but I knew he would not disobey an order from an officer, even a cavalry officer. The grenadiers only had Major Lefevre left, the rest of their officers were dead. They had all led from the front' that was what made them grenadiers. I suspected the sergeant would soon be promoted. "There you go lieutenant, you can now send them ashore."

The disgruntled men trudged off the ship and the sailors quickly began to swab the decks. "Thank you for that captain. Sailors hate to have a dirty ship."

"It is my pleasure. How is Pierre?"

"He is awake and demanding food and wine."

I laughed, "Then he is back to normal and he will live."

Pierre was, indeed, much better and he grinned as we entered the orlop deck where the wounded were being dealt with. "Well sir, did you miss me?"

Tiny answered, "We managed without you sir and we didn't lose a man. How's that?"

"You see, sergeant major, it was my training that enabled you both to do that. So you see it was my victory. Where is the major?"

"Getting cleaned up and into uniform. We assume he will be wanted by the general. That is the advantage of being a minion; no one is bothered about you."

In the end no-one came at all for a whole day. We ate and then slept while the city was invested. I think Major Lefevre was under the impression that the actions of his men merited a visit from the general. He did not know Bonaparte as we did. When the relief troops did arrive they were gunners and engineers who were completely indifferent to our efforts. We said goodbye to Francois, collected Pierre and our belongings and marched to the edge of the town. We headed to the headquarters, marked by the tricolour, to find out what our next orders would be.

Chapter 2

We were greeted by Colonel Bessières. He beamed at us. "Well done gentlemen, you did all that was asked of you. The general is delighted."

Major Lefevre grumbled, somewhat sulkily, "We did wonder why no one came sooner, sir."

Bessières looked a little shamefaced. "I am sorry about that but the general was very busy taking charge of the port. He has much to do. Major Lefevre if you would take your men to the camp south of the town you will find the rest of your regiment there."

The major turned and shook Jean's hand and then mine. "Thank you. It has been a pleasure to serve with you and I will think better of the chasseurs in future."

"Good luck major."

As they marched off we looked expectantly at Bessières. He smiled, "As you might expect the general has other orders for you four." We noticed that he had completely overlooked the fact that one of our numbers was no longer with us. To the general's staff, we were a tool to be used and then discarded. "Your regiment is camped to the east of the town, about half a mile away, with the rest of the cavalry. If you follow your noses you can smell the horses. When you have recovered your horses return here, Major Bartiaux and Captain Macgregor. The general will have your new orders ready for you. And if you bring Lieutenant Bouchard with you that would expedite matters."

As we walked back I asked Jean. "What do you think he wants with Pierre-François?"

Jean shrugged. "You know him as well as I do Robbie. He will have some skill which the general needs."

I noticed as we walked that Pierre was struggling with his breath. "We had better slow up. Pierre is not finding this easy."

"I will be alright. Don't worry about me."

"We will have the doctor take a look at you when we reach the regiment. Although I am no surgeon that looked like a nasty wound to me."

"You saved my life sir and that is enough."

Bessières had been correct, we could smell the horses. There were more cavalry that I had seen before. They were mainly dragoons but there was also a regiment of hussars too. The general intended to defeat whoever the Ottomans threw against us. We soon found our tents and the colonel was pleased to see us. "We wondered how your mission had gone." He suddenly realised there were only four of us. "What happened?"

We told him, and he nodded, "That is war. It is a shame; he was a good sergeant." He saw Pierre's pale face. "And what happened to you, Lieutenant Boucher?"

"A pirate stabbed me in the back."

"Can the sergeant major take him to the surgeon sir?"

"Of course. Off you go." When they had gone the colonel poured us a beaker of wine each. "This campaign promises to be difficult. We already have men fainting with the heat and the horses are not coping well either. It is like nothing I have ever experienced."

We showed him the clothes we had stolen. "The locals wear these and they keep you cooler even if you wear them on top of your uniform. It is strange."

"Well that won't help us; they won't keep the horses cool. And we are having problems with the water. That is why we are drinking wine; it is safer. We have only been here little more than a day and we already have men going down with dysentery and diarrhoea."

"Sir, the general wants to see the two of us again. I think he has another mission in mind."

Albert gave a wry smile, "Your trouble, Jean, is that you are too good at what you do. You need to make mistakes a little more often."

"And he wants to see Lieutenant Bouchard."

"Really? That seems strange. He is a good officer but a little bookish really. He seems an academic rather than a soldier. Still…" He shrugged and then grinned, "The stable detail will be glad to see you, Captain, Killer has been living up to his name."

"With your permission, sir, I will go and see to him."

"And I will find the lieutenant. I don't think that the general likes to be kept waiting."

Killer was glad to see me and the stable detail was overjoyed. "He is as mad as a fish sir! He can be nice as pie one minute and then try to take your hand off the next."

"He does take some getting used to. Come on boy, let's go and visit with the general."

It was good to be on his back again and I headed for the officer's tents. Jean had told me that when my father had served in the regiment then every officer had a servant. Since the revolution all that had changed but we did have a trooper for every two officers to put the tents up and see to our needs. "Ah Trooper Lannes, did all my equipment come ashore?"

"Yes, sir. Your chest is under your bed and your musket is on top of it. I gave it a good clean this morning. The sea air does them no good at all."

"Thank you for that." My best uniform was in the chest. The attack on the harbour had not merited a good uniform but a meeting with General Napoleon Bonaparte did. When I stepped out of the tent I saw Jean and the lieutenant there with their horses.

Pierre-François asked, as I mounted Killer, "Why me sir? I am not like you two officers. I am not suited to sneaking around behind the enemy lines."

Jean winked at me, "Oh and we are the sneaky officers who are, are we?"

The flustered lieutenant said, "Oh no sir. You are both legends in the regiment. The things you have done…"

"He is teasing, Pierre-François, but we were not chosen originally because we were sneaky but because we had skills the general needed. He must have a skill of yours in mind."

"But I just studied books, sir."

I laughed, "Which in this regiment is something of a rarity."

"Come on you two, the sooner we get there the sooner we will solve this mystery."

As we had predicted we had to cool our heels in the antechamber to the general's office. At least it was cool. Eventually, Bessières came out with an armful of papers. "You can go in now."

Bonaparte did not look up as we entered. "Close the door behind you."

He leaned back on his chair and peered at Pierre-François. "I suspect you are wondering why you are here with these two warriors eh lieutenant?"

"Er yes, sir."

"Someone at the Commission of Science and Arts thinks highly of you. It seems you have some skill in archaeology and the study of the past?"

A look of relief washed over the young man's face. "Oh yes, sir. It is my passion I…"

The general put a hand up to stop him. "Spare me the details. Tell me what you know of Alexander the Great in relation to Egypt."

"Er, he founded Alexandria. He visited the oracle at Siwa and Ptolemy had his body buried at Memphis."

"Good. I have made the right choice. I want you to find his body." Pierre-François' mouth dropped open but the general was studying his papers and maps again. "And of course, if you find any treasure whilst you are doing so then so much the better. Captain Macgregor seems to have a nose for such things."

"Are we going too, sir?"

"Of course, is that not obvious? You leave as soon as possible. You are to take a squadron of your troopers for protection. Bessières has your orders. You will travel with the army while we head south to secure the land around the Pyramids and then you will be detached."

With that, we were dismissed. I put my arm around the lieutenant's shoulders. "That is the way he carries on Pierre-François. Do not worry we will manage."

"But what if I cannot find it?"

"Then the general will be angry so if you cannot find it then please find something which is as valuable to him. Take heart, we will not be doing this immediately anyway."

When we reached the camp we were greeted by Captain Alaine and Pierre. They both looked glum. "What's the matter with you two? Isn't it hot enough for you?" The temperature was so high that shades had had to be rigged over the horses.

Pierre looked too upset to speak. Claude put his arm around his old friend. "He is to be given a discharge from the army. He will fight no more."

I was almost bereft of words. Jean nodded, "I feared it was a bad wound. What did the surgeon say?"

Claude spoke for Pierre. "He said the lung had been punctured. He will always be short of breath. The colonel knows."

I found my voice, "What will you do?"

"I do not know. The army has been my whole life."

"You could always open a bar. That would suit you."

"Where would I get the money from for that?"

"The regimental fund?" We all paid into a fund for just such an occasion.

"The colonel has been more than generous but it would not buy a decent tavern."

I looked at Jean and had a sudden flash of inspiration. "Julian! It is perfect?"

"Of course!"

Claude and Pierre looked at the two of us who were grinning as though we had just had the best news ever. "What are you two going on about? Who is Julian?"

"You met him at Montenotte. He was the son of the gardener at home but he lost his legs in the Italian campaign and we helped him to buy a tavern close by Breteuil. He needs a partner and you would be perfect for each other."

"O course it is in the north and far away from the warm sea and the fine wine… but."

"Would he be happy about this?"

Jean and I looked at each other and nodded. "I will write a letter for you to take." Jean suddenly looked at him. "When do you leave?"

"This evening; I am to sail on the 'Carillon'. We are taking all the wounded back to Toulon with despatches from the general."

I felt sick. "So this is goodbye then?"

"In an hour or so, yes. I will go and tell the others and meet you in the mess tent."

He wandered off looking suddenly frail and less confident. First, it had been Michael and now it was Pierre. My friends were getting fewer in number. I went to my tent and sat on the bed. I could not abandon Pierre with nothing to show for our friendship. I took out the purse of coins given to me by Sir John MacAlpin, the Knight of St.John. He had given it to me to pay for my journey back to Scotland but I had plenty. I took out four of the gold pieces and returned the purse to my money belt.

I felt a little lost and so I went to the mess tent. I found Pierre-François poring over a book. "Where did you get the book from?"

"Colonel Bessières gave it to me. The general thought it might be useful."

"Well do not forget we have a large part of this land to subjugate before we can dig up the past."

"I know sir but I do not want to let the general down."

That was how Bonaparte worked. He made you feel you were doing it for him and for France. No wonder his Guards were fanatically loyal to him. Jean came in with the letter. I told him of my decision to give some of the money to Pierre. He smiled and showed me the small purse he also held. "I had some spare coins left over from the trip to Vienna. We will make him take them." Both of us knew that Pierre might let pride get in the way of good judgement.

Most of the officers who had served with Pierre and all the sergeants were there to say goodbye. Tiny looked even more upset than Pierre. He looked up to Pierre, almost like a father. The colonel said goodbye first. Albert regarded all of us as his sons and Pierre had served with him a long time. Jean and I waited until the end. The wagon to take him to the harbour was outside when it was our turn. We gave him the letter and the coins. As we had expected he tried to refuse them.

"No Pierre, you looked after me when I first joined and I want to repay you. This isn't goodbye anyway. We will be home sometime and I am looking forward to seeing the changes that you and Julian make to the inn."

"You take care of yourself, Robbie. You are too reckless for your own good. Let others do some of the dangerous stuff." He looked at Jean, "I know you'll look after him, Jean."

"Of course Pierre."

As he climbed on the cart he leaned down and said quietly, "And don't trust that bastard, Bonaparte. He is sneaky and cunning. He just looks out for himself."

"I will. Take care."

As the cart headed north I felt sad. A few months later I was pleased that he had escaped the horror which was yet to come. He would be a survivor from this war.

We had no time to feel sorry for ourselves as the whole army headed south the next day. It was one of the toughest journeys I have ever undertaken. The heat, the dust and the sand all combined to make every mile a living hell. What was worse was the effect it had on the animals. Four horses went lame and had to be destroyed. When you added that to the fact that we had lost eight men to dysentery too it became obvious that we were becoming weakened by this land and we had not even lost a man in combat yet! I was luckier than most because Killer didn't seem as affected by the heat as the others did but we still had a hundred and eighty miles of the torture to endure.

The general had the rest of the regiment as scouts but had told the colonel to spare us as he was saving us for his special mission. It did not make it any easier for us to watch the others coming back exhausted each day. We felt as though we were letting the regiment down. It became even worse when they began to suffer casualties. The Turks laid ambushes for our patrols and soon the other squadrons were becoming decimated. It was like a slow death for the regiment as the troopers were taken in ones and twos.

Claude was the one who, after a week on the road, found the enemy. He reported to us after he had seen the general. "Well, we have an interesting battle coming up. They have fifty thousand men." He paused, "And they are all cavalry!"

I turned to Tiny, "As we only have twenty thousand men that should make it interesting."

We left the little town of Cairo and we halted within sight of the mighty pyramids. I wondered how they could be so big and yet so ancient. They were enormous. The general had a unique plan to cope with the fifty thousand horsemen called Mamelukes. We were gathered into huge hollow squares. The infantry made the sides and the cavalry and artillery were in the middle. When we were formed General Bonaparte addressed us. We were the largest army I had fought in but we were still dwarfed by the hordes of Turkish horsemen who were hidden by the distant dust cloud.

As we were close to the front we heard his words as he addressed us. "Forward! Remember that from those monuments yonder forty centuries look down upon you." It was the first time I had heard him try to inspire his men. It appeared to work as the infantry all looked at these huge ancient tombs and cheered as though we had built them in times past!

We marched in these squares towards the enemy. Our left flank was anchored on the Nile and there the battalions had a target of the fortified village of Embabeh. We were on the right close to the desert and the feared hordes of Mamelukes. Suddenly the enemy began to advance and the general ordered us to halt.

The horsemen who came towards us were of two types. There were the irregular horsemen and camel riders and then there were the Mamelukes. These were the elite warriors of the Turkish army. They were all superb horsemen, as we came to learn, and they were the best armed of any of the opposition. On that hot day in July, they faced the most modern army in the whole of Africa.

I had never witnessed a charge of so many cavalry. It was terrifying. Their hooves drummed loudly on the sand so that the very ground beneath our feet appeared to shake. Clouds of dust and gravel were thrown into the air making it look like a sandstorm was approaching. I admired our battalions of infantry who stoically stood to await this onslaught. Our cannons boomed and the muskets of the infantry rippled with the volley fire of the line companies. Soon the five squares were shrouded in smoke. The Turks were brave horsemen but their curve scimitars were no match for muskets and bayonets, not to mention the cannons which cut swathes of death through the Turkish horsemen. When the order to cease-fire was given and the smoke dispersed we saw the ground before us littered with the dead and the dying, horses, men and camels.

We had no time to congratulate ourselves as the Mameluke cavalry suddenly raced towards the Nile and General Desaix's detached garrison. General Murat ordered all of the cavalry into three huge lines. We were on the right flank. We began to trot towards the Mameluke horsemen who were desperate to achieve some sort of victory from the battle. We could hear Desaix's cannons blasting at the fanatical warriors who assaulted them. When General Murat gave the order to charge we were but a hundred and fifty yards from their rear. As ordered, my squadron was in the third line, and so I was able to see the effect of two thousand cavalrymen crashing into the unprotected Mamelukes; they stood no chance. As I thundered over the bodies of those slain and those wounded I saw pathetic figures trying to drag themselves away from the battlefield, only to be crushed beneath unseeing hooves. The Mamelukes had had enough and they threw themselves into the Nile. As they tried to swim I saw a frenzy in the water as the fearsome crocodiles of the river enjoyed a feast and they gorged on thousands of brave horsemen. We turned away unable to watch such an end to courageous soldiers. Once again we had won and Egypt was conquered. It seemed to be over so quickly. We had landed but a couple of months earlier and now there were no Ottoman armies remaining in Egypt.

Chapter 3

The battle had a profound effect on Lieutenant Bouchard. He looked white as a sheet and was shaking slightly. "Sir, is every battle like that? The only other battle I have seen so far was Malta. This one was nothing like that." Malta had not been a battle it had been a victory parade. I wondered how many other young soldiers had been deluded into thinking that was the true face of war.

"I have never seen one with as many men as that before but Rivoli was as bloody." I looked at his young face, beginning to redden in the hot African sun. "I am not sure that you are cut out for this. Have you not thought of changing to say the engineers? They have less chance of having to fight."

He became a little indignant, "I am no coward! I will fight for France."

"The engineers fight for France, Pierre-François; you do not wish to kill do you?"

He looked down and shook his head. "No sir, not really. My readings have shown me of the horror of war but I am a patriotic Frenchman."

"I know. Let us find this tomb and then you can ask the general. He might be able to do something for you if you bring him some treasure. Do you know where to look?"

"Memphis has been abandoned for over a thousand years. The tomb we are seeking should look different from the rest of the buildings. For it was built by Greeks and not Egyptians. I am not sure that it is here to be found." He shrugged. "I know where to look and I know what to look for but I have no idea what we will find there after some many years left to the desert, the sand and the wind."

It was the most confident I had seen him. It boded well for our mission. I turned to look at the one hundred men in the squadron; I was less sure how they would cope with the heat. Jean, Tiny and I had brought our stolen clothes and all of us were tempted to wear them. We knew we would be cooler but it would not look right to allow the men to suffer. It sounds macabre but I was hoping to fight some desert nomads just to get their white cloaks for our men. We had, with us, one small wagon for the food and the digging equipment. As Bessières had said it was more of an engineer's role but we were so far from the army that cavalry might be the best option. Jean had also told me that the engineers would be needed to build forts to house the garrisons the general was going to use to control the country. We would have to learn to improvise.

I rode forward to speak with Jean. Tiny and two troopers were ranging far ahead. "Sir, I have been talking with Bouchard. I am not sure he is cut out to be a cavalryman."

"I totally agree but he is here now so he will have to learn to adapt. We can have no passengers. I expect the same standards from him as I do from my other officers."

"I think we ought to ask the general if he could become an engineer. He is a clever man and his skills would be better used."

"That's a thought. Let us just get this job done first and then we can think about his career eh Robbie?" With Jean, the regiment always came first.

We were lucky in that we travelled next to the Nile and had no problems with water. We camped, the first night about halfway between Memphis and the Pyramids. "Sergeant Major Barriere, have the men dig a ditch around the camp. We are a little to close to the enemy for comfort. Make sure you keep the horse lines well protected."

"Yes, sir."

Lieutenant Bouchard came up to Jean like a schoolboy with a question. "Sir, if I might suggest? I think we should boil the water." He pointed at the dirty looking river. "My researches indicate that drinking the Nile water can result in some unpleasant diseases."

"Well done Pierre-François. That is a good suggestion. We will do it for the horses too. We don't want to be afoot in this desert. Sergeant Chagal, I want all the water for the animals and the men boiling before we use it. Do not let them drink it straight from the river."

Charles looked nonplussed. "Sorry sir, a couple of them just drank and let their horses drink!"

"Idiots! Put them on a charge and make sure no-one else does anything as foolish."

The desert was as cold at night as it was hot during the day. I had the middle watch, along with Tiny. Neither of us was looking forward to getting from under a warm blanket and then to freeze in the chill and damp Nile air. It would be just as bad for Jean whom I would wake. We were both being kind to the lieutenant. He would have the dawn watch which was not such a problem. With Pierre now discharged we were an officer down. Jean and I would have to work out who to promote. Until we did so, Pierre-François would have to pull his weight. I was grateful to slide into my blankets and find some warmth and I pitied Jean.

I was awoken by the sound of muskets. The squadron was well trained and we all slept with a loaded musket. I jumped up and looked out into the black of the night. I saw the flashes of gun barrels and heard the screams of the wounded. I ran towards the flashes. I almost tripped over the body of Trooper Sagan. As I ran to reach where the firing was I suddenly saw a Turk trying to steal the horses. I fired from the hip. The range was less than twenty yards and it threw him from his mount. I ran and grabbed the rope he had dropped. I heard a whinny and saw another Mameluke trying to mount Killer. I turned my musket around to use it like a club. Killer bucked and reared despite the whip being wielded by the Ottoman. The man might have been a good rider but this was Killer and the unfortunate thief was deposited at my feet. I swung the musket and heard the sickening crunch as the side of the man's skull caved in.

By now the whole camp was awake and the raiders were fleeing, largely empty-handed. I heard Tiny's voice. "Everyone grab your musket and get to the horses."

Jean appeared next to me. "What happened?"

"I have no idea, sir. I was woken by the noise but it looks like they tried to steal the horses." I pointed to the Trooper Sagan. "It looks like we took some casualties."

"Check the wounded Robbie. Lieutenant Bouchard!"

As I knelt down to check the trooper who was nursing a cut arm I saw a shamefaced Pierre-François wander up. "Sir?"

"What happened lieutenant?"

Before he could say anything, Charles snapped, "I'll tell you what happened, sir. This officer fell asleep. The section he was supposed to be watching was where they came in!"

"Is this true lieutenant?" Pierre-François nodded. "That is a serious offence. You will have to consider yourself under open arrest until we return to the army. What were you thinking?"

"I was reading sir. I didn't mean to fall asleep, I just did."

Jean pointed to the body of Trooper Sagan and the other five troopers who had been killed. "Well tell them that! I'm sure they will understand!" Jean's voice was filled with anger and I felt sure he would strike the academic.

"Sorry."

"Get out of my sight and find something useful to do!"

When dawn broke, we saw the full extent of the damage. We had lost six horses and gained two. Apart from the six dead troopers another five were wounded although none seriously. We had killed just ten of the Turks. The only bright spot was the haul of fine swords we accumulated. Normally we would have offered them to the officers first but Jean was in no mood for kindness towards the lieutenant. He gathered the men around after we had eaten our breakfast.

"Last night should not have happened. You have to remember that everyone and everything out here is going to hurt you; the soldiers, the heat, the scorpions, the snakes and the animals. There are crocodiles in that river who will think nothing of creeping out to make a meal of you." He flashed an angry look at Pierre-François which conveyed the impression that he hoped they would take the academic first.

"Now we are short of officers and this would have happened later but events mean it is going to happen now. Sergeant Chagal you are promoted to sous-lieutenant and Sergeant Major Barriere you will become lieutenant. Sergeant Leblanc, you will assume the duties of First Sergeant until we return to the regiment. I hope that from now on everyone does his duty."

It was obvious to everyone where the blame lay but we all liked Pierre-François. It just confirmed to me that he was in the wrong branch of the service however it had cost good men their lives to find it out properly.

"Captain Macgregor will you take our academic and four troopers and find this Memphis. The sooner we get this job done the sooner we can get back to doing the job we were trained for."

If there had been a hole deep enough then Pierre-François would have crawled into it. "Snap out of this. You need to find these ruins so it is no good you feeling sorry for yourself. It will not bring the dead men back. Do your job. What are we looking for?"

"Er, there may not be anything visible above the ground; the sand may have covered up the ruins but the ground should look lumpy?"

"Lumpy?"

"Yes, sir, as though there is something underneath. Imagine a badly made bed with things hidden underneath." Now that he was talking about his work he sounded like his old self. "There might be ruins by the river. The sand can't cover them there."

"Good that's better. You two ride to the river and follow its course. Look for big quarried stones in the water fire your pistol if you find anything. And don't get eaten by the crocodiles."

Trooper Manet laughed, "We'll try not to sir."

"You two ride to the right for a few miles. If you see nothing then cut east and head for the river. If you hear the pistol then head for the river anyway. We will carry on this way."

"Yes, sir!"

The lieutenant appeared happier when we were alone. "What will happen to me, sir?"

"I am not sure. This has never happened before. A court-martial I should imagine. It will depend on the colonel."

We rode in silence for a while and then he asked, as though he didn't really want an answer, "And the punishment?"

"That is up to the colonel." In truth, I didn't want to say.

"What is the worst then sir?"

"Firing squad."

He paled, even with the red cheeks burned by the sun. "Thank you for being honest sir. Then I suppose I had better find this tomb for the general although I think the body was moved."

"Why didn't you tell the General?"

"I did. I said that there were rumours it was moved to Alexandria and further west into the desert but he seemed convinced it would be here."

Once again the general's ego had got men killed. Just then we heard a pistol. "Well, Manet has found something at any rate."

We kicked on towards the river. We soon saw the two troopers waving at us. We halted by the river and Manet pointed at what looked like steps under the water. Pierre-François leapt from his horse and, typically, did not bother to tie his mount up. "Trooper, grab the lieutenant's horse. Otherwise, he will be walking!"

The grinning trooper shouted, "Yes sir."

Bouchard was oblivious to it all. He began to sweep the sand away at the edge of the river. He shouted excitedly, "This is it! These are…"

Before he could go any further a huge crocodile launched itself from the water towards Pierre-François. He had quick reactions and tried to get away. The reptile's teeth locked onto his scabbard and started to drag him back into the water. I drew my pistol and fired. I was only ten feet away and I could not miss. The animal continued to drag the lieutenant towards the murky waters of the Nile. I drew my second pistol and, leaping from my horse, placed it to almost touch the foul-smelling beast's head. I fired and this time it let go and began thrashing around furiously. "Manet!"

The trooper grabbed the lieutenant and I drew my sword in case the beast had survived. Suddenly the water became a maelstrom of foaming bodies as the other crocodiles tore the would-be killer to pieces.

Pierre-François was in shock. Trooper Manet also looked as though he had seen a ghost. "I thought you were joking sir. They take some killing don't they?"

"They certainly do. We will move further away. Trooper Didier, ride back to the major and tell him we have found the ruins." I looked at the lieutenant and he was shaking. "Are you hurt?"

He shook his head. "Just terrified. Thank you."

"It would have been a wasted trip if you had ended up inside a Nile crocodile but just take a little more care eh?" He nodded vigorously. I looked around. "So this is it is it?"

"I think so." He began to regain some of his colour. "If you look over there you can see where the ground rises unnaturally. That will be where some of the ruins are but the steps were the biggest clue."

The other two troopers reined in. "Sir, there are lumps and bumps for at least half a mile in that direction." He pointed west. "We rode in along the line."

"Good, dismount and have a rest but stay away from the water."

They laughed, "Why are there crocodiles there?"

Trooper Manet said, as he pointed to the water which still bubbled, "You had better believe it. Captain Macgregor needed two shots at point-blank to discourage it!"

Pierre-François wandered off to explore the ruins. "Manet go and follow him. Don't let him get bitten by a scorpion or a snake."

He grinned and began to load his pistol. "Will do sir."

By the time Jean and the rest of the squadron arrived, we had uncovered some of the stones. There were pillars with pictures on them which the lieutenant said were called hieroglyphics. He seemed impressed but the couple that we saw looked to be the work of a child. The major ordered the men to dig deep ditches and he sent others to find some wood to make a palisade. There appeared to be little around.

"I hear you met a crocodile?"

"Yes, sir. It scared the lieutenant a little."

"Good, he might start to act more responsibly."

"I don't think so, sir. He appears to be in his own little world."

We made sure that the guards were more alert as we camped by the Nile. The next day the lieutenant began to give orders and the men were soon shifting sand to reveal the ruins. Jean had them move the sand to make a barrier behind the ditch. The men complained until Jean pointed out that it made a more effective defence than just a ditch and we had to move the sand anyway. Rather than just watching I joined in with the troopers. I enjoyed the physical work and I have never been a watcher. I stripped down to my shirt and felt much better than sweating in the hot woollen uniform. I was quite impressed with the finds. The sand appeared to have protected them and the colours were remarkably vibrant.

At the end of the first day, we made our most exciting discovery. We found a long piece of stone which had been shaped and then covered in hieroglyphics. The lieutenant said it was an obelisk. "The general will like this."

"Why, does it tell us where Alexander's tomb is?"

"Well no, but it is full of information and it is old."

"Keep looking Pierre-François we need the tomb."

"If we can find the Temple of Ptah then we should be closer to finding it." I had spoiled his discovery. He had forgotten the purpose of our trip.

Jean took the opportunity of scouting the surrounding country. He was amazed at how fertile the land was close to the river. "But then you get a line and it is the desert and there is nothing. It is an amazing land."

Five days into the dig and we found the Temple. I was intrigued by the way that the lieutenant managed to uncover the stones and then piece together a picture of the city. This was definitely his forte and not soldiering. Jean had every man not needed for guard duty working to uncover the ruin. We worked solidly for two days.

I had been out on patrol and, when I rode in I saw a despondent Lieutenant Bouchard talking to Jean. "Problems?"

"The tomb was here. You can see where it was and I saw the Greek word for Alexander next to some hieroglyphics. They moved it."

"So back to the general tomorrow?"

"Yes."

The lieutenant looked distraught. "But you can't! We have so much to do and…"

Jean's voice became cold. "Lieutenant, you forget yourself. Our mission was to find the tomb. You said it is not here. We leave in the morning!"

I am not sure that our academic lieutenant slept at all that night. He was busily scribbling in his notebooks recording all that he had found. He could be as obsessive as the general at times. The men were glad to leave. We had lost two men to snake bites and those who had drunk the Nile water when we had first arrived had still not recovered. They did not mind the work but I know they all wanted to be back with the regiment.

When we reached the scene of the battle the soldiers guarding the camp told us that the army had headed north, back to Alexandria and the general had set up his headquarters there. It meant an even longer journey back to our regiment. We left our sick and wounded at the hospital in Cairo and the rest of us trudged north along the river. August in Egypt is a dreadful time to travel. The heat and the flies made everyone short-tempered. Even the horses began to become fractious. I wondered if the rewards were worth the discomfort. I hoped the general knew what he was doing.

We found the regiment well to the south of Alexandria and Jean and I dropped the men and the wagon off there. The major explained about the charges against the lieutenant. Albert shook his head sadly. Dereliction of duty was the most heinous of crimes in the old colonel's eyes.

"I just heard that the fleet has been sunk and all the treasure with it."

"We are unable to sail home?" I recognised the implications straight away. My hand went to my money belt unconsciously. Sir John had done the right thing in giving me the seal.

The colonel nodded and added, philosophically, "It would appear that, for the moment, we are trapped in Egypt."

Pierre-François, who had said little on the journey north suddenly said, "Trapped? But surely we can get more ships."

Jean laughed, "It was that little admiral Nelson who did this. I do not think he will allow any more ships to come. We may be marching home."

We rode through the crowded streets to the headquarters. There was a buzz of noise. Part of this was normal but a greater part was the gossip about the battle and what it meant for the French Army. There was an air of revolt which seemed to permeate the dusty streets filled with the wretched and the desperate of Egypt.

The general was busy meeting with his senior officers and the three of us sat in a, thankfully, cool antechamber. The lieutenant clutched his books and papers as though his life depended upon them. Bessières appeared glad to see us. He was philosophical with the news that we had not found the tomb. "It was a gamble but now that we have the scientists from France we can begin to discover more about this ancient land." He glanced at the books in the lieutenant's hands. "They will prove useful. This could mean a promotion for you, young man."

"I am afraid that he is facing charges of dereliction of duty. He fell asleep whilst in command of the camp and men died."

"Ah." Bessières shook his head sadly, "We had such high hopes for you. Such a pity." He disappeared back into the meeting and we waited again. Jean and I could understand the delay. The loss of the fleet was a disaster and General Bonaparte would need all his skill and luck if he was to extricate both himself and his army from this far off land.

Murat and all the other officers nodded to us as they came out. They might not have recognised the lieutenant but Jean and I were known to them all. Once inside the general pounced eagerly upon the books held by our colleague. "So lieutenant, did you find anything of interest?"

Pierre-François suddenly broke into a grin as he forgot protocol and almost tore the book from the general's hand. He flicked through the pages explaining what his notes and drawings meant. I think Bonaparte was amused. When Pierre-François paused for breath the general laughed. "Excellent. You can take some engineers and recover the treasure. This is excellent work."

Jean coughed, "I am sorry, general, but this officer is facing charges."

Almost absentmindedly the general looked up, "Ah yes Bessières mentioned this. Why was he in command?"

Jean looked confused. "He is an officer, it was his duty."

"I knew there would be a simple explanation. You misunderstood the orders I gave to you. This young man was not to be given duties. He has done all that I asked of him," he pointed at the books. "The charges will be dropped."

"But general the troopers…"

"Bonaparte held up his hand. "He is to be transferred to the engineers with the rank of captain." He smiled at us as we were summarily dismissed. "Well done you two. You may return to your regiment."

As we rode back I could see that Jean was fuming. "Every time I see that man he sinks lower and lower in my estimation of him! He is a soldier and you would have thought he would have understood that military discipline takes precedence over tombs and stones! Troopers died because of that young imbecile!"

"Jean, Ssh! Men may hear."

"I care not!"

Luckily the streets were so full of street hawkers and sellers that we could not be heard. What worried me was how angry Jean was. Normally he was calm, almost placid but not now. The general had angered him.

"The sooner we get back to being real soldiers the better."

We did not have much time to reflect on the meeting. For when we returned, there were our neglected duties to perform. When we told Albert of the general's decision he shrugged. "He was a pleasant young man. Do you think that the firing squad would have helped our morale? The other troopers on guard that night also bear some responsibility. Think on that."

Before Jean could reply a rider galloped in to the camp and leapt from his horse. "Colonel Aristide, General Murat requests your presence at headquarters."

"I'll be right with you. Major, you had better prepare the men for a move. General Murat is a little impetuous and likes things done yesterday."

With something military to do Jean was much calmer. "Right Robbie, get Claude and organise the men to check their horses and muskets. With the fleet destroyed we will be struggling to get supplies. Get as much as you can from the quartermaster's stores. I am not sure where we will be operating this time."

I found Claude and gave him his instructions. "I'll take Lieutenant Barriere and visit the quartermaster."

Tiny drove the wagon and I rode next to him as we headed for the warehouse which had been commandeered for the quartermaster. He knew us from our trip into the desert. "Ah, you have come to return the wagon eh? Very thoughtful of you."

"No, we have more orders from General Bonaparte. I am here to fill it up."

The mention of the commander was like oiling a greasy wheel; it worked instantly. "Ah, the general. Right, what do you need?"

"Musket balls, powder, canteens, blankets."

The quartermaster nodded to the sergeant who wandered into the warehouse with three bored privates following him. I suddenly spied some of the white cloaks we had found so useful.

"What are they?"

The captain looked up from his list and said, "Oh they were in here when we commandeered it. I will get rid of them soon."

"We will take them off your hands?"

"Why?" the suspicion was back in his voice.

"Well, when the general sends us out into the desert we sometimes need to be in disguise. Besides I am doing you a favour by clearing space in your warehouse."

I could see him working out how we were robbing him. He obviously couldn't see a profit in it and so he shrugged. "You are right it gives me more room although when our next supply ships will reach us is anyone's guess."

"Tiny, stick them in the wagon."

Tiny grinned, "You are getting sneakier, captain."

"I think it is being around the general that does it."

By the time we reached our camp with our treasures, the colonel had returned and Jean had prepared the men to move. We were summoned to a briefing. The colonel had two troopers hold up a map and he pointed at it with his dagger. "The general wants a screen of cavalry to the east of the river. There are no more Turks on the western side. We are sending a couple of requisitioned river cruisers to patrol the Nile and we will be stationed to the east of the Nile. Each regiment will have a sector to patrol." He jabbed his finger at a dot close to the sea. "This is Kolzum on the Red Sea. This is the southern edge of our patrol. The 22nd Dragoons will be there. We will be thirty miles north," he pointed to the map, "where there is nothing. The cavalry has a hundred and twenty miles of frontier to cover if the mapmakers are to be believed. This is where any Turkish army will come. There is a lake, here, but the water is, apparently, undrinkable. We will have to fetch our water from the Nile on a daily basis. As we know, to our cost, the water is almost poisonous and so we will have to gather firewood every day. That means we will need wagons. "

He looked at me, "Did we return the quartermaster's wagon captain?"

"No, sir."

"Good then we have three in total they will have to suffice. I want one troop a day on firewood detail and one troop a day on water detail."

Jean frowned, "That only leaves two troops to patrol sir."

"A troop and half. We have half a troop in the hospital; some with dysentery and others with a kind of coughing disease." He shrugged. "You know how it works, major. If it is any consolation the general's precious Guides are being assigned an area too. They will have to earn their precious red and green uniforms."

"What about infantry support and artillery?"

"There is a brigade building a line of forts behind us to protect the road from Alexandria to Cairo but we are the front line."

I held up my hand, "Sir, I managed to get some white cloaks from the quartermaster. We used them as a disguise when we arrived but they keep you cool. They might be useful."

"Good, how many?"

"Well I thought we would be short but if we only have three and a half troops then we will have enough."

"Good. Issue them, captain."

Chapter 4

The troopers all named our new camp, Versailles. It was their dark humour at work. The Bourbon palace of canals and water features was as far from the rock-strewn, sandy, scorpion and snake-infested camp as you could imagine. We chose the best site that we could but it was still grim. Every rock seemed to hide a scorpion, a snake or some insect which enjoyed feasting on cavalry flesh. I was pleased that Jean and I were assigned to lead the first two patrols. It got us out of camp and I did not desire to be the carter carrying water or firewood. Jean had Charles as his lieutenant and I had Tiny. I was comfortable with the ex-sergeant major. I had made Trooper Manet the first sergeant of the troop. He was dependable and reminded me much of Tiny when he had first been promoted. We had just fifty troopers in the patrol but I felt sure that we would be able to deal with whatever the enemy threw at us. The Mamelukes might be brave but, compared with us, they were ill-equipped for a modern war and the irregulars were even worse. The only advantage some of them had was that they rode camels, which our horses hated and shied away from. The strange beasts could also go for longer without water.

"Sergeant Manet, make sure the men all have two canteens. Check that they haven't any alcohol with them. That will dehydrate them faster than anything."

"Sir."

I had made the men wear white cloaks. At first, they were unhappy about the extra weight but they soon relented when they found out how cool they were. The huge hoods also afforded more protection to their heads than our hard helmets.

I led the patrol to the east. It was all enemy country to our fore. The sergeant sent out four men ahead of us to give us early warning of any enemy. It was not good cavalry country. The rocks threatened to send you skittering down the slopes and you would suddenly find patches of soft sand which seemed to drag you down. I had decided that we would halt during the noon sun. There was little point in frying. Each step seemed to take twice as much effort during the heat of the day. Our maps were poor but it looked as though there might be some shelter some five miles ahead. I turned to Tiny. "I expect the four scouts back soon to tell us there is water and shade. The map seems to show something."

Tiny looked up at the sun, It was his way of telling time. "I would have expected them back by now. Suddenly Sergeant Manet shouted, "Sir, up in the sky. Look!"

I could see, over the next rise, the circling buzzards. There was something dead ahead. I felt a sick feeling in my stomach. "Take out your muskets and be ready for trouble. Gallop!"

As soon as we crested the rise I saw my scouts, or at least what remained of three of them. Their severed heads had been stuck on the hilt of their swords. Of the fourth and their horses there was no sign. "Lieutenant Barriere, take ten men and form a skirmish line. Sergeant Manet, send five men to look for the fourth trooper and tracks."

I dismounted close to the bodies. They had all been hacked to death. "Trooper, get some men and dig graves for these brave troopers."

I tied Killer to a scrubby looking tree and began to scour the ground for clues and evidence. One advantage of the lack of moisture and rain was that you could track a little easier. Even when it was soft sand you could see where someone had stepped. As I knelt to examine some ash I could hear the shovels as they dug the graves for the three troopers. I rubbed the ash between my fingers. It felt warm and I knew they had been here recently. There were darker patches which showed where the men had bled. The Ottomans would pay for their cruelty. I finished my examination and returned to the others. Everyone was there and the men had fashioned three crude crosses. I was not sure that the Committee would approve but I did.

I took off my helmet and the others did the same, "Lord, take these brave men into your care. I know not what religion they were but I know that you would not shun such brave troopers. Amen."

I put my headgear back on. "Well?"

Sergeant Manet said, "The tracks head east and there is no sign of Trooper Denoire. There was a trail of blood and then it stopped."

I nodded. I looked at each of them in turn as I spoke. "This is what happened, the Ottomans were hiding here. They smoked their pipes and they dug pits in which to hide. One of them must have been over there." I pointed to where the bodies had been found. They did not know it but it was a trap. When they approached the Turk they were surrounded and… well, you know the rest. I realise it is too late for them but get this into your head. Out here everything is a potential enemy and killer. Take nothing at face value. I am sorry the three of them died but they were careless and stupid." I almost spat the word out in my anger. "If there are four scouts and one of you sees one man then only one trooper needs to look at him. The rest should be watching for danger. Use your nose. I could smell the tobacco when I arrived. They should have smelled it too. Listen for noises and use your horses. Killer was unhappy even before we saw the buzzards." I let my words sink in. "Mount. Sergeant Manet, take four men and ride half a mile behind us. Let us get well away before you follow. I do not want to walk into another trap."

I could see the puzzled look on his face. "They knew we were coming. They know we will follow. What I don't want is for us to find them and then discover that we are surrounded." He grinned. I snapped a reply to wipe it from his face. "And that is the last explanation I give. Just follow orders and I might get you back to France alive."

We mounted and Tiny and I led the column. Tiny snapped, "Keep your muskets handy."

I looked at the clear trail left by the Ottomans. "What worries me is that they want us to follow. I am not going to hurry."

"But, sir, what about Trooper Denoire? Shouldn't we try to rescue him?"

"Trooper Denoire is dead. They have taken his body to make us follow. That is why the blood stopped."

"How do you know, sir?" This was curiosity and I answered.

"I cannot see them seeing to his wounds. See how much blood there is. He died...," I pointed to the ground, "right here where the blood stops. They want us to charge in and get ourselves killed." A movement in the sky attracted my attention. "See the buzzards in the sky? We have denied them a meal and they are following another one. That is where the Ottomans are. Take ten men and ride south for a mile and then east for another mile. You should be able to catch them or get ahead of them."

"And then what do we do?"

"Come to our rescue when we ride into their trap." As Tiny rode away I thought about the changes I had seen in me. Three years ago I would have ridden back to the camp, fearful of what might happen; now I was courting death to try to avenge my dead troopers. Working for General Napoleon Bonaparte changed a man.

"Corporal Degas." The corporal rode next to me.

"Sir?"

"I want you at the rear of this column. I suspect we will be ambushed. Take charge of the rear of the line in case I am hit. The lieutenant and the sergeant will join us with their men once the firing starts."

"Sir."

Degas was a new appointment but he had potential. I liked the way he hadn't bothered with any superfluous questions. I checked both my horse pistols. I would not be using my musketoon when we were attacked. I wanted to fire as soon as I saw a Turk. As I looked ahead I saw that the buzzards had now stopped moving away and were flying in lazy circles. There was a defile in a rock-strewn valley. That would be their killing ground. I turned to the four men behind me. When we get to those rocks dismount and tie your horses. Make your way through the rocks. The Ottomans will be waiting there for us. Outflank them and use your muskets."

"Sir." My little speech earlier on had eliminated questions anyway. I had just twenty-nine men with me. I hoped that would be enough. I deliberately slowed as we neared the defile to allow the men to dismount. As they did so I turned and said quietly, "We are about to be ambushed. When we are attacked I want you to dismount and take cover in the rocks. Pass it on."

The message slipped down the column and I led us into the valley of death. I could see the buzzards. I knew that the ambush would be in the ground in front of the buzzards. I scanned the rocks for a sign but it was Killer who alerted me. He whinnied and I caught the reflection from the metal of a weapon. I yelled, "Ambush!" and slid from Killer's back.

I raised my pistol and fired at the Turk who had stood less than ten paces from me. His lifeless body collapsed in a heap. I put the pistol back in the holster and took out my second. There was no point firing into the rocks, it would be a waste of powder. I had quickly realised that their musket balls were not even coming close to us. I suspected they were ancient ones even worse than those used by the Maltese. A Mameluke ran at me from his place of concealment. He was just twenty yards from me. I caught the movement, turned and fired. He had moved quickly and was almost within a sword's length when my ball took off his head. I took out my sword. I could hear the pop of muskets from behind me. My four skirmishers were doing as ordered.

I turned to the men crouching behind me. "One man in four, watch the horses and guard our backs. The rest of you come with me." I was trusting that Tiny would be to the south of me. I led the survivors of the ambush up the northern slope. We stood more chance than down in the defile. I bent double as I scrambled towards the ridge. I could see the puffs of smoke from their guns and made my way towards the closest. As soon as the gun had fired I ran, knowing how long it took to reload.

When I was a third of the way up a movement to my right made me turn and I saw a Turk trying to load his gun. I raced to him and thrust my blade into his side. I could see that some of my men had fallen; the blood from their wounds staining their white cloaks but I saw more dead Turks as we climbed higher. A musket appeared from the rock ahead and I grabbed hold of it. The barrel was hot but I pulled anyway and a surprised Turk forgot to let go and was impaled on my blade. I had just withdrawn the blade when a second Ottoman ran at me with his sword aimed at my head. I knocked the blade aside and punched him as hard as I could in the stomach. He doubled up with the force of the blow. I smashed the hilt of my sword on to the back of his head and he slumped in an unconscious heap at my feet. I picked up his sword in my left hand and shouted to the nearest trooper. "Watch this man and reload your weapon!"

It was easier to move up the slope as the firing became more sporadic. I could see the Turks begin to move away from my chasseurs. We were eager for revenge. Two of the enemy rushed towards me and I was forced to use both swords. I barely fended off the man on my left. I used my superior strength in my right hand to spin around and force one of my opponents to fall towards the man on my left. Rather than retreating I went on to the offensive. I stamped on the knee of one Turk and heard a satisfying crack as it broke. As he screamed, I plunged my sword into his neck. The second man slashed at my leg from a prone position. I barely had time to block it with the Mameluke sword. Even so, it bit into the leather of my boot. I raised my sword and chopped down on him. He put his hand up in defence but it merely slowed the blade up. I sliced through his hand and into the side of his neck.

Sergeant Manet joined me. "I think they are on the run."

"Good. Get the bugler to sound recall. You check the bodies and try to find Denoire. I'll go and find the lieutenant."

The sergeant grinned. "I think I saw him and his men charging after the Turks sir."

By the time I reached the bottom of the defile, the horse holders and the horses had arrived. I mounted Killer, much to the relief of the trooper holding him. "First ten come with me. The rest, cover the troopers up there."

I led my ten men down the defile. I could see bodies dotted on the rock-strewn slopes. Suddenly I heard the clash of weapons, "Draw sabres!"

The hiss of metal sliding from scabbards was a reassuring sound, and, as we turned to follow the valley we saw Tiny and his men engaged with some Turkish horsemen. We had no bugle with us and so I roared, "Charge!" I leaned forwards over Killer's head with my sword held before me. My mount was the best in the regiment and soon outpaced his peers. I did not even need to move my hand as Killer slid next to the rear of a Turkish horse and my sword pierced the back of the robed Ottoman. His sudden scream alerted the exultant Turks to the new danger from their rear. They turned in time to be spitted on the sabres of my men. The eight survivors threw their arms in the air. I could see the fierce anger on the faces of my men and I feared that they would take their revenge on these prisoners.

"The prisoners must remain unharmed. We are not savages." I saw their weapons lower.

"Thanks, sir, just in time!"

I shook my head, "Lieutenant, next time wait for me."

He looked hurt, "But sir they would have got away."

I rode next to him and pointed to the bodies of the three dead troopers, "And they would be alive. Where do you think we will get replacements from? We have no fleet."

Realisation dawned on his face. "Sorry, sir."

"Never mind. Get the dead troopers on their horses and then collect the equipment and horses of the dead Turks."

It was sometime later when we rode back down the defile with our eight prisoners. A grim-faced Sergeant Manet was waiting for me with the rest of the patrol. "We found Denoire sir. We wrapped his body in a robe. He is whole and…"

"And you thought to bury him at the camp. Good. We have three others to bury."

"Six, sir." He pointed to the horses standing forlornly with their robe covered cargoes.

We had lost ten men on this patrol. That was a fifth of the force and this was but our first outing. "Sergeant, take the rear. Lieutenant, you watch the prisoners. Let's go home."

Versailles looked a little more welcoming as we rode towards it. We could see the smoke from the cooking fires and smell the food in the pots. After the horror of the morning, it would do the men good to have hot food and talk to try to rid us of the memories.

I made my report to Albert as the prisoners were taken by Lieutenant Chagal back to Cairo. I idly wondered what would happen to them but then dismissed the thought. It was not my problem.

"So they ambushed your scouts."

"Yes, sir. This is a different country from Italy and these are not Austrians. They are sneaky and, " I added coldly, "cruel."

"I know and it must be distressing but I do not think they would have suffered and dead is dead, captain."

"I know."

"Any other signs of the enemy?"

"No, sir. It is a treacherous land out there and they know it." I pointed to the east. "They were waiting for us and they must have scouts watching for us."

The colonel knew me and smiled, "Go on Robbie out with your idea."

"If we went out at night we could find them, sir. They wouldn't be expecting that."

"A good idea, but not tonight. Your men can rest tonight and tomorrow you can get the water so that your men will be able to take the night patrol."

"Yes, sir!"

As we ate in the mess tent I told the other officers of the Ottomans and what they had done to the troopers. They were all appalled. Jean was more phlegmatic. "But if the Turks had come to our land and conquered it, what would we do?"

"We wouldn't chop off their heads!"

"I think that if you are dead it does not matter." He looked at me. "And do we not chop off heads in the Place de la Revolution? Where is the difference?"

Tiny shivered, "It just seems, I don't know, barbaric."

"War is barbaric but do not let the blood rush to your head. From what Robbie said you charged after superior numbers today with a handful of men. Why?"

The lieutenant blushed, "I was angry and I wanted…"

"You wanted to get back at the men who had done that to your troopers. You are an officer. Think with your mind and not your heart. You will save more troopers' lives that way."

Jean was right, of course, but it was hard to be dispassionate when you had seen young troopers treated that way. When Charles returned after delivering his prisoners he told us that what he had experienced was being duplicated all along the line of outposts. It was hit and run. The Turks knew we could not reinforce and were wearing us down. It would be a war of attrition. They were making the desert red with the blood of our horsemen.

The water detail did not seem so bad after the horrors of the previous day. All we had to worry about were the crocodiles and they were easier to spot than Turks hiding in the rocks. The water butts were emptied into the huge cauldrons and boiled before being placed in new water butts. We were able to rest during the heat of the day and then, in the afternoon, we planned our night time patrol. I had Tiny and the sergeants and corporals around me as I explained what we would be doing.

"I pointed to the two sergeants, you two along with the lieutenant and I will each lead ten men out tonight. We will split up as soon as we leave the camp. Half will go south with the lieutenant and the other half with me, north. We ride four miles east and then the four columns will work their way back to a point here, " I gestured to a line on the map. "It is about a mile from the camp. Sergeant Manet has been out while we were getting the water and placed a line of white stones in the shape of an arrow where the line is." The sergeant's biggest problem had been collecting enough white stones. He had seen no one but it was daylight and I suspected that the Turks hid during the day and closed with the camp at night time to observe our patrols leaving at dawn.

"Horse holders will stay with the horses and then we will move forward. I am sure they have men watching. I want us to capture or kill those men. Muskets will be no good so leave them here. Pistols and swords will be all that we will need. Make sure your men know what to do. No spurs tonight, they will only trip us up."

When Jean returned, he too had casualties as had Charles. Between them, they had lost five men. "I think you are right Robbie, they are waiting for us. Good luck tonight." He looked thin and drawn. The war of attrition was not just about dead bodies; it was about damaged minds and spirits too.

I lead Sergeant Manet and eighteen others to the north. It had been slightly cooler during the day and the September evening was much cooler. For once we were glad of our woollen uniforms. There was no moon and we had to move carefully to avoid injury to our horses on the rock-strewn desert. The sergeant knew where we were and he suddenly pointed to the ground. There was an arrow. "There sir!"

"Well done sergeant. You take your men towards the camp. I will move further south."

The sergeant's patrol dismounted and we rode half a mile towards the lieutenant's men who were, hopefully, ahead of us. With two men watching the horses we only had eight of us to find the enemy but I was fairly certain that the watchers would be few in number.

It was my nose which alerted me to their presence. It was the now, unmistakable smell of camel. Once you had smelled camel you never forgot its pungent aroma. I held up my hand and my men froze. I could see nothing ahead but there appeared to be a rise. I crept forward and then slithered along the ground. I hoped I would not disturb a scorpion or a snake; that would be an inglorious way to die. I took off my helmet as I neared the rise. I peered over the top with just my forehead and eyes showing. There, below me were five camels and their riders. One was watching the camp and the others were sleeping. I slipped back down the slope and gathered my men around me. I held up five fingers and they nodded. I pointed to two and gestured for them to go to the right. I gestured for two more to go to the left and the others I pointed to me. They nodded and we crept forward.

I led my three troopers up to the rise. I put my helmet back on as I needed both hands. I drew my pistol and the others did the same. We were just descending the slope when there was a crack of pistols to the south. My other men had made contact. Of course, the four sleeping men awoke. There was no point in being silent any longer. I fired my pistol at one of the Ottomans as I yelled, "Fire!"

The pistols all cracked together and I drew my sword. One of the enemy soldiers had not fallen to a musket ball and he ran for a camel. A camel is not a horse and you have to mount whilst it kneels. It gave me the time to race over and to stab him in the side. "Secure these camels!"

I had a half-smile on my face as the troopers warily approached the camels. The ones we had met so far appeared to be bad-tempered, flatulent, spitting machines; it was no wonder our horses disliked them. "Corporal, check that the Turks are dead and take charge here."

I ran back to the horses and mounted Killer, "Take the horses to the corporal and then head back to the camp with the bodies and the camels. I will go and find the others."

As they obeyed I headed south towards the sounds of the firing. I discovered Tiny and the rest of the southern patrols. "There were six Turks sir. All dead. We had two men wounded." I frowned. I had hoped to avoid any casualties.

"Very good. Take the bodies and the camels back to Versailles. I will follow. I will find Sergeant Manet."

I headed north in case the sergeant had found any other watchers. The lack of firing suggested not. I intended heading back to the first arrow just to make sure. I was close to that point when I felt Killer falter and whinny. That meant trouble. Even as my hand went to my sword a figure leapt from the rocks to dash me to the ground. My sword fell from my hand and the wind was knocked from me as the Turk crashed on top of me. His hand came towards me and there was a wicked-looking blade in it. I made a feeble attempt to deflect it with my fist. I managed to turn it but the edge scored a deep wound in my right hand. I punched as hard as I could with my left hand and felt it connect with the side of his head. It was powerful enough to knock him from me. As I jumped to my feet I grabbed the stiletto from my boot. I could feel the blood dripping from my wounded hand. It felt like a bad wound and I needed to finish this quickly.

Although my assailant was not as tall as me he was stocky and powerfully built. This would not be easy; especially with only one hand. I took in the way he was dressed. He had light shoes and baggy trousers. That gave me an advantage. I feinted with my knife, held in my left hand. He countered with his knife. As we closed I stamped with the heel of my boot on his foot. I heard the crunch of bones breaking before he screamed in agony and fell backwards. I dived at him and plunged my knife into his throat. His body shivered and then fell still.

My hand was bleeding from the deep cut and I had to stop the flow. I grabbed his headdress and wrapped it tightly around my bleeding hand. I whistled and Killer galloped over. I took the dead man's knife and thrust it into my belt. I dragged myself up on to Killer's back and looked to see where his mount was. I was relieved to find that it was a horse and not a camel. I rode next to it and, tying my reins around the pommel of my saddle led the horse with my left hand. I kicked Killer in the flanks and he trotted off towards the distant camp. He knew the way back to the camp and I could just concentrate on staying upright. I had been lucky and I knew it.

The vedettes saw me and shouted, "Halt who goes there?"

I answered, "Captain Macgregor," and then everything went black as I tumbled to the ground.

Chapter 5

I dreamt that I was falling from a high tower. I seemed to tumble over and over. Even as I descended there were knives and swords hacking at me and birds pecking at my eyes. I was trying to scream but no sound came from me. I could hear the maniacal laugh of Mama Tusson and the ground was rushing up at me.

Suddenly there was an acrid smell in my nose and I found myself coughing. I heard a voice say, "There you. Smelling salts, they work every time.

I opened my eyes and saw Jean and the colonel looking at me with concern written all over their faces. With them was an officer I did not recognise. The colonel clapped him on the back, "Thank you, doctor. We were quite worried there and wondered if we had lost our Scotsman."

"It was touch and go. He lost a great deal of blood but he is strong and young. He will recover. I want no duties for him for at least two weeks. When I take those stitches out we can consider giving him a light duty."

"Don't worry. He will not move."

After he had gone Jean shook his head. "Reckless Robbie! Why did you go off alone?"

"I wanted to make sure that all the other troopers were safe."

The colonel tut-tutted, "Next time take a trooper with you. What happened?"

"I was jumped by a Turk. If it had not been for Killer then I would be dead. How did I get here?"

"Luckily for you, the sentry knew what to do. He applied a tourniquet and brought you into camp. He saved your life. That was three days ago."

I struggled to rise, "Then I must thank him."

Jean put his arm on my shoulder and shook his head, "Trooper Carnet was killed on patrol yesterday."

I sank back and closed my eyes. Another dead trooper and debt would now go unpaid. I heard Jean say. "Let us leave him alone. I think sleep may be the best medicine."

After they had gone I reflected that sleep might be the best medicine but it would not come. I could barely remember the trooper and yet he had saved my life. I thought of all the others who selfless actions had saved me in the past, Guiscard, Madame Lefondre, even my father and I had not thanked them or done anything in return. I resolved as I lay in the tented hospital, that I would begin to live life differently. Each day would be as though it was my last and I would tell those around me that I valued them and I would thank them. I would make up for the omissions so far.

I decided that I knew best and, the next day, when I awoke I was determined to ignore what the doctor had said. The problem was Jean. He had known me since birth and knew all of my ways; sometimes I believe that he knew what I was thinking. As I left my tent he strode up to me with a smile on his face that, in itself, was disconcerting. His smiles were rare. "Ah, Captain Macgregor I am pleased to see that you are up. You are to be attached to the general's staff for the next month. You are to become a temporary Guard for the general." He pointed to the cot next to mine. On it was the red and green uniform of the Chasseur of the Guard.

"What is this?"

"Your new uniform until you recover and the general sends you back to us."

I slumped on to the bed. "But sir!"

"It is for the best. That was a deep wound. With the heat and the dirt, it could become infected. The headquarters building is cleaner and they have Bonaparte's doctor on hand. I think you will enjoy it. Besides he asked for you. He has need of someone who can speak English. The wound means that the colonel and I can let you go without regrets."

I was defeated and I knew it. I pointed to the uniform. "And this?"

"The general wishes you to look the same his other Guards. This was made for an officer who died before he could join the army. It is new and we have had it altered to fit you."

"When?" I knew we had men with sewing skills in the regiment but I did not expect this.

"It was done while you were unconscious. Now get into the uniform. Lieutenant Barrier and his troop will escort you to Cairo."

"His troop?"

"Until you are well enough to command again, yes, it will be his troop. Why do you think he is not competent enough to run the troop? You promoted him."

"Of course I trust him but you make it sound permanent."

"Oh no, Robbie. You will be back here soon enough."

By the time I was dressed in my new uniform, Killer and my escort were waiting for me. Sergeant Manet looked quite concerned. "Sorry about your wound sir. I feel terrible about it. I should have sent a rider to tell you we were safe. Sorry. It won't happen again."

"No sergeant, I have learned my lesson. I am not immortal and I cannot win this war all by myself."

I heard a chuckle from Tiny. I shot him a look which, in times past, would have made him shrivel but he just shrugged. "The troopers were worried sir; all of them. I am pleased that you have realised how close you came to death." He appraised my uniform. "I like the uniform sir; very smart."

The lieutenant had grown up from the diffident and awkward youth into a confident leader. The troop would be in good hands. I wondered just what was in store for me at headquarters. My life, hitherto, had been one of action; how could I become a cypher? I looked at my right hand in a sling. I would not even be able to write. Would I just be a flunky for the general? I resigned myself to a boring month.

General Bonaparte's headquarters was quite obvious from the outside with the huge Tricolour and the large number of red and green guards. The sentry outside sharply saluted my new uniform. As I dismounted I said to Tiny, "Well lieutenant, you will need all the luck you can get. In my tent are the knife and the Mameluke sword I took from the men I killed. Take them. I shan't need them for a while and I have learned that extra weapons are always handy."

"Thank you, sir. I will put them to good use."

After they had trotted off I asked the sentry, "Where are the Guard stables?"

He looked at me as though I had spoken a foreign language. "Sir? Just leave it here and someone will take it for you."

I looked at the trooper who was dressed as I was. He was not a real cavalryman. A real horseman looked after his horse. "Just point me in the right direction, trooper." There was a snap to my voice I had not needed since my days as a sergeant.

He snapped his heels together and pointed north. "Just around the corner sir."

After I had made sure that Killer had been fed and watered I returned to the trooper who was rigidly at attention as I entered the white building. Bessières smiled from his desk when I stood before him with my colpack in my hand. It felt insubstantial after the Tarleton helmet I had been used to "It suits you, captain. I hope that you come to like us. We would like you to become a permanent member of the squadron."

I held up my bandaged arm which gave me the appearance of an injured bird. "I can't see what use I would be like this."

He stood and led me out of the building. "And that is where you are wrong for we intend to have you working right now." He turned to the lieutenant who was writing at the other desk. "Send Sergeant Delacroix to us. We will be with the prisoners."

Although I had only been in the building for a few minutes the bright sun and the white buildings were blinding as we left. I was just grateful that winter was almost upon us and it was much cooler than it had been when we had fought at the pyramids.

"You are able to speak English, captain and we have captured some sailors from the English fleet. Even though our fleet was defeated we still managed to capture some of the men who survived in the sea. There are eight of them in the prison. We need you to question them. The general wishes to find out as much as he can about their fleet and their bases."

I remembered my times in prison. I had been in prison in San Marino as well as the dreaded Conciergerie and I felt some empathy for these sailors. "What will happen to them, sir?"

He gave me a puzzled look. "What do you mean captain?"

"Are they to be exchanged? Sent to a prison hulk? What is their fate?"

I could see that nothing had been planned for them beyond the basic questioning from me. He looked confused and puzzled. "I am not sure. What a curious question. We have no ships left never mind hulks and there are no English nearby with whom we could exchange them." He paused and looked at me. "What would you suggest, captain?"

"They may well be reluctant to speak with me unless I can offer them something in return. They will cost money to feed. If I promised them their freedom then they might give me information in return."

We continued walking as the colonel considered my words. "Your idea has merit. I suppose we could send them to Cyprus or Naples on the 'Carillon'. " He smiled, "We have at least retained the lucky sloop of yours. Yes, you have my permission to make that offer. Who knows the young lieutenant on the 'Carillon' may be able to gather intelligence when he lands them."

I was not bothered about any intelligence. I doubted that they would know much unless they were officers. I just did not like the idea of men rotting in a cell. The prospect had terrified me on two occasions and I would be able to do something to alleviate someone else's suffering.

There were armed sentries on the main doors. I guessed that this had been a Turkish prison and the general had taken it over. Bessières took me to an empty room. It contained only a table and three chairs. "This is yours to use to interrogate the men. When the sergeant arrives he will act as your scribe to keep notes. The general will want daily reports but I expect this task to take you but a couple of days." He looked at my hand and saluted. "I shall leave you now. The sergeant will bring you to the quarters you will be using." He chuckled, "Here, we do not sleep in tents there are some benefits to serving in the city!"

I looked down the corridor. "Where are the cells?"

"Down there. They are the only prisoners. The general had those who were criminals executed and so each man has his own cell. They talk to no-one." I realised that these men had been in solitary confinement since the battle some weeks earlier. It might make my task a little easier. "Well good luck captain."

With that, he left and I looked at the bare office. I decided to wander down and inspect the men. The guard at the end saluted. The smell of human faeces hit me as soon as I walked along the dark and disturbingly damp corridor. I wondered how often they slopped out their waste. Perhaps I could do something about that and get the men on my side. They would be resentful. To them, when I spoke, I would appear a traitor. The last time I had interrogated a prisoner he had resented my uniform. I peered through the grille of the first cell. It was so dark I was not sure if it was occupied but a movement from a shadowy shape showed me that it was. The smell from the grille was even more powerful than the smell of the corridor. While I interrogated them I would see to it that their cells were cleaned.

When Sergeant Delacroix arrived it was like meeting Albert Aristide again. He was of an age with the colonel and had the same look with the fine queue, pigtails and moustache. I wondered what he thought as he looked at this young officer he had to call sir.

"Hello, sergeant. I am Captain Macgregor." I pointed to the table. We will be in here."

He nodded and said, "Sir." There was no trace of any feelings in his words or his look. This soldier was a professional.

I summoned the sentry. "Bring me the first prisoner and while we interrogate him, have some of the workers clean out the cell." I saw his mouth begin to open as he glanced at the sergeant. "Just do it trooper or I will have you and the rest of the detail doing it instead." He snapped to attention and left. I caught the ghost of a smile from the sergeant.

I turned to him. "I will tell you what to write in French. I am assuming they will not know French and it will mean you have to write down less. Much of what they say will be irrelevant anyway."

The first sailor I interrogated I would have guessed was in his twenties although, beneath the matted hair in which I could see the head lice crawling and the dirt on his face, it was hard to tell. Even though he did not appear to be wounded there were many scabs and scars on his hands, arms and legs. I suspected rats. I gestured to the seat and he sat down.

I saw him blinking in the bright lights. He had been in the dark for so long he was almost a mole. I waited patiently until his eyes had adjusted and he looked at me. When I spoke I kept my voice calm and quiet. I remembered the Regent of San Marino when he had spoken to me in his prison. It had been his calm voice which had reassured me.

"What is your name?"

I saw him start as I spoke in English without an accent. "Er, Jamie Webb sir."

"My name is Captain Macgregor. What ship were you on?"

It was an easy question to start and I already knew, from the information given to me by Colonel Bessières that they had all come from two ships. "The Orion sir."

"Good." I pointed to his arms. "How did you come by those wounds, Jamie?"

"Rats sir. The cells are filled with the little buggers."

"Ah." I would do something about that too. "Who commanded the fleet?" Again I knew I was on safe ground here but I needed confirmation.

"Our Nel, Admiral Nelson sir." There was clear pride and affection in his voice.

I deliberately chose not to tell anything to the sergeant yet. As soon as he began to write then the prisoner would realise he was giving away information. I could see Jamie relaxing as we chatted. He had been on his own for so long I must have appeared as a saviour rather than an enemy. "Your Nel, he captured many ships, where would he take them?"

"Leghorn or Naples those are the ports we sailed from."

This was much easier than I had expected. In my mind, I determined that I would still tell the colonel that I had offered them their freedom. This young man before me was a sad picture of what could have happened to me but for fate. "And the rest of the fleet is still at Gibraltar?"

"Sir? Should I be telling you all this?"

I turned to the sergeant. "Their bases are Naples and Leghorn. I believe their fleet is at Gibraltar." I looked the young man in the eye. "Do you want to get home, Jamie?"

His eyes filled with tears. "Of course I do."

"Then just answer my questions and I give you my word that we will put you in a ship to take you to Naples."

He nodded, "Yes sir Gibraltar."

It became much easier then and he gave us the names of the captains and the ships. As he left he turned and asked, "Sir, did you mean what you said about going home?"

"Yes Jamie, I did."

"Then God bless you, sir."

The next five sailors all said roughly the same and the sergeant had a sheet of paper filled with the precious intelligence we had gathered. I decided that I would only interview the sixth man as I was certain that the information would be the same. The guard had told me that the sixth man was some sort of officer. As he came in I could understand why. His clothes looked to be of a slightly better quality but I suspected that he was not an officer but a naval version of a sergeant. He had tattoos and a scowling face. He was the antithesis of Jamie. He sat and stared sullenly at me.

"What is your name?"

As soon as I spoke he launched himself across the table at me. "You traitor!"

He took the sergeant by surprise but I had seen the flicker of anger in his eyes and I had already begun to move out of the way. Sergeant Delacroix fell off the chair and crashed to the floor. I punched the sailor on the side of the head with my left hand as he lost his balance over the table. The guard rushed in with his musket levelled. I waved my hand. "We are safe. Drag him back to his cell." The sentry called for aid and the two of them bumped the unconscious sailor back to his cell.

As I helped the sergeant to his feet he grinned. "Well sir, you are deceptive. I thought a young officer like you would have been felled by that animal, especially with the injured hand. That was a hefty punch!"

"Thank you, sergeant. I grew up working hard. I think we have gathered enough information for the colonel."

He nodded, "You ought to think about doing this regularly, sir. You got more information out of those prisoners than most officers would have managed."

I shook my head. "I did not enjoy the experience. I have been a prisoner and I understand what they are going through."

The colonel was more than pleased with my speedy work. "Well done captain. This is useful information." He leaned into me and spoke quietly, "Since your visit to Naples the general has become interested in that region. I believe that this will further pique his curiosity."

As Sergeant Delacroix handed the report over he saluted, "Good working with you sir. I hope you enjoy the posting."

The colonel said, "I am afraid we will be moving tomorrow and heading back to Alexandria. The general has business there."

"And the prisoners, sir? I promised them…"

"Of course and it means we will no longer have to maintain a guard." He scribbled on a piece of paper and handed it to his orderly. "Requisition a wagon for tomorrow and inform the guards that the prisoners are to be made ready to move when we leave in the morning."

I chose not to eat in the mess with the others but found a local place which served some of the indigenous food. It was not that I did not wish to socialise with the officers of the Guard but I missed my comrades. I also did not relish the questions I knew I would have to endure. The food was cheap and wholesome. It was also far spicier than any food I had eaten before. I enjoyed it.

Before we could head for Alexandria the populace rose in riot and revolt. We were in the old part of the town, called Old Cairo but Dupuy, the general in charge of the remainder of the garrison, was amongst those killed by the rioters. We were all ordered to present ourselves to the general. He was in no mood for any dissent. Colonel Bessières gave us our orders. "We are to drive the rioters back into the city. The infantry and the artillery will be there by the time we arrive."

General Bonaparte noticed me. He pointed to my hand, "I heard about your escapade Scotsman. Take care." He tapped the leather satchel Bessières carried, "Thank you for that information."

"I just did my duty sir."

"True but you did it efficiently and I like that. I think the news of the freedom for the prisoners should come from you."

I wondered how much use I would be with one hand but I rode next to the sergeant and the colonel. The rest of the squadron rode behind us. I thought this strange as the general was in the fore. If we were attacked then he would be the first to be in danger. I surreptitiously checked that my pistol in my holster was loaded. The sergeant saw my movement. "Never had much use for them before sir. Do you like them?"

"Like? No. Use? Yes. The trouble is once you have fired they are useless although they do make a nice club!"

He laughed. "I'll bear that in mind."

General Bonaparte turned around and smiled, "It seems you two are as calm about this as I am. My officers fear we will all be killed by these rioters."

I felt he wished a comment and I gave him one. "They are not soldiers and will not stand up to discipline sir."

"Quite right. Just like in Paris eh?"

Before we could reply we saw a mob appear at the Boulaq gate. Without drawing his sword, he shouted, "Charge!"

We rode at them. My injured hand prevented me from drawing my weapon and so I just gripped the reins and roared. Killer was next to the general in a couple of strides and he was flanked by me and Colonel Bessières. They both looked exultant. I sensed the sergeant's mount coming next to mine and felt happier; he was a good soldier. The mob had never seen charging horses and they just fled before us. Even though they outnumbered us they still ran. Once we were through the gate the general reined in. "Bring the guns forwards!"

The horse artillery galloped through the gate and quickly unlimbered. The general was an artilleryman and he knew his business. "Grapeshot. Keep blasting until they flee I want them driven into the centre of the city."

I almost felt sorry for the rioters but the dismembered bodies of the French soldiers hardened my heart. It took just two rounds to disperse them. Bonaparte did not halt. He was relentless. We charged again until they all took shelter and refuge in the Great Mosque. I wondered what he would do at this point. It was their equivalent of a cathedral. General Bonaparte was the most ruthless general I have ever known and he ordered all his artillery to fire. I could not see the effect as ball after ball crashed into the old building but it must have been terrifying. The sky turned black and a great thunderstorm began. With the cannons firing and the thunder and lightning, it was like a scene from hell. It was no surprise that they surrendered within a very short time.

Bonaparte was deliriously happy. He turned to the sergeant and myself; we had remained at his side throughout the engagement. "Thank you, gentlemen. That was like the old days in Italy! Tomorrow I will punish the leaders and then we can leave for Alexandria!"

The day we left I went for my Killer myself. I received many strange looks from the troopers sent to collect the mounts for the other officers. I could not understand how an officer could let someone do that for him. For me, it was a pleasure to saddle Killer and it helped to reinforce the bond we shared. The result was that I reached the general and his carriage first.

I rode to the prison where the wagon was waiting. Sergeant Delacroix was there with the ten troopers who would act as escort. As I rose up he turned to the trooper next to him. "Right Trooper Royan, go and fetch the prisoners. The rest of you, be on your guard until the officer has told them what will happen to them."

As the prisoners shuffled slowly out they all held their hands up to the skies to shield their eyes from the bright winter sun. Trooper Royan nodded as the last man was brought up. It was the man I had hit and the side of his head showed an angry bruise.

I began to speak with them. "Sailors of the Royal Navy. General Bonaparte has agreed to set you free." I saw the surprise on their faces. The sullen sailor still scowled and I suspected he distrusted me and my words. "We will take you to Alexandria and put you on a ship to take you to a port which will get you home."

Jamie shouted, "Thank you, sir." The sullen sailor spat on the ground. I smiled as Sergeant Delacroix smacked him on the back of the head. "Of course, until we reach the port you will still be prisoners and be guarded so…" I looked at the spitter, "I would behave until you are aboard the ship."

He looked up at me defiantly, "I am not afraid of you. Traitor."

I shook my head, "You are a sad specimen. I have never set foot in England and I was born in France. Am I a traitor because I speak English better than you? Tie this man's hands and get them in the wagon."

The sergeant and I rode ahead of the wagon as we headed north to the port. I had to admit that the troopers of Bonaparte's Guards were both smart and well trained. The sergeant barely had to issue an order on that journey. We headed straight for the harbour. "Sergeant, watch the prisoners and I will try to arrange passage for the men."

I was looking for a ship which had the flag of a non-combatant. I walked along the quayside but saw none. Then I had a stroke of good fortune, I saw the 'Carillon'. François was on the deck.

"Ah captain what brings you here?"

"I need a favour."

I went aboard and explained what we needed. I expected a refusal but he grinned. "Excellent. I have been asked to sail and scout out Naples and Leghorn. This gives me the opportunity to enter the harbour legitimately and land the prisoners. They might even thank me and I can work out how we can capture it. Bring them on board."

It is strange the way that fate works. I think that some of the prisoners still thought that there would be some sort of trick until they finally stepped on to the gangplank. The prisoner who had tried to hit me was last and he held out his hands for us to sever the ropes. I laughed and shouted to Francois. "I tied this one's hands as he is a little violent. It is up to you what you do with him. The others seem like good fellows."

The lieutenant waved, "Do not worry; my men know how to deal with officers such as him."

For my pains, I received a look of pure hate as he was taken on board.

"Now sergeant let us rejoin the squadron and find out what we are about."

The general had taken over the old governor's palace in Alexandria and that meant that we had comfortable quarters to stay in. We used the Janissary barracks where the best of the Ottoman soldiers had been housed. We rode directly to the stables. Sergeant Delacroix said nothing as I took off Killer's saddle and rubbed him down. I always had something special for him as a treat and I had acquired a couple of apples from the 'Carillon' when I had visited the lieutenant. Killer nuzzled me as I fed her and I turned to leave.

"You began life as a trooper did you not sir?"

I laughed, "Yes. Does it show?"

"What does show is that you are a cavalryman through and through." He pointed to Killer. "That mount will die for you and carry you when others falter. I can see the bond." We turned to walk out of the stables. "I had heard of you and I did not know what to expect, sir."

I was curious, "What had you heard?" He hesitated, "You can speak freely sergeant I am not precious about my position."

"I had heard that you were a death or glory merchant, sir." He gave me an apologetic shrug. "I can see that I was wrong but you were spoken of as one of the general's killers. I am sorry for misjudging you. I should have known better. Old Albert Aristide is a good judge of character and he would not have promoted one so young if you had been reckless."

"You know the colonel then?"

"Yes. sir. I served, briefly in the 17th and then left to join the 15th for promotion."

"How did you end up here then?"

He looked at the ground and then around him as though he did not want eavesdroppers to hear his words. "I had a disagreement with the adjutant when he sent a troop to their death by giving a poor order." He shrugged, "The colonel liked me and recommended me to Colonel Bessières. He is a good man."

"He is. sergeant. Thank you for the confidence and it will stay that way."

"I never doubted it, sir. I can hear in your voice that you are an officer with integrity." We were at the entrance to the barracks. "A word to the wise sir, not all the officers in the squadron are like Colonel Bessières."

I smiled, "Thank you, sergeant. I appreciate the warning."

When I entered the officers' quarters there was a corporal seated at a desk. He looked up as I approached. "You must be Captain Macgregor. Your room is at the end of the corridor on the next floor, sir. Your name is on the door and your chest is in there." I must have shown surprise for he said, "It arrived this afternoon sir. The evening meal begins in an hour, sir." He pointed to his right. The mess is in that direction sir."

I reached my room and opened my chest. I only had the one uniform and it was dirty. I knew that I would be judged on my appearance. I took the uniform off and knocked as much dust and dirt off as I could manage. I took off my shirt and filled the basin with water. It was cold but it refreshed me when I washed. I then took a face cloth I had in my chest and used the water to clean as many of the stains from the uniform as I could. I then cleaned the boots with the cloth which looked filthy when I had finished but at least I looked a little better. I put a clean shirt on and then dressed. I used the oil Pierre had brought me from Paris, all those years ago and oiled my moustache. I was then ready for the ordeal that would be the dinner.

Chapter 6

There was just a squadron of the general's guards at that time which meant a smaller number of officers. Even so, I could hear the hubbub of noise from the mess as I approached. When I entered the room I could see that there were ten officers, including the colonel and the adjutant. As I stepped through the door silence descended on the room and I wondered if there was something amiss with my dress. I had been quite careful that I was dressed appropriately.

Bessières gestured me over. As I began to walk to the empty place he had kept for me I heard a voice say in a haughty manner, "I see the stable boy has finally made it!"

The younger officers all laughed but Colonel Bessières, snapped, "That will be quite enough, Captain Hougon."

I stared at the man who had spoken. He was older than I was and he had a duelling scar running down his cheek. When Charles had been wounded in Italy he had boasted that his wound would look like a scar of honour but this one really was. He obviously disliked me for some reason. I had no idea why for I had never met him. Then I remembered Sergeant Delacroix; perhaps it was my reputation he disliked.

"This is Major Armandiere, the adjutant. You have already met one of the captains, the rude and ungracious Captain Hougon. The other is seated next to the major, Captain Tenoir. Then we have the lieutenants Dubois, Sagan and Lettoir. Finally, we have the three sous lieutenants Callas, Besoire and Gallas." He smiled, "You will forget their names I know but at least we have been introduced. "Gentlemen, for the next month we have Captain Robert Macgregor on detachment from the 17th Chasseurs. I hope you will make him welcome." He shot a pointed look at Captain Hougon. "I know that the general thinks highly of him. Some of you younger officers would do well to ask this modest young man about some of the missions he has undertaken for the general. They belie his years."

I wished that the colonel, well-meaning though he was, would not have built me up so much. Looking at the two captains, who whispered to each other like coquettish young women, I suspected that they would take great delight in making fun of me.

I found the adjutant a really pleasant man. He had been the colonel of the 18th Chasseurs and when they had been disbanded he had been unemployed until the guards were formed. He regarded this as a chance to do something useful for France.

"I remember old Colonel Armande. Our young officers used to take great delight in the similarities of our names and the fact that the numbers of our regiments were so similar." He smiled fondly at the memory. "I was sad to hear he died. Soldiers should never grow old. A good cavalryman dies with his boots on." He lowered his voice, "The two captains are good soldiers but both are a little arrogant. They have seen little combat as yet." He looked at me seriously, "I pray you to be patient with them. They may make good officers." I must have shown my feelings in my face. "Do not be modest Captain Macgregor, I have read the reports of your exploits. You are a killer and I am just pleased that you are a killer for France."

I was able to enjoy the rest of the meal and the conversation with the major and the colonel. However, when I saw the looks on the faces of the two captains, I could see the resentment written all over them. I had done nothing wrong and yet I had made two enemies. It was not a good start to my secondment in the Guards.

As I made my way back to my room I realised that I missed my old comrades. Pierre was many miles away in France but both Jean and Tiny might as well have been. I looked ruefully at my wounded hand. The colonel had been right. I had been reckless and had I not been so I might still be with them and not here. I was so engrossed in my thoughts that I did not hear the two captains approaching me from behind. The first I knew was when Captain Hougon sneered, "I hope you do not find your quarters too comfortable. You must be used to sleeping in a stable, stable boy."

I turned and with my left hand grabbed a handful of tunic. I thrust my head as close to his as I could manage. "Have a care captain. I know not why you insult me but I do not take insults well."

I am a powerful man and Captain Hougon could not break free. I also saw fear in his face. "It is a good job you have an injured arm or I would call you out! Not that you would understand that."

I laughed and pushed him into Captain Tenoir. The two of them almost fell over. "I could take you with my left hand so do not use that as an excuse."

They both had anger in their red, wine flushed faces, "Unlike you, I am a gentleman and I will wait."

"You will excuse me if I do not hold my breath captain." I went into my room. I now had another reason to heal.

Thankfully the squadron and the general it protected were on the move the following day. I wondered what my role would be. There were just two troops and each was commanded by one of the captains. I decided I would just present myself and await orders.

Sergeant Delacroix was in the stables when I arrived. "Morning sir!"

"Morning sergeant. Any idea where we are off to today?"

He tapped his nose. "If I was a betting man I would say east." I nodded and began to saddle Killer. "He is a fine animal sir. I hear he is called Killer."

"It was a joke amongst the men as no-one could ride him but he suits me."

"I agree, sir. Find the right horse and this job is quite easy." He frowned at some of the men who appeared to be struggling to control their horses. "The trouble is a lot of these lads joined because of the uniform, not because they liked horses."

I saw a few of the troopers I had known in the 17th. "I thought that you had to be invited to join this squadron? Isn't that why they wear the elite uniform?"

He lowered his voice. "Between you and I sir that is supposed to be the case but some of the officers and troopers have political influence. Still when we go into action then we will see." He suddenly noticed my sword. "That isn't standard issue is it sir?"

"No," I took it from its scabbard and gave it to him. "I took it from an Austrian officer I killed."

"This is a fine weapon. It is little longer and straighter than ours."

"Yes, sergeant. The one I was issued broke in combat. This one will not. I also have a Mameluke scimitar I took. That is also a fine weapon. I left that with my lieutenant."

"That is something else that marks you as different sir. You have killed, and it shows."

We rode from the stables and I saw the ten troopers leading the officers' horses. When the officers mounted I noticed that they almost ignored the horse they were riding. None of them greeted the horse or showed any affection towards the animal they would have to rely on in battle. That was a mistake in my view. The horse was just as much a weapon as their sword or their pistol. As we waited for the general to appear I tried to flex my fingers. The wound did not ache any longer but the fingers were stiff. I resolved to exercise the hand without putting pressure on it. The last thing I needed was to have a weaker right hand.

Colonel Bessières rode over to us with the major. "We will be riding just behind the general. He has some questions for you and he needs you to be close."

"Where are we going, sir?"

"General Murat is camped close to Suez and I believe we are going to journey to Arabia."

We rode into General Joachim Murat's camp. His tent was obvious as soon as we rode in and I hid my smile. It was adorned with flags and looked like the quarters of an Eastern Potentate. The general's ego was like the sun; it just grew and grew. He embraced General Bonaparte as though he had not seen him for years. The colonel entered the tent and the major stayed outside with me.

"Have you served with General Murat, captain?"

"No, sir. I was on detachment when the regiment was brigaded under him."

He lowered his voice. "He is quite brilliant but unpredictable. I am hoping that the general can manage him."

When Colonel Bessières came out, alone, it was to inform us that we would be camping with the cavalry for the night. He also told us that there would some civilians from Paris; scientists, engineers and historians and they would be travelling with us as well. The resourceful Sergeant Delacroix had already picked out a suitable campsite which was upwind of the horse lines. He set the troopers to erecting the tents and to prepare the food. I stayed close to the major. This was not because I was afraid of confrontation with the two captains but I preferred the company of the major and I did not think any good would come from such a confrontation.

The major and I wandered over to the dunes to look out on the Mediterranean. It was cooler and there were fewer flies. "You would prefer to be with the 17th wouldn't you captain?"

I nodded, "Yes, does it show?"

"A little. I know that the two captains are unpleasant but, for me, I appreciate having an experienced officer. Last week when you charged boot to boot with the general and with an injured arm I could see that you were a born cavalryman. We need that in the squadron. This could be the finest cavalry unit in the French army but it needs people like you and

Sergeant Delacroix," he shrugged, "and, I dare say, people like me. Do not desert us too soon eh?"

The squadron was ready to move before the civilians arrived in their ponderous wagons. The general cast an impatient look at them. He turned to an aide who scurried off and then he announced, "Gentlemen the path we take has few roads. You shall ride, as I do, camels. They are the ships of the desert and we shall sail a course to the Red Sea."

Such was the general's reputation and power that none could gainsay him and when the spitting and snorting animals were brought we watched with amusement as the civilians were manhandled aboard their new vessels. Killer did not seem to mind the flatulent creatures as much as the other horses and I was able to be quite close as the enormous beasts rose into the air. It must have been alarming for the rider as first one end pitched them forwards and, as the animal stood, the other end threw them backwards. As they moved off I could see the metaphor. The action of the camel was a swaying one like a ship in a sea swell. One thing was certain; we would not be slowed up by the men from Paris.

One troop ranged far ahead of the small column. There were but three hundred of us to guard the general and his party. Although there were French soldiers ahead of us, there was no continuous line of defences. As we had discovered to our cost the enemy could easily slip through this treacherous land and ambush you from nowhere. I had made sure that both of my pistols were loaded.

After three days we reached Suez where the civilians began their work. The general had heard a rumour of a canal which once connected the Red Sea to the Mediterranean and he was anxious to see if this was possible. After a few hours of watching them painstakingly study the ground, dig a little and then discuss matters he grew impatient. He gestured to the colonel and the ten of us who had stayed close to the works. "You ten, come with me. Let us do some soldiering."

We rode to the small garrison at Suez. The soldiers there had the look of men who are aware that they were on a frontier and they were vigilant. The little general dismounted and took us with him as he marched around the town and its environs. I was amused when he sent troopers into the desert to march towards us. I knew why he did that, he wished to view a potential enemy, but the troopers were bemused. It did not take him long to make the town defensible and then he became bored with the visit to Suez. I saw him looking longingly to the east.

As we rode back to the diggings he rode with Bessières just ahead of me and I heard his words. "You know that Alexander the Great stood here and looked to the east. He conquered as far as India. Quite an achievement eh?"

The colonel nodded his agreement, "That was many years ago though general."

"Yes but we now have the finest army the world has ever seen. How much more likely that we could do more than even he did. Perhaps we could even reach China."

As we rode I pondered his words. The French soldiers I had seen in the Low Countries in the early days of the war had been raw and ill-disciplined. They were now better but, as far as I could see, the opposition we had defeated was poor. How would we fare against a well-drilled and disciplined army?

We left some of the civilians working on the canal with some of the local garrison as guards. The general was anxious to cross into Arabia and see the famed fountains of Moses. I think he was desperate to emulate his hero, Alexander. We crossed the Red Sea at low tide and the general joked, "See, we have parted the seas, much as Moses did!"

He was in good spirits. He had not been defeated and he had subjugated this land very easily. I could understand his elation but the further we went into the oven that was Arabia the less confident I became. Sergeant Delacroix caught me flicking my head from side to side as we rode.

"What are you looking for sir? There cannot be anyone out here. I don't even know why we are out here."

"There are Ottomans out there sergeant." I held up my bandaged hand. "This is evidence of that. They live here and they understand the desert. They do not wear wool but linen cloaks which are cooler. They are watching us and I do not think for one moment that our scouts would spot them. This is their land and they understand it. They are part of the land whereas we are intruders."

I could see that I had alarmed him and he too began to scan the horizon for the enemy who waited and watched. When the scouts returned minus one of their number my fears were confirmed. His head was lobbed into the camp that night and few of the troopers enjoyed a good night's rest as they feared the knife in the night.

I suggested to the major that we use double guards at night and, although it meant less sleep, we were all happier. The disturbing part was that the general seemed indifferent to the loss of the trooper. He just wanted to see the fountains of Moses. Although they were impressive I thought the journey a waste of time. They had not been worth the loss of the single trooper who had died. The general, however, was satisfied and we headed west once more.

All of us were glad when we set off back to the Read Sea and Suez. The general confidently rode towards the crossing we had used. As we stepped into the sea I was worried by the fact that the water appeared to come up higher on our horses than when we had set off. The general was on a camel and did not seem to notice. As we were at the halfway point the water rose alarmingly, Killer was a good swimmer but I could see that some of the younger troopers were beginning to panic. Even Bonaparte and his scientists showed concern. Sergeant Delacroix shouted to the troopers. "Keep your horses swimming towards the western bank; do not let them turn back! They can swim."

It was then that Captain Hougon slipped from his horse. I do not know if he was trying to keep his boots dry or if he panicked but, whatever the reason, he fell into the sea and his horse fled without him to the safety of the other shore. I saw the captain's head dip beneath the waves. I jerked Killer around and swam the horse towards him. The captain was flailing around in a desperate attempt to stop himself from going under but he only succeeded in tiring himself out. I was forced to hold the reins of Killer in my injured hand and then grab hold of the back of his jacket. As soon as I had hold I turned Killer around and we headed for the shore. He was still struggling. "Keep still or you will drown us both!" I am not sure he heard me but he suddenly went limp, for which I was grateful. I felt relief as Killer's hooves struck the bottom and then the sergeant and the major helped to drag the unconscious officer ashore.

I leaned forward to stroke Killer's mane. "Well done boy!"

The captain was turned on to his front and he began to cough and splutter. I noticed that none of his friends had bothered to come to his aid. "Well done captain. That was bravely done." The major nodded up at me.

"I had little time to think sir, I just reacted."

"And a good job too. This officer would have died otherwise. I trust he will be suitably grateful."

When he came to and glared at me I knew that he would not. He struggled to his feet and stormed off to his horse. He mounted it and then dug his spurs into its side whilst beating the animal with the scabbard of his sword. Sergeant Delacroix just shook his head. "It is no wonder the beast dumped him in the water. He has not made a friend of that animal that is for sure."

The general had not even noticed the accident and was already heading towards Suez. I shrugged and we followed. "I can never understand mistreating horses, sergeant, but then I was brought up caring for them and not abusing them."

When we entered the town we heard the mullah calling the faithful to prayer. General Bonaparte seemed oblivious to it all. Perhaps he was still thinking of the fountains of Moses. He halted, quite close to the mosque and turned to speak with Colonel Bessières. I kept Killer moving as there was a press of people suddenly I saw an open blade appear from beneath the voluminous cloak of a man waiting to go into the mosque. I was already drawing my pistol as he launched himself at the general. Even Bessières was transfixed. Everything seemed to move slowly as the scimitar arced towards General Bonaparte. The Turk shouted something and I pulled the trigger. He was less than six feet from me and his head exploded and the scimitar crashed to the ground. Another three swords appeared from beneath the cloaks of some of the faithful but the rest of the squadron had drawn weapons and Sergeant Delacroix shouted, "Fire!" The ten people closest to the general fell dead. I drew my sword and forced Killer between the general and the crowd. Bessières and the major joined me. The sight of two hundred guns being levelled at the crowd had the desired effect and they edged away and allowed us to make the safety of the fort.

General Bonaparte was white. It was the first time I had ever seen him shaken. He turned to his interpreter who was also shaking with fear. "What did that man say?"

"He shouted, 'death to the destroyer of Islam!'"

The general seemed bemused, "Why?"

"I believe it is because of the mosque in Cairo when you destroyed its walls. They are not happy about the sacrilege."

He shrugged, "Then they should not revolt should they?" He turned to me. "Once again, I am in your debt captain, thank you." That was as much as he ever said. Then he turned and rode off towards his quarters. He was never disturbed for long.

Our trip was broken by the news that a Turkish army had left Syria and was on the coast at El Arish less than a day's ride from Alexandria.

We rode hard to reach the army. The general deserted the scientists and sent messengers to bring the army from Cairo.

"Well sir, this might be just the experience these lads need."

"Will the general risk his guards, sergeant?"

The major had been listening to us and he nodded. "I think so, captain. We need to eliminate all opposition. The general has been waiting for this."

I had misjudged the general. I thought he had thought we had already won and was enjoying the fruits of his victory. As he rode hard through the scrubby barren land I saw that his mind was like a razor and he had been just giving the illusion of torpor.

We returned to the camp of General Murat where there were, already artillery and infantry gathered. The scouts who had seen the approach of the three armies had then been sent by General Murat to bring reinforcements. I looked at my injured hand. Would I be part of this or be forced to be an onlooker? I was not good at watching.

Colonel Bessières was delighted to be given command of a division for the battle. He gathered his officers, and me, around him in the mess tent. "This is a great day for the squadron gentlemen. We will no longer be merely bodyguards but we will be attacking the enemy." For once everyone, including the two sulky captains, was delirious with excitement. "We have been assigned six horse artillery pieces. Captain Macgregor will also be delighted to learn that we are to be brigaded with his old regiment, the 17th."

I smiled but inside I was perturbed. Although I was pleased to be with my former regiment again I did not like the comment 'old regiment.' It implied I was now in a new regiment. I decided to wait until things were a little quieter before I said anything. I did not wish to give Captain Hougon any more ammunition.

"Our job will be to see that the Turks do not reinforce El Arish. The general is busy organising siege guns so tomorrow we will leave the camp and head east where we can be in a better position to thwart the enemy."

The rest of the evening was spent in the logistics of movement which were of little concern to me as I was almost a supernumerary. However, once the rest had departed I asked the colonel what his comment meant.

"It is nothing bad, Robbie. The general has another task for you but you will not need to undertake it until after we have finally subjugated this land. He was reluctant to allow you to be part of this action; he wished that you be close to him but I persuaded him that you would be needed in this battle. I knew that you would not wish to cool your heels at headquarters. I promise you that you will be returning to the 17th. You have my word on that."

Despite my initial impressions of the colonel I had come to learn that he was a man of his word and I trusted him. Although things did not work out as I might have wished the colonel kept his word.

Three days later and we were to the east of El Arish in Syrian territory. We waited for the 17th to arrive. I saw a cloud of dust to the south and one of the troopers reported that it was the 17th. When they halted next to us I was disappointed to see that they had only brought half of the regiment.

Colonel Aristide, who looked a little drawn, and Jean rode up to us. "Sir, we have brought the 17th as ordered."

Even Bessières looked surprised, "Where are the rest?"

"I am afraid they have been laid low by disease sir. Forty troopers have died and the rest have been sent to the hospital. This squadron is all that remains of the regiment."

I saw the haunted look on Jean's face and knew that there was a story here. "Well, Colonel, even a squadron of your troopers are worth a regiment of many others. Welcome. Your men can take the place of honour on the right. We have scouts patrolling and we hope for action soon!"

As things turned out, no enemies were sighted and we camped for the night. I took the opportunity of joining my old comrades. Jean was pleased to see me but he checked my hand to make sure that it was still healing. "Good. I was worried that you would be using it."

"Never mind my hand. What happened, sir?"

"It is as the colonel said we lost men to the Turks but we had an outbreak of the pestilence and it took many men. Captain Alain and Sergeant Chagal both succumbed to it and they died." I was lost for words. Claude and Charles were gone. With Pierre back in France my old comrades were becoming fewer. "The sick should now have a better chance of recovery. They are aboard the L'Italie on the Nile. They have good doctors and it is cleaner on the ship than it would be in Cairo believe me."

Tiny joined us and I saw how thin he had become. "The lieutenant here had the disease but he recovered. It was as well that you were away for with your wound you might have been at a greater risk."

"We will be in action soon anyway. We are here to stop the enemy reinforcing the fort."

"Are you not rejoining us, sir?"

"I am sorry lieutenant. As much as I wish that the general still has tasks for me to complete. However, I will be with you for this campaign."

It was the scouts from the 17th who found the Mamelukes under the command of General Iphrahim. Colonel Bessières heaped praise on Sergeant Manet who brought the news. "Excellent! As ever the 17th does not let us down." A messenger was sent to General Murat and his division of cavalry. This would be a cavalry battle!

We lined up in two lines on the foothills overlooking the road. The 17th were to the right of our squadron. Our six cannons were above us and would be able to fire over our heads at the enemy. When Bessières explained his plan to Albert I was pleased to see him nod his agreement. This would be no disaster; not with two such heads in charge. And then General Murat galloped up with his nine hundred strong division of horse. He placed himself on our left. I was with the two colonels when the general explained his plan. "I will charge at them and then you will sweep around their rear and envelop them." I could see that neither colonel was happy but at least our squadrons would be together.

The approaching dust cloud told is of the arrival of the enemy. There were many more of them than us. Because they did not fight or even travel in neat lines numbers were hard to estimate but I knew that it would be a hard-fought fight. I had acquired some gloves and I decided to risk my sword. I could not charge with just a pistol for defence. I knew that if Jean discovered what I was about he would try to stop me and so I kept my sword sheathed.

The twelve cannons we had begun to pound the enemy. The dust and the smoke made it hard to estimate how many were killed but so long as it weakened them it would suit us. I heard Murat's bugles sound and then the ground shook as his horsemen galloped towards the Mameluke army. When we heard the clash of metal on metal we knew that battle had been joined. Then we heard the bugle which signalled our movement. I rode just behind the major and next to Sergeant Delacroix. Killer took some controlling as he fought me to get to the front. It was always that way with him. We were travelling blind because of the dust but we heard the clash of arms from our left. Colonel Bessières waved his sword and we began to turn to our left. The timing of the charge would be a test of the skill of the two colonels. We began to trot and I heard the noise grow. Suddenly the bugle sounded the charge and I drew my sword. Although it was painful to grip the hilt, it was not impossible and I determined to try. Even before the last notes had died away we saw the rear of the Mameluke army. The two squadrons gave a roar and we crashed into the rear of their horses.

I leaned forward, eager to find someone to strike but the troopers before me cleared the way. I wondered if I would get to use my sword at all when the trooper next to the major fell in a bloody heap. I saw a scimitar flashing at me and I raised my own blade to parry the blow. My whole arm juddered and I felt a rush of pain in my hand. Killer's head came round; he was always an aggressive horse. The Mameluke's horse also had a fiery temper and he turned to try to bite Killer. The result was that the Mameluke turned slightly to bring his scimitar to bear and it was his left side which faced me. I slashed down with the sword and saw it rip his arm open from the shoulder to the wrist. The horsemen fell from his mount and Sergeant Delacroix's horse trampled him. My hand was hurting me and so I sheathed my sword. I had been lucky and there was little point in pushing my luck. I held the reins in my left hand and drew a pistol.

All semblance of order had now gone. It was a series of individual combats. Suddenly I saw two Mamelukes attacking the major. I urged Killer on and fired at one of the men who fell from his horse. The major despatched the second. I took out my second pistol to look for another target but there was none. The enemy before us was dead and I saw the dragoons from General Murat's division sabring the last of the Mamelukes.

As recall sounded, I peered through the dust to see which of my comrades had survived. I was delighted to see the colonel, the major and Tiny all lined up with the squadron but I could see that the numbers were depleted. The Guards had also suffered but it appeared as though they had fared slightly better. It was inevitable. The 17th had fought since the day we had landed while the Guards had not. The pestilence had taken its toll too.

General Murat was fulsome in his praise of our charge. "Your two squadrons fought like two regiments today. None of the Mamelukes escaped. You have done well!"

We had done well for the garrison capitulated when the relief force failed to arrive. The seven hundred and fifty Albanians who surrendered were all conscripted into our army. The loss of the fleet meant that we could no longer be sent any reinforcements. But we had no time to rest on our laurels. Having defeated two armies the general was determined to take Jaffa and Acre. I think he actually had designs on Constantinople!

Chapter 7

The greatest advantage of being a Guard was that we travelled with the van and did not have to suffer the dust as the army snaked its way towards Jaffa. This was to be another siege which meant we would be protecting the general once again. The port was quickly surrounded and trenches dug. The general's tents were erected close to the sea and the sea breezes were quite pleasant. I was taking advantage of a stroll in the evening as the mess was still an unpleasant place for me when I almost bumped into the general who was also walking.

"Ah, my Scotsman. I have not thanked you properly for saving me in Suez. You are quick thinking. I will find a way to reward you."

I took a breath, "You could reward me general by allowing me to return to my regiment."

Instead of the anger I expected, he laughed. "Still trying to get away from me eh? I promise you that I will let you return but I have another task for you. I cannot tell you yet as events have not fallen the way I wish them to. Suffice it to say that one way or another you will return to your regiment when we have captured Acre."

I knew that Acre was the most important city in Syria. If we controlled that city then the road to the heart of the Ottoman Empire was open.

"Thank you general."

He waved a dismissive hand and then that seemed to trigger an idea in his head. "Come with me, we will see my doctor."

The general had his own physician, although why I have no idea for he was never ill. I followed him. Doctor Etienne-Louise Malus was a strange little man but a brilliant doctor. In the aftermath of the siege of Jaffa, it was thanks to him that so many men survived who would otherwise have died.

"Ah doctor, would you be so good as to examine this officer's wound. He suffered it some time ago and I suspect he has not had the bandaged changed in all that time." He was of course correct.

"Come with me, young man."

As I left the general said, "After Acre, Scotsman, and you will be free."

He took me to his tent. He put a kettle of water on the fire to boil it and then cut through the bandages. The wound was red and angry but there did not appear to be a foul smell. He shook his head. "Sit there." He pointed to a seat. He sniffed the bandages. "Have you immersed this in the sea?"

I was going to say no and then I remembered the rescue of the captain. "Yes, sir."

"Good, then you might have saved your hand. The saltwater has cleansed the wound but I am not happy with the colour. I think it is infected. I will soon discover if that is so." He briefly left the tent and then returned. The water had boiled and he poured some in a shallow bowl. He rolled up his sleeves and then poured some more of the water into a deeper bowl and added some cooler water. He washed his hands. "Always have clean hands when dealing with a wound young man." He then dropped a pair of scissors into the bowl of boiling water.

Once he was satisfied with his hands he took some forceps and removed the scissors. He carefully cut the stitches and then, with the forceps, threw them into the fire. He took a clean cloth and dipped into the boiling water and began to clean the wound. Although it hurt I did not make a sound. The count, my father, had taught me never to show that you were hurting. Once he had done that he nodded. He was, apparently, satisfied. "Good. You are a brave young man, I would have yelled for all I was worth if it had been my hand." An orderly came into the tent. "Ah good, Richard, just place them here." He held out a clean bowl and the orderly deposited into it a handful of squirming maggots. He gave me an evil grin as he stood and watched. "Now wash your hands Richard and prepare a bandage for me."

To my horror, the doctor then took the maggots and placed them around the red and angry wound. I tried to recoil but the doctor was remarkably strong. "This will not hurt so trust me!" His voice was kind and I let him finish putting them in. They wriggled and they squirmed. It was not a pleasant experience. Then he and Richard wrapped and tied the bandage tightly around the wound. "The maggots will eat the dead flesh and then they will die. When the arm itches then return to me and I will remove them. Now off you go."

The next days and weeks were desperate. The battle for Jaffa was a brutal affair. The cannons pounded the walls and when the infantry assaulted they were ruthless. However, none of us were prepared for the next few days when the general had every single one of the prisoners, all two thousand five hundred of them, executed. He even sent to Cairo for an executioner. I still do not know why he did so. It backfired on him, especially when he assaulted Acre but the general did have a ruthless streak in him. At the same time, bubonic plague broke out. The army did not know it was the plague, this was kept from them but, as I returned to the hospital to see the doctor I was privy to that knowledge. I went with the general who wanted to see his sick soldiers. It was, probably, the bravest thing I think he ever did but it was pitiful to see brave soldiers suffering. What made it worse for me was that I saw that many of the sick were from the 17th and they were dying. The stench of death hung over the hospital like a cloud.

Although the doctor was busy he found time to see me. He said, "The hand, has it been itchy?"

"Yes sir, last night and today."

"Good then watch when I remove the bandage." As he cut the cloth away the dead creatures fell to the floor. What had been red and angry was now slightly pink and healing. "You will be able to use it normally in a day or two. Either wash it in the sea or pour brandy on it for a few days. It will keep it clean. Now you will excuse me I have some brave men to minister to." He was a noble doctor and I was pleased to hear that he survived the plague- my comrades did not.

We headed north to Acre. As soon as I saw the city which was attached to the land by a tiny strip of soil I knew that this would not be easy. We could not get close with our trenches and the siege guns struggled to punch holes in the walls. The plague and the battles had decimated the regiments. The 17th was down to less than a hundred and fifty and that included the forty who were still recovering on L'Italie. The only bright spot was the fact that we were at Acre which meant I would soon find out what I had to do for the general and then I would be able to return to the 17th. What worried me was that there might not be a regiment to return to the way things were going.

Jean and the remains of the regiment were in a camp some miles from the siege lines. This was partly because of space and partly to give the army protection from uprisings. The destruction of the mosque had made the Egyptians unhappy about French rule. They might not have liked the Ottoman Empire but they hated their churches being desecrated. The 17th were patrolling the land between the Nile and Jerusalem. I only got to see them when they arrived at the general's headquarters to report on their work. The general liked to know everything that was going on.

It was on one of their visits during the first week in April that we heard about the massacre on the Nile. The hospital cruiser, L'Italie, had been attacked and all five hundred men on board had been massacred.

Another forty of my comrades were dead. Most of my first troop had died. The only one who now remained was Tiny. I felt as sad as I had when my mother had died. The three of us reminisced about the brave men we had fought alongside and who were now dead. To die in battle was one thing but to be massacred in your bed was entirely different. The general's ambitions were hurting the army and, as far as I could see, to no good effect.

Jean shook his head as we talked of the disaster. "I am just glad that Pierre is out of this."

"He thought that the wound was the worst thing that could have happened to him but we now know that it was the best." I lowered my voice; the general had banned any mention of the plague. The men who were now dying in their hundreds had died of many diseases. "I have seen this plague that men die of and it is a horrible way to die. It is far better to be killed in battle. It is over much quicker."

Albert had not known of the disease, "It is the plague then?"

"It is sir, and I have been in the hospital and seen the deaths."

Jean gave me a concerned look. "Was it safe for you to do so?"

"I had to have my wound seen to but I think so. I feel no ill effects."

"If the wound is healed then can you return to the regiment?"

"I am sorry sir. The general has another task for me and then I can."

All three of us were reluctant to leave and so we sat in silence and watched the sun set over the Mediterranean and then darkness enfold the water. I walked alone to my tent. I had few duties as a Guard of Bonaparte but I would have traded that for a night as a vedette with the 17th.

We moved out of the camp when the general decided to try to draw some of the Ottoman forces to the north of us to battle. We headed for the Holy Land. The general tried to appeal to the local population as the one who would save them from Islam. I do not think he convinced them. Colonel Bessières had been promoted to general now and we had the 15th Chasseurs as well as the 17th brigaded with us. I did not think that Bonaparte would find much use for cavalry in the hilly land around Mount Tabor but I was wrong.

The Ottomans had many horsemen. While their infantry came from the Balkans and Greece their horsemen came from the desert plains to the east. This was the land of Persia and the major explained to me that their horsemen had destroyed vast Roman armies in times past. "They are wild warriors and ill-disciplined but they are not to be underestimated." He was right to warn us.

The brigadier commanding the leading battalions found that to his cost. Whilst marching in column a huge host of Mamelukes and mounted fellahin charged them. The rocky and uneven terrain, aggravated by a lack of discipline meant that they did not form square in time. Many of the soldiers were cut to pieces before they could even get a shot off.

General Bonaparte was not happy and so our brigade was sent to be the advanced guard. Now that my sword hand had healed I was no longer a supernumerary and I could fight. I was still acting as General Bessières' aide but, as I knew from his days in the 17th he liked to lead from the front. Sergeant Delacroix and I rode just behind him and the bugler. There were ten scouts out ahead of us but that means nothing. The twisting roads and the rocky defiles meant that you could be attacked even with scouts out.

We were surprised by the enemy when they charged the middle of our brigade between the 17th and the last troop of our squadron. They charged in and hacked at the troopers before riding back up the defile. All would have been well had not Captain Hougon charged into the defile with his troop behind him.

General Bessières cursed. "The damned fool. Sound recall!"

The bugler blew recall but nothing happened. He turned to me. "Ride to the 17th and take a troop of them to find out what has happened to the idiot."

I reined in next to the colonel and gave him the orders. He nodded. "The young man struck me as an arrogant and reckless officer. Major, take the First Troop and try to extricate them."

I did not ask permission to join them I just drew my sword and rode next to Jean who gave me a smile. "Good to have you back Robbie!"

We could hear the clamour of battle as we entered the defile. The troopers were surrounded and fighting desperately for their lives. They could not retreat as the enemy were to their rear. Jean took it all in and then shouted, "Column of ten!" The narrow pass was just wide enough to enable that formation and it would allow us to hit them with a mass of superior and heavier horseflesh.

I leaned forwards as Jean shouted, "Bugler, sound the charge!" The strident notes alerted the enemy but they also told the beleaguered troopers that help was at hand. The Arab irregulars we hit had poor swords and no protection. Our front rank smashed and dispersed them as though they were not even there.

I could see the green and red of the guards. "Guards to me!" Some of the heads turned and they began to hack and slash at the attackers who were between us. We gradually whittled down their numbers until we joined with the rearguard.

"Bugler sound recall!" This time it worked and the red and green horsemen began to work their way back to us. I saw Hougon being helped by a lieutenant. Beyond those two there were none. I urged Killer forwards as a Mameluke launched himself at the wounded pair of officers. I leaned as far forward as I could manage. The Ottoman was so focussed on his prey that he did not see me coming in from his left. My sword went through his neck and, as I gave a flick of my wrist, it severed it all together and the headless corpse crashed to the rocks. The man must have been a leader for the enemy halted and I turned Killer to follow the last of the Guards back to the main trail and the safety of the army.

Albert smiled and nodded as we rejoined the column and I rode back to General Bessières. "Did you manage to extricate them, captain?"

"Yes, sir. They had been surrounded but the Ottomans were ill-disciplined."

He glanced down at my blade. "I see your sword arm is healed." He looked over his shoulder. "I will have words with Captain Hougon."

"He was wounded, sir. I think he was taken to the surgeon."

That was the last ambush before we reached the top of Mount Tabor. Although it was not an important site it was strategic and General Bonaparte himself saw to our dispositions the next day. The infantry were arrayed in lines with the cavalry guarding the flanks. Over twenty thousand horsemen hurled themselves at our lines but the lines held and the horses could not break the wall of steel. At the end of the day, the field was ours and the Ottomans headed north. Acre would not be reinforced that day.

General Bessières was unable to have a word with the disobedient captain as he had been sent back to the hospital. The general brooded all the way back to the siege lines. I could hear the conversation with the adjutant and it did not bode well for Hougon. He had made the cardinal sin of failing to obey an order and not coming back victorious. Many generals would forgive a disobedient officer if he was successful but Captain Hougon had lost eight troopers.

The siege had not improved since we had left for our foray north. The British Fleet were supplying the city and I could hear Bonaparte berating the Admiral who had lost him his ships. As long as the Royal Navy was there we were, effectively, hamstrung. The next few days were spent recovering and burying those who still died from the plague. It was distressing to see brave men dying helplessly of a disease which seemed to spring from nowhere. With the total force in the 17th down to less than a hundred, it was decided that we would work with the Bonaparte's Guards permanently. We had no base to supply new men.

When Captain Hougon came back he did not appear to have learned any humility and, even before he was summoned to his commander, he was insulting Jean and the men of the 17th as cowards who had refused to follow his lead. He called us all stable boys. His sycophantic acolytes took it all in and hung on his words. He was sure that if they had followed him then he would have defeated the whole Mameluke army.

It took all of Albert's personality to restrain Jean who wanted to show the captain the edge of his blade. I too would happily have fought him but it was unnecessary. Jean and I were summoned to General Bessières' tent. The adjutant was there as well as Captain Hougon. I could see the resolution on the general's face but Hougon appeared oblivious to it.

"Captain Hougon, I have heard that you have made disparaging comments about these officers. That is unacceptable, especially as you disobeyed an order. I want you to apologise for those comments."

The captain looked appalled. "Apologise? I am a member of the Guards and I apologise to no-one."

He was about to have that superior look wiped from his face for I saw the smile appear on the adjutant's face. The general nodded, "I see. Normally this would involve a court-martial but, quite frankly you are not worth the time and the effort. The 15th lost some officers to the plague. You are hereby transferred to the 15th Chasseurs. Perhaps now, as you are no longer a Guard, you might reconsider an apology."

"You cannot do this!"

Bessières was enjoying the captain's discomfort. "I think you will find that I can and before you speak of talking to General Bonaparte, I have to say that he endorses this decision. I do remember telling you the high regard he had for both the captain and the major. It seems you did not listen."

He snarled at me as he left the tent. "This is not over, stable boy. When my arm is healed, I will teach you a lesson."

"Do not worry captain. I will be waiting."

After he had gone the general said, "I am sorry about him. He is a bad one. Perhaps the others might be straightened out now."

The adjutant nodded vigorously. "They will be, believe me."

Jean nodded. "Thank you for that sir. I am not afraid of that whelp."

"I know but it would not do the morale of the army any good to have two officers fighting. It is better this way." As we turned to leave he said, "General Bonaparte wishes to see you, captain. He has a task for you to complete."

Jean's look showed the worry he felt. I shook my head, "Do not worry Jean. I know all about this." In truth, I did not but I was confident that whatever the task was I would perform it and get back to my regiment.

We were alone after Bessières left us. The general looked at me for some time before he spoke. "I have asked you to perform many missions for me before Scotsman but the one I am giving you now is the most important, the most dangerous and the most secret. Not even General Bessières knows what it entails. I know you are of noble blood and I know you to be a gentleman. All I require is your word that you will not speak of this mission to anyone, ever."

I did not know what to say. I had never seen him so serious. I had no choice but to nod and say, "Of course sir. You have my word."

He seemed visibly relieved at that. "What I am about to tell you has been in mind for some time." He sighed, "Since our fleet was destroyed our position here is untenable. Things are not going well in Italy and the fools there have lost many of the gains I made. I need you to go to Naples and speak with the British there."

He knew he had astounded me by the look on my face and he waited. Was he talking surrender? "And how would I get there general?"

"The sloop 'Carillon' still sails and her Captain, like you, bears a charmed life."

I nodded. I could understand why he had chosen me. My Italian was rusty but still serviceable, I knew the area and I could speak English but what was my task? "And what do I say to the English?"

"You will deliver this letter for me." He handed over a document which had been sealed with wax. "If this letter looks like falling into anyone else's hands but the British representative in Naples then you must destroy it. Is that clear?"

"Yes, general."

"If the eventuality occurred then you would need to speak with the representative and tell them what I request." I could see that he was in a difficult position. He had to trust me with something so delicate that even Bessières knew nothing about it. "I want to return to France aboard a French ship with my Guards and generals. There is one frigate left in Alexandria, the, Muiron and I want them to leave her alone."

He was deserting the army! I had to ask the question. "And the army?"

He sighed. "I wish safe passage for them too but not yet. I think the British might allow me to leave but not my army." He shrugged, "It will take away the threat to India but for the present, they will not allow the army to leave but eventually…"

"Do you trust them, sir?"

He laughed. "An excellent question. The short answer is yes. They are a people who still believe in giving their word and keeping it. I am hoping they would rather I was in Italy than Egypt."

I tried to take this in. I was not even certain that I would last more than a day alone in Naples let alone do what he requested. He allowed me to think for a while and then he said. "The 'Carillon' will return each day to the rendezvous point. You will have six days to complete your task and after that, the sloop's commander will assume you have been captured or killed." He could be quite cold when he wished to be but I understood that. "You will, of course, travel in civilian clothes."

"And when do I leave?"

"Tonight. The 'Carillon' is at Jaffa. You will not return to your regiment. There are clothes and money in the next tent. There is a chest on board the 'Carillon' with spare clothes and money for you." He stood and I noticed how small he was. He normally sat or was mounted but when he stood he barely came up to my chest. He put out his hand. "You do this for me and you do this for France. I shall be in your debt if you succeed."

I had no choice but I did think that I was going to my death. I changed into my new clothes and left the uniform on the cot. I went outside to Killer and the two generals came to see me off. Bonaparte seemed genuinely concerned when he said, "Good luck Scotsman. My fate is now in your hands."

Napoleon's Guard

Chapter 8

When I reached Jaffa, I went to the garrison commander. I had met the colonel during the campaign and he was a good man. I asked him to stable Killer with his own horse. I did not trust the locals and I knew that he would be cared for. Paul was a horseman too but events had made him an artilleryman. He also seemed to like the spirit of Killer although I cautioned him about riding the black beast. He laughed, "No captain, I will just exercise her with my own horse. Horses get lonely and it will do her good to have another horse close by."

Satisfied that Killer was taken care of I took my horse pistols and headed for the harbour. I had already seen the masts of the 'Carillon'. She was the only vessel in the harbour. The crew had not changed since we had scouted Malta two years earlier. François, the lieutenant who captained her was waiting at the head of the gangplank. He had aged a little but he still looked like a pirate.

As he shook my hand he said, "I do not know who is more the fool; you for landing and spying or me for landing you. I fear we are both in mortal danger."

I shrugged, "The sea and the battlefield are both dangerous places. We are young and we take our chances."

He laughed and shook his head. "Older and now philosophical; how you have grown!. Let's get under way. Your chest is in the cabin. Prepare to get to sea First Mate!"

"Aye aye, sir."

As I descended into the stygian gloom that was the accommodation on the ship I heard the commands being given to slacken ropes and loosen sails. By the time I had found the dimly lit cabin I could feel the movement of the ship as we headed out to sea. One advantage of being the only ship in harbour was the lack of obstacles to strike and we made swift progress into the open water of the Mediterranean.

I never like being below deck and I joined the lieutenant at the stern. His crew were young and efficient. They went about their business competently and without fuss. I did not disturb him as he conned the ship towards the setting sun. I looked back at the lights of the land as they flickered and flashed. I wondered when I would return. I laughed to myself if I returned. I could end up in a prison hulk or even shot as a spy. I was not wearing a uniform. General Bonaparte was relying on the British being gentlemen and honouring their word. My mother had told me tales of General Wade slaughtering highlanders who had surrendered. Patently not all of them were to be trusted.

When the lights from the land faded François lit his pipe and joined me at the rail. He gestured with his pipe at the now invisible land we had just left. "I will not ask you what you are about for I was told not to but I wonder why you are alone this time and why Jean, Tiny and the others are not with you."

"All that I can tell you is that you are landing me in Naples and my English will come in handy."

He tapped his nose, "Then that is enough."

We watched the sea for a while and then I ventured, "Do we have many ships now that the fleet has been destroyed?"

"Just frigates, brigs and sloops. We have to be fast enough to evade their ships. That is easy enough with the battleships but they do have quick frigates too. Luckily the 'Carillon' is faster than them all. We avoid them if we can but that is not as hard as it might sound. They lie off Alexandria, knowing that our main army is there. They have other ships at Acre for they know the general is there and the rest harass the south coast."

"Suppose I wanted to get to France by boat. Could I do it?"

"I could have you there and no-one would be the wiser but if you wanted to, say, bring your squadron then we might struggle. For that, you would need a frigate."

"And how many men could a frigate take?"

"More than you might think. If they were prepared for cramped conditions then it would be a couple of hundred but a hundred would be easy." He tapped out his pipe and the sparks dropped to disappear into the sea. "Are you thinking of running then?"

"No, but I wondered how we would get the army back to France."

He laughed. "We could probably get many of the soldiers but not the horses and certainly not the guns."

I nodded. I now saw what Bonaparte intended. He could escape with his generals, his scientists and his guards on a frigate. The rest of us would rot in Egypt until we all died of the plague or ran out of ammunition. At least I knew, in my own mind, where I stood. "Have you decided where you will drop me and how?"

He gestured at the flagstaff. "We will try the Maltese flag again and I will try to land you in the port itself."

"Aren't the Maltese allies of us now?"

"Yes, and the British are in Naples."

"How about Sorrento? It is just down the coast and I could make my own way north?"

He shook his head, "No for I need to pick you up as well. I will try to go in under another flag perhaps. One the British might think twice about firing upon."

"Is there one?"

"The Stars and Stripes, the American flag. They might not like their ex-colony but the Americans are precious about people firing on their flag and the British would be wary of doing so. We will try that." He looked up at the pennant. "It is a good wind. Let us go down to my cabin and we will eat."

François was good company and we ate and drank well. It would be six days before we would reach our destination and I needed that time to prepare myself. I spent part of each morning practising with my sword and my stiletto. I became quite adept at throwing at a target and hitting it. I had the sailmaker fashion me another canvas belt like the one I wore beneath my clothes. This one was for the precious letter I carried. I spent each afternoon studying the maps and charts of the town and the coast. If anything happened to the 'Carillon' I would need to make my own way home. When I looked at the money provided by the general I saw that the coins were not French but a mixture of Austrian, Spanish and Italian. I would, at least, not look French. The clothes, too, were similar to the ones I had worn when travelling to Vienna as an Italian. General Bonaparte certainly knew how to plan.

As we headed up the Italian coast François and I worked out how we would rendezvous. "I cannot keep coming back into port that much is obvious."

I suddenly remembered our story on Malta. "Could you not say you have repairs you need to make. That should buy you a couple of days. You could sail out and then back saying that it had not worked."

He stroked his beard. "That would work but could you get your task done in such a short time?"

I was not certain. "I do not know. This is unlike the other work I have done for the general and I am not sure how this one will progress. How about this; if I am not back before you sail then sail down to Sorrento and I will make my way there."

"That leaves you on your own doesn't it?"

The silence seemed as big as the sky. "Yes." The simple word was filled with a thousand thoughts. I had no-one else to rely on. For the first time, I would not have Jean, Tiny or any of the men I had shared hardship with over the past few years. My nearest friend would be François and he, too, would be in danger on board the ship.

The next day we sailed along the coast and saw the tiny port of Sorrento. There was nothing in the port larger than a fishing boat but the fort bristled with guns. François seemed satisfied. "That should not be a problem."

"Good. I will leave my chest on board. I need to travel light but if you have a leather bag it will hide my brace of pistols." The sailmaker had such a satchel and the guns fitted snugly inside.

The three huge ships in the harbour of Naples all displayed the Union Jack which made my heart sink. I suspected that Royal Navy officers might just be more belligerent than a diplomat. I just had to play the cards I had been dealt. We had timed it to arrive just after dawn so that I had the maximum time ashore. The American flag did not appear to arouse any interest and I was delighted that there were no other American flagged ships in the port. François found an empty berth at the end of the harbour where he could flee quickly and he would be out of the way of prying eyes.

When I stood on the gangplank it felt like I was stepping into an abyss. François put his hand on my shoulder, "Do not worry Robbie. You are resourceful; Jean says you have the quickest mind of anyone he has ever known. You will do well."

As I walked towards the town, I pondered Francois' words. Jean had never said that to me but then again, he had told me I should not always be looking for compliments. It did make me feel better about what I was undertaking. Naples was just coming to life when I walked into the town. I walked slowly allowing my ears to attune themselves to the Italian I had not spoken for some time. I found a bakery and went in to buy some bread just to speak it again and hear it spoken. It did not sound as alien as I had expected it to. Once I reached the market square, I went to buy a drink. I was neither thirsty nor did I need the courage of alcohol but I needed to ask questions. The bar I chose had been the one we had entered when seeking English sailors all those years ago. I did not think they would remember me but it mattered not anyway. The last time I had been in here I had stunk of fish. Now I was a young man about town. I discovered that the town was filled with the crews of the ships and that the Neapolitans were thinking about war with France. Neither pieces of news was what I wished to hear. After I had discovered where the British Residence was I set off. Delay would not help me.

I saw that there were two red-coated guards at the entrance. From their headgear, I knew that they were marines. I took a deep breath and stepped up to the one with the stripes on his arm. "I would like to see the British Resident please." This was the first time I had spoken English since I had interviewed the prisoners those weeks ago. It sounded like a foreign language to me.

"And who the hell are you?"

I was taken aback by the coarseness of the words and the aggression. "I have a message for him."

"Well give it to me and then piss off."

I had only recently heard this phrase and knew it was an insult. I steeled myself. "It is not written down I need to speak with him."

"Not today, sunshine, now bugger off before I stick my boot up your arse."

He was a bully I could see that and he was trying to impress the young marine next to him. I had no doubt that I could have dealt with him but I didn't think that would either get me inside or ingratiate me to those who I needed to see. I made a tactical retreat. As I left, I heard his voice laughing, "I hate Jocks I do. They are all piss and wind!"

I did not move far. I crossed the street and stood in an alleyway to watch the door. No-one came out for a while and then I saw a well-dressed middle-aged gentleman exit. He nodded, absent-mindedly at the two guards who saluted him and then headed towards me. As he passed, I turned and followed. I had to get a message inside the residence and if the marines would not let me in then I would have to find another means.

The man called at a shop selling, amongst other things, writing paper. His purchase was wrapped and he went further towards the port. I was intrigued as he did not wear a uniform and yet he walked with a military gait. He stopped at the gangplank of the Vanguard, the flagship of the squadron. He took something from his pocket and gave it to the sentry. He said a few words and I took the opportunity of glancing down the harbour to see if the 'Carillon' was still there. She was.

The man turned and walked back into town. When he stopped at the bar I had used I followed him. He went to one end of the bar and I went to the other. I was served first and I sat with my drink at a corner table and I watched as he had a conversation with the barman. When the barman looked at me and spoke with the man I knew that I was in trouble. They both looked at me. The man paid and then strode purposefully towards me with his drink in his hand.

He placed his wine on the table and smiled as he asked, in Italian, "May I sit sir?"

I nodded and as he slid next to me a small pistol appeared in his hands which he jammed into my ribs. "Now why were you asking about the British Residency and why were you following me?" He spoke to me in Italian.

"I need to speak with the British resident."

He still held the pistol to me but the pressure lessened. "Then why did you not approach the front door?"

"I did but the marines there sent me away."

"Ah, the inestimable Sergeant Tobias. Now I see." The gun moved away from me but was still pointed at my middle. "But you are not Italian, are you?"

I shook my head, "French." It was a gamble but I would have to tell them at some point that I was an envoy from Bonaparte. I would just keep secret the fact that I could speak English until I knew what they were planning.

"Brave then to come here where Naples is about to declare war on France and the town is filled with the sailors who just destroyed your fleet."

I suspect he was trying to see if I lost my temper but I just smiled. "Brave or foolish; it depends on who you speak with."

He tossed off his drink. "Then get to your feet and let us go to see what you are about. I will take you to the British Resident, Sir William Hamilton. Be careful young man my gun will be close to your spine all the way. Lead on, I know that you know which way to go."

As we wove our way through the throngs, I suddenly remembered that the sergeant had heard me speak English. My deception might not last long. As we approached the guards the sergeant began to raise his weapon. My companion waved it away. "No need for that Sergeant Tobias; the young man is with me but we will have words after this."

Sergeant Tobias shot me a filthy look as I entered the grounds. I had made an enemy there. He would have to join the queue; later, I seemed to be losing friends and making enemies with alarming speed. The building was cool after the heat of the street and so clean that I felt dirty. I resisted the urge to smell myself. We walked across a marble floor to a room with another marine outside.

My companion spoke to the marine in English and I kept my face impassive. "Is Sir William in?" The sentry nodded, "Then keep your eye on our friend here. He is French but he appears harmless."

"Sir." After the door had closed the marine lowered his musket slightly so that the bayonet was at neck height. He had a cheerfully evil grin on his face. "Now you behave yourself Froggy or I'll stick you like a pig!"

I seemed to stand for an age and then the door opened and I was invited in. "Sentry, come into the room and watch him from the door."

Sir William Hamilton looked to be about sixty years old but his eyes belied his age. They were sharp and missed nothing. He appraised me as soon as I entered. His French was as good as my English. "Take a seat." I did so and the man who had brought me sat next to me. "Now my aide, Colonel Selkirk here, tells me that you are French and you need to speak with me." He leaned back in his seat. "I am intrigued. Pray tell me why."

I began to open my jacket and the pistol appeared next to my side again. "I smiled, "I am just getting out the letter I was asked to deliver."

"Do it carefully then."

Sir William chuckled. "Colonel Selkirk here was a soldier and I think he misses guns."

"No my lord, it is just that there is something about this young man that does not ring true." He spoke in English and Sir William replied in the same language.

"He cannot escape and I cannot see what he has to gain from this."

"He looks to be a fit young man and he could be an assassin."

"Then why did you leave him his sword?"

"The sword is not the weapon of an assassin. By the time he drew it McIntyre behind us would have shot him. Isn't that right marine?"

I heard McIntyre's cheerful voice from behind me, "Yes sir. It would be no trouble at all."

I kept an impassive face so that they would not know that I had understood their words. I had recovered the letter from my belt and I was pleased that it was still sealed. I handed it over. "This is the reason I asked to see you, Sir William."

I relaxed as I leaned back in the chair relieved that I had achieved my objective. As he opened it Sir William said, "He is a cool customer for one so young."

"And that is why my gun is still ready. There is something about him…"

Sir William waved an impatient hand to silence the colonel. "By Jove. It is from the Boney fellow, General Bonaparte."

"The one in Egypt eh. Isn't he the chap who fired on the French mob?"

"That is the fellow and this starts to make sense. Sentry, ask the Admiral to join us. I think he is entertaining my wife in the garden."

"But sir, the prisoner…"

"I think we can handle him, McIntyre. Now off you go."

Once he had left the room, Sir William read the letter. His only reaction was a slight widening of the eyes. He folded it and handed it to Colonel Selkirk. Sir William asked me, "Do you know the contents of this letter?"

I nodded, "Yes sir. The general told me."

"Then he must trust you very much. This is a powerful letter and, were it to fall into the wrong hands…"

"I have done work for the general before. He trusts me."

"Do you mind me asking you sir, how old are you?"

"I am twenty-two."

"You are a soldier?"

"Yes sir, the 17th Chasseurs. I am a captain."

The colonel finished reading the letter and handed it back. They both reverted to English. "I think we wait until the Admiral arrives before we discuss it."

"I agree, Sir William and what do we do about him?" He inclined his head at me.

"I think he can stay at the moment. According to the letter, this is not imminent. He can stay here as our guest for a few days."

My heart sank; so much for a speedy escape in the 'Carillon'. On the other hand, the fact that they had not dismissed the idea out of hand meant that Bonaparte had judged the matter well. I wondered who this Admiral was. The door behind me opened as the sentry allowed the Admiral to enter. Sir William said, "You can wait outside McIntyre."

"Admiral Nelson, we have a letter from General Napoleon Bonaparte. This soldier has just delivered it. We have sent for you as it directly concerns your ships."

I turned my head and saw the famous Admiral Nelson. All of the sailors I had interrogated had mentioned him and all seemed in awe of his skill as a sailor and as an admiral. I was surprised. He looked to be the same height as General Bonaparte but the difference was the general was inclined to be stocky this admiral looked like he was so frail he would blow over in a strong wind. I knew he had lost an eye and an arm but you hardly seemed to notice. Despite his diminutive stature, he held the room with his power.

He seated himself next to Sir William and read the letter. When he had read it twice he put it on the table and then looked at me. "And this fellow? What of him?"

I found it fascinating, almost amusing, that when they spoke about me in English it was as though I was not even there.

"Interesting chap. A cavalryman and he seems to be resourceful."

"Hmm. I wonder how he got here."

This Nelson had a sharp mind. The other two had not even bothered to ask me. Sir William asked me, in French, "How did you reach Naples?"

I pointed vaguely to the south; the port was to the north. "I landed by ship."

Colonel Selkirk nodded, "Probably north of Sorrento. There are little coves there. Perhaps his ship is still there Admiral Nelson. Maybe one of your ships could..."

Nelson laughed and it was a piping little laugh. "I do not think it would have hung around. A more pertinent question would be how does he intend to get back to Egypt with our message?"

"Good point, but does he need to go back at all? What is in it for us?"

"Let us not be hasty Colonel Selkirk. We should not dismiss this out of hand."

I could see that the man, who had captured me, was shocked and surprised at Admiral Nelson's suggestion. This was the first time I began to believe that General Bonaparte's plan might just work.

"Let us look at the facts. This general could well be stuck in Egypt for some time. I have Sir Sydney's latest reports. Although Acre is still holding firm, mainly due to our ships, this general has defeated every Ottoman army sent against him. Apparently, he defeated twenty-five thousand Mameluke horsemen with just four thousand of his own men. This is a dangerous general. If he stays in Egypt who is to say he could not conquer the Ottoman lands?"

"But surely that is an argument for not bringing him back to France."

I noticed that Sir William was allowing the two men to argue between themselves which allowed him the luxury of hearing both sides of the argument. My face remained stoically impassive, almost bored. I fiddled with the edge of the table and I looked at the paintings as though interested in them but I took in every word they were saying.

The little admiral shrugged. "I have heard that he has royalist leanings. He put down the mob in Paris savagely enough as he did in Cairo. This man is not a revolutionary. He is someone who would like things the way they were."

"The admiral is correct, colonel. The politicians in London want the revolution destroyed and not France. France has always been a buffer against the ambitions of the Hapsburgs. The Prussians are now flexing their muscles too. If we leave him in Egypt he might well conquer that land and that would mean the Russians would move west. We just need to know more about this new general."

"Why not ask the messenger?"

"A good idea. Do you speak French Admiral Nelson?"

"A little and badly but I will try to follow."

Sir William smiled at me as though he had noticed me for the first time. "Now then er…"

"Robert." I pronounced it the French way.

"Well then, Robert, what is this general of yours like? If you have performed such tasks as this before you must know what kind of person he is. Does he support the revolution?"

This was not what I had expected. If I spoke with them would that make me a traitor? I decided that as the general's envoy I could tell them things which were in the public domain and not private.

"He is hardworking and rarely sleeps. He is the most efficient man I have ever met and he is a great organiser."

I could see that my answers were not what they wished to hear. "Yes, but his politics? What of them?"

"I am a soldier I know nothing of politics."

Admiral Nelson slapped the table with his good hand and roared with laughter. "Just like my sailors. They care not a jot who runs the country just so that they get their prize money and beat the enemy." He shook his head. "The general is a political creature else he would not have lasted this long. He is pragmatic. In the letter, he says that he desires peace with Britain and that makes sense to me. The Austrians are a ripe plum for the taking and Italy can soon be his."

Although I understood all that they were saying and wished to reply to the admiral I kept my dumb silence.

"But can we let him have free rein in Europe?"

"I am not a politician either but if he leaves Egypt then my ships can then rule the Mediterranean and we can keep his fleet in port. We have to keep ships off the Holy Land and Alexandria and yet there are no French ships for them to watch; the remainder of their fleet is bottled up in Alexandria. With this general out of the way then the army will atrophy and wither and we will have won."

"I will have to think on this. Colonel, could you look after this chap? He is a soldier and you were one until recently. Have Caruthers find him a room and put a guard on his door."

I could see that Colonel Sinclair was not happy but he smiled ruefully and said, "Yes Sir William."

"See that he is scrubbed up and brought to dinner. Lady Hamilton might find him diverting."

"Come with me, captain."

Leaving the diplomat and the sailor to continue their discussion I was led up the stairs. We ascended the wonderfully ornate staircase to the third floor. I suspected this was where minor officials slept in this Palazzo Sessa. It was still an opulent home. Colonel Sinclair opened the door. "While Sir William makes his decision you will stay here. As an officer do I have your word that you will not try to escape?"

"Of course."

"Good," he smiled, "although I will put a guard there." He hesitated, "For your protection. You will dine with the family tonight. I will send up a servant to clean your clothes a little."

"It is not a problem."

"I know which is why I have a servant to do it for you. This is not France you know."

After I had taken off my jacket and shirt I washed. I wondered how long it would take Sergeant Tobias to tell them that I could speak English. I was not worried; it was not as if this would jeopardise the negotiations after all.

The servant came to my room and knocked discreetly. He tried speaking English to me and I feigned ignorance and then answered in Italian. He was delighted that he would be able to speak to me in his own language. Carlo was a fussy little Neapolitan; he was almost effeminate but the best gentleman's servant I have ever met. He shook his head at my clothes and left the room. I was at a loss. He returned with a dressing gown. " Sir, please take your clothes off and put this on and I will make you presentable. You cannot go to dinner smelling of fish!"

I suppose I was used to the smell but I had been on the ship for some days and the odour must have clung. I did as he asked. When I emerged from the dressing room he said, "Follow me!"

He marched imperiously down the corridor to the bathroom. My marine guard followed. Carlo opened the door and said, "I will bring towels in half an hour. It will take that long, at least, to get rid of the smell." He sniffed the perfumed water and nodded happily. Then he left.

The bath did feel good and I fell asleep. I was awoken by a gentle tap on the arm and Carlo stood there with towels. As he shaved me, then dried and dressed me in the clean clothes he went prattling on about the Neapolitan Revolution. "I cannot understand it. In France, it was the peasants who wanted rid of the king. Here it is the aristocracy. I have heard that they have invited the French army here! What a thing. No offence sir, but you can keep your revolution in France. Here we know our place and we like it. If they succeed then I will return with Sir William to London, which is, at least, a civilised country."

He stepped back when I was finished. "There. You clean up quite well sir." He stroked the lapels of my jacket making me feel most uncomfortable but I think he meant nothing by that. It was just his way. "I will take you to the terrace where they are gathering."

The house looked out on the Bay of Naples and the terrace afforded a magnificent view. The others were already there and speaking English when I arrived. There was a sudden silence at my appearance. It gave me the chance to look at the most famous woman in Britain, Lady Hamilton. She was stunning but more than that, she made you like her at first sight. I do not wonder that Admiral Nelson fell in love with her. That much was obvious to me from the moment I saw them. It was as though they were the couple rather than her husband, Sir William. The diplomat did not seem to mind.

"Ah, my dear may I introduce Robert, our guest." He spoke in English and I just stood. He then said, in French, "Robert this is my wife, the Lady Hamilton."

My mother had been a lady and taught me how to speak to and treat ladies of quality. I bent one knee and, taking the proffered hand, kissed it lightly and said, "I am enchanted, your ladyship."

Her smile lit up the room. "How delightful! What a charming young man."

Carlo was hovering in the background and I saw the happy nod and smile. He walked over with a glass of a yellow liquid. He said, quietly in Italian, "That was well done, sir."

I said equally quietly, "And what is this I am drinking?"

"Limoncello. It is an iced lemon liqueur. Sip it and you will enjoy it."

He slipped away as quietly as he had arrived. I did sip it and found it pleasant and refreshing."

The only person missing was Colonel Selkirk. The door opened and he suddenly appeared. He ignored everyone else and stormed up to me. "You speak English! You are Scottish!"

Before I could say anything Sir William said, "Steady on, Colonel. What has upset you?"

"Sergeant Tobias told me that this man arrived this morning and he spoke English with a Scottish accent."

Sir William looked at me. I noticed that the Admiral and Lady Hamilton seemed faintly amused at the colonel's tantrum. "Is this true? Are you Scottish and can you speak English?"

"Yes I can speak English," I said in English, "but I am only half Scottish and I was born and raised in France."

Sir William seemed exasperated. "Then why didn't you tell us?"

I shrugged, "You never asked."

While he and the colonel looked lost for words Lady Hamilton and Admiral Nelson fell about laughing. The dinner gong sounded just in time.

Chapter 9

The colonel was so flabbergasted that he could say nothing. We were led into the dining room and seated. Eventually, Admiral Nelson leaned across the table to me and asked, "So, captain, what is your name and what is your story?" He turned to Lady Hamilton, "I think that we may find this quite interesting and it will allow Colonel Selkirk to regain his composure."

"My name is Robert Macgregor. I never lied. I was born to the Count of Breteuil and Marie Macgregor, the granddaughter of a Jacobite supporter of Bonnie Prince Charlie. My mother died some years ago and my father was executed at the Place de la Revolution. I joined the cavalry and now I am a captain of the 17th Chasseurs serving in Egypt."

Sir William seemed happy with that. "Now I can see why Bonaparte picked you. You are the perfect choice." He wagged an admonishing finger at me. "You were less than honest with us about your knowledge of our language although I can see why you did so. You heard what we said. Had we known we would have been more guarded in what we said."

The colonel had recovered his voice. "It was deception, plain and simple!"

I spread my arms. "There was no deception when I came to Palazzo Sessa. I spoke English but I was thrown out by Sergeant Tobias and then had a gun stuck in my ribs. Would you have behaved any differently?"

I saw the first hint of a smile creep across the colonel's face. "No, I suppose not. But no more lies and no more secrecy. Tell me now where the ship you came on is at present?"

"I will not tell you."

"What? Then your words mean nothing. What of honesty?"

"I said I will not lie and I am not lying now but I will not put in jeopardy the brave men who brought me here."

"Then how will you return to Egypt?"

It was my turn to smile as I looked directly at Admiral Nelson. "I believe the Royal Navy has more than a few ships. I suspect they could easily take me."

Nelson and Lady Hamilton were joined in their laughter by Sir William. "By Jove sir, but you have wit. The general chose well."

Despite the fact that we were enemies I did enjoy the evening. Lady Hamilton was both vivacious and funny. She had a great sense of humour and Admiral Nelson had a great sense of fun. It was bizarre but Sir William was more like a parent than a husband. I also managed to talk to Colonel Selkirk. Once he got over his outrage at my deception he saw why I had done it. He too came from Scottish stock and he had been a cavalryman. "Aye, I served with the Scots Greys. We all rode bonnie grey horses."

"Are they Dragoons sir?"

"Aye, heavy cavalry." He seemed to see me for the first time. "I can see why you joined the French army but Bonnie Prince Charlie has been dead for some years. Why not come home? I could get you into one of our regiments."

I shook my head, "Think about it, sir. Could you serve in any other regiment than the Scots Greys?" His head dropped. "It is the comrades I have fought with that keeps me there."

His head suddenly turned, "Will you not be leaving with General Bonaparte?"

"I could but I will not leave my regiment."

"You have honour sir but not much hope. If the general leaves you will either all die or become prisoners."

"I will not leave my friends." I said stubbornly.

He laughed, "You are a Scot, through and through! Mad as a hatter!"

As the evening drew to a close Sir William tapped his glass for silence. "Firstly, I would like to thank our guest. He has been an unexpected pleasure this evening. Secondly, I have made my decision but," he held up the empty bottle of port, "I will tell you of that choice in the morning."

I was satisfied. The colonel escorted me to my room. "Just to make sure you didn't escape," he joked.

"You can't be too careful." As I closed the door I thought that as prisons go this one was the best I had ever enjoyed.

I rose early, as was my want and descended the stairs. I noticed that the guard followed me. I smiled at his diligence and sense of duty. Had I wanted to escape then the climbing plants which were on the wall near to my room would have afforded me an easy egress.

I sat on the terrace and watched the sea, a cold blue at this time of day. It was pleasant although I knew that it would be uncomfortably warm later.

A soft voice wafted over to me, "Enjoying the view captain?"

I leapt to my feet and bowed. "Yes, your ladyship. It is not often that I have the opportunity to witness such views."

"Quite. Marine, you may go."

"But your ladyship I have been ordered to watch the prisoner."

Her voice changed from soft to authoritative. "Do you think he will leap from the walls? Do as I say?" He snapped to attention and left. "Soldiers," she muttered and then as she realised I too was a soldier she giggled. "I am sorry captain, perhaps it is only English soldiers who are like that." She gestured for me to sit and waved the hovering servant over. "Coffee?"

"Yes, your ladyship. Thank you. And I can tell you that we have soldiers just such as he in the French army."

As the delicate cups were filled she asked, "How long have you been a soldier then?"

"About five years."

"Five years? Then you must have been a child when you joined."

"If I was then I was a big child, your ladyship."

She laughed and became suddenly serious, "We have much in common, you and I for I too began to work at a young age." Then she smiled, "But it does no harm does it captain?" She hesitated and then leaned forward, "Forgive my questions and, if they are impertinent then pray do not answer but were your mother and father married?"

I liked her frankness and felt no shame in answering. "My mother was the count's father's ward and when the old count died my father took my mother to his bed. He took others too."

"But you were his only issue?"

"I believe so."

She gave me a shrewd look. "When the revolution is over then you will have the title and the land of your father?"

I shrugged, "Perhaps. I have a lawyer making a claim but…"

"Quite. I now see another reason for the general's choice of envoy. You are almost an Englishman," she giggled, "sorry, Scotsman."

"Let us go and breakfast. You look as though you have a healthy appetite." As we went in she linked my arm and leaned into me. She exuded a sensuous aroma and I could see how she could bend men around her little finger. I was hooked already.

Sir William looked a little red around the cheeks but he smiled genially. "Well, I think that we can accommodate your general. Colonel Selkirk will write a letter for you to take back with you. You do not need to know the contents but, should anything happen to prevent you from returning to the general you must destroy the letter. Is that clear?"

"Yes, sir." I smiled. "The general told me the same with the other letter."

He nodded his approval. The admiral and the colonel joined us. "Now then as to how you will return home to Egypt."

"I will arrange that sir, with your permission of course."

"Hmn, I will be intrigued as to how you do that."

Admiral Nelson sipped some of the orange juice and said, "I rather fancy there is an American flagged ship in the harbour which might do the trick."

For once I was unable to keep my impassive face and I stared at the admiral who laughed. "The sea is my world young man. My officers told me of the American ship crewed by Frenchmen who did not go ashore and were repairing a fine ship which was perfectly seaworthy." He saw my shoulders sag. "Oh do not worry. You can sail and we will not pursue. Apart from the fact that your sloop would lead my battleships a merry dance, it suits me to let you return. Besides, I now know the ship and if I see it again, I will know it for a Frenchie eh? But a word of advice young man, once your ship leaves the harbour then she and you will be in danger. My frigate captains are hungry for plunder."

After I had eaten, I said, "If I might have the letter, my lord, then I will be on my way."

He handed it over but added darkly, "I hope this Bonaparte is as honourable a man as you are Captain Macgregor."

"So do I, my lord, for if we are both wrong then this war could last our lifetimes."

We shook hands. Lady Hamilton gave me a chaste kiss on the cheek but she lingered close to me so that I almost drowned in her perfume. Admiral Nelson shook my hand, a little awkwardly, and said, "I enjoyed your company young man and I hope we might meet again under better circumstances eh?"

Colonel Selkirk said, "I will take you to the door. I believe Sergeant Tobias is on duty again. As we walked through the house he said, "If you ever tire of your regiment and wish to join the soldiers of your mother's and grandfather's people then please contact me."

I asked, "Here in Naples?"

"No captain. I normally operate in London; at Horse Guards in Whitehall."

"I think it is unlikely sir, but I will do so should I ever make it to London."

"You are a resourceful young man and whether you know it or not you are an accomplished spy. I could use you."

As we exited Sergeant Tobias and the other marine snapped to attention. The colonel held out his hand for me to shake. As he did so I noticed a smirk on the sergeant's face.

"Good luck, captain."

"And to you, colonel. Thank you for your hospitality." I leaned in to the sergeant. "And the next time I see, you ape I will acquaint your ugly face with my fists and believe me you will not be smirking then. This Jock will teach you a lesson, lobster. If you were a real soldier you would be on a ship not guarding a palace."

I could see him reddening as the marine, next to him, grinned at his discomfort. The colonel said, "I will be having a word with the corporal myself."

As the portent of the words sank in I thought that the ex-sergeant would have an apoplexy. I turned and headed for the harbour. With the letter safely ensconced in my hidden belt, I wanted to be away as soon as I could. Now that I knew that the navy was aware of the identity of the 'Carillon', I felt nakedly exposed as I walked alongside the huge battleships with the gawking sailors. I kept my head down and walked purposefully towards the end berth. I felt a wave of relief wash over me as I saw that she was still there. The crew must have had someone watching the harbour for me; even as I was walking up the gangplank the ropes were being untied and the sails were being lowered. I knew better than to bother François and so I stood by the wheel watching Naples become smaller as we headed south-west. Surprisingly I had enjoyed my stay and yet when I had landed, I had feared for my life.

"Well, Robbie was your mission successful?"

"It was and I still cannot tell you about it but I can say that I met Admiral Nelson and he knew you were a French ship."

"But how? None of my men went ashore and we flew the American flag."

"And that is the reason. The Americans speak English and they like to go ashore. As soon as you did not they were suspicious."

"Then why did they not capture us? It would have been simplicity itself."

"I cannot tell you all but it suited the admiral to let me leave aboard your ship but he did warn me about frigates eager for prize ships. I think the Battle of the Nile gave them a taste for it."

He shook his head. "You live a charmed and exciting life. I bet you stayed in the residency itself."

"I did but how did you know?"

"It is you and your luck but I am pleased that we escaped and escaped so quickly. Now we will make a swift journey home. This time, however, I think we will avoid the straits of Messina and travel around Sicily. It is a longer journey but we have sea room if we need it. If there are frigates hunting us then we will need to run and run fast."

"Well, I will go to my cabin and change out of these clothes. They were cleaned for me…"

He held up his hand. "I wondered why you smelled like a Paris tart! You bathed as well?" I nodded. He came and sniffed my coat, "And there was a lady unless you have taken to wearing expensive perfume."

"Lady Hamilton was a beautiful and hospitable hostess."

He shook his head. "As I said, I would like a tenth of the luck that you seem to enjoy although I think there will be a payment at some time. Your luck must run out some time."

After I had changed and returned to the main deck I saw that there were some black clouds to the west. I pointed at them, "Inclement weather François?"

"Just a squall I think and it will speed us home but it will make sailing around Sicily more difficult. You had better stay on deck and we will see if some of your luck can rub off on us."

When the storm struck it was savage. I daresay they are worse in the Atlantic but this one was bad enough for me. The ship seemed to heel over so much that I thought the ends of the cross trees would touch the water. François had me tied to the rail as he feared I would be washed overboard. I did not mind. I wished to stay with a deck beneath me and not above me. It blew all day and into the night. I could see the salt-crusted beard of the weary helmsman glowing in the dark as he fought the ship and the elements. It became so tiring that François had to order two men on the wheel. I was terrified that we would lose someone overboard but, thankfully, when a damp dawn broke, we were still intact.

Francois ordered the galley fire lit. "We need hot food and then I need to find out just where we are."

As the First Mate ordered men to repair and replace the damaged masts, sails and rigging, I went below deck to wash away the salt. The clean clothes I had put on the day before were now so soaked that I would have to put my others on.

This time when I emerged on to the main deck I saw that we had almost stopped. "What is the problem, François?"

He pointed to the mainsail, which hung in tatters, "We need to replace that urgently. I have taken a sun sight and we are quite close to the African coast. Malta is not far to the north and the English are now there with their ships."

I took his words in. We were too far south and were too close to the frigates Nelson had warned me about. I scanned the horizon for the sight of a sail. Whilst all hands were needed for repairs, the lookout and I watched the thin distant line to see a speck appear. It was, of course, the lookout who spotted them. "Sail Ho! To the north." It was the direction we had expected. When we had been attacked by xebecs they had approached from the south. The Barbary pirates liked to dart out from their lairs and attack unsuspecting victims. I stared north but could see nothing. Part of me wondered if I had been tricked by the admiral but I could not see what they had to gain from the deception. Had they not wanted me to return home they could have just thrown me into a cell.

"Two more sails. A frigate and two brigantines!"

I saw the lieutenant's shoulders sag as he came up to me. "That is the worst possible news. The brigs will be as fast as we are and will be the terriers. The frigate can pound us to matchwood. The only thing in our favour is that the British like to take prizes and so they will attempt to dismast us and then board us."

"Could we not head inshore?"

"The pirates are there, remember. No, we will try to outrun them. The wind is blowing from the west and we are ahead of them but we will need to use every inch of canvas. Hoist the stuns'ls." He strode over to the helm. "I think I will need to be here for this voyage." He glanced over his shoulder. "If we can avoid them until dark then we have half a chance. Hopefully, there will be no more ships ahead of us."

I knew what he feared. There was a squadron blockading Alexandria and another at Acre. If either of those had patrols out they could bump into us and capture us without even trying. I felt better when the extra sails were used and the ship leapt forward like a greyhound released from a trap. My face must have shown my expectation for François said, "Do not get your hopes up Robbie; those brigs can do the same and they have the advantage that there are two of them. If it was just one ship we could turn and lose them but they will be like sheepdogs nipping at our heels until the frigate is close enough to fire."

A battle on the land is one of preparation where the armies manoeuvre and get into position. Once an attack is started then it is obvious what will happen. At least in the battles I had fought that was true but at sea, nothing seemed to happen for a long time. I was not aware of the three ships closing but they were. I went below decks to get my sword and pistols. I would not need them for a long time but it gave me something to do. I was a spare part on the ship and not a particularly useful spare part at that. Yet I had to get back with the letter and my news. If not then the whole venture would have been a waste of time.

I saw the sun begin to slowly dip behind the three ships. All three of them were now clearly discernible and I could see just how big the frigate was. Not as big as a battleship she still had a lot of guns. Looking at the scene in a positive way I could see that we would be hidden by the dark before they were. The sun was setting behind them and made them as clear as day. The captain of the frigate must have worried too for suddenly there were two puffs of smoke and them the distant crack as he fired his bow chasers.

François laughed. "He must think I am a novice and will wet my pants when he fires his guns. He expects us to change course. The captain must be a fool. If I did that I would be caught. Our only hope is use every breath of wind there is." He must have realised that I needed a task. "Robbie, load the swivel guns. We do not have spare crew so if they close you will have to fire them all."

I laughed, "A one-man army! I like it. It will keep me occupied at any rate."

I went to the powder magazine and brought up the powder and the musket balls. I knew nothing would happen for a while and I loaded the guns carefully. If I did have to fire them then I would have little chance to remedy mistakes. After I had finished I looked up and saw that the two brigs were much closer. The Frigate still popped ineffectually away with her bow chasers. The water spouts were getting closer but we appeared to be in no danger.

"Gun crews run out the guns."

I could see that the brigs had both closed to within a mile of us. I could see that they had three guns a side. We had four but we did not have enough crew to man all eight. If they came at us from both sides then we would struggle. The light was now deteriorating quickly. One of the brigs began to turn to starboard and I knew what that meant, they would rake our stern and take out the rudder. We would be helpless. Surprisingly this seemed to please François. "At last, they have made a mistake. Larboard guns, be ready to fire as you bear when I turn. I want that brig dismasting. Use chain shot."

I knew our guns were the smallest in the navy and we could never hope to batter an enemy into submission but we could use accuracy. "Robbie, when they fire then fire the larboard swivel gun; we may get lucky."

I waved an acknowledgement but I was not hopeful. Although the range would be less than half a mile when we fired the swivel gun would be like firing a shotgun at range. Some of the balls might strike home but the odds were not in my favour.

"Ready!" Suddenly François turned the ship to port, towards one of the brigs and the frigate. The darkness was already working in our favour and they did not see the manoeuvre for a precious few minutes. The brig was head on to us and the chain shot was bound to hit a mast if fired accurately. The first gun fired and then, as the second one cracked I pulled the cord on the swivel gun. Once again I was deafened as I had forgotten to tie a cloth around my ears as the gunners had. I entered a silent world. As the smoke cleared I saw that the brig had slewed around. The brig only had two masts and the foremast had been sliced in two and now hung over the side like a huge anchor. The gunners fired a second time with ball and I saw all the balls strike home.

As François turned to starboard once more the frigate tried a broadside but they were hampered by their own brig drifting towards them. Even so, one of the guns was upended and two of the crew hurt as a ball struck us. Holes appeared in our new canvas and I felt the thud as balls hit the side of the ship. Before they could fire again we had turned and presented a tiny stern to their guns. As darkness enveloped us we heard the crack of cannons but did not feel the strike of any balls. The captain turned once again to port. I thought it was a risky move and I made my way back to the stern. As I did so he turned again so that we were heading directly east again.

"Aren't you worried we might run into them?"

He shook his head. "They will expect me to head for the coast. Look," he pointed to the flashes in our wake. They were firing blind.

"First Mate, get those men below deck. Robbie, take some men and see if you can get that gun working. We have too few as it is."

I joined the other gun crews as we struggled to repair it. It was the trunions and not the barrel which was damaged and the carpenter's mate brought some wood to repair the gun. It would be awkward to fire but at least it would fire. I suddenly felt exhausted. None of us had slept the night before and now it looked as though we would have a second night without sleep. François had other ideas. "Port watch get some sleep. Starboard watch we will rest in two hours. Robbie, you are with me and the starboard watch. Go to the galley and get something hot for us to drink."

I did not mind as it gave me something to do and I went below decks to find the galley. In the darkened ship it was like descending into Hades. The cook was a cheerful Creole. "Hot drinks for the watch."

"Coming right up, soldier boy." He poured a milky looking liquid into a jug and then emptied a small bottle of rum into it followed by a ladle of sugar. Finally, he took a poker from the fire and thrust it into the liquid. It steamed and hissed. "My own recipe; you take a little cocoa, a little coffee, a jug of milk and some rum from my island home!"

I grabbed some mugs and the jug and went on deck. François shouted, "Serve the crew and then bring it aft to me." There was plenty left for the two of us. "Cookie is a magician when it comes to drinks. This will keep the men going."

"Any sign of pursuit François?"

"They have stopped firing but they will be after us again in the morning and we still have a long way to go. We have to slip through the blockade at Alexandria and hope that the general hasn't lost Jaffa." That had never occurred to me. I had thought that the hard part was getting to see Sir William. I was wrong. The two hours sleep I managed to get did not seem to refresh me but I knew that with four men dead we needed every man we could get.

François took us well north, almost to Acre before he headed south. We had managed to get one night's sleep since the encounter with the British but we were all exhausted as we saw the distant coastline of the Holy Land appear in the distance.

"Now we hug the coast and hope that any guns are our own."

When Jaffa hove into view I, for one, was heartily glad for I had been certain that we would either be sunk or captured. Someone had been watching over me again.

Chapter 10

François shook my hand as I descended the gangplank. "I will spend some time repairing the ship what do you wish for your chest?"

I shrugged. "It was sent by the general. Keep it, you can sell the clothes or use them. It is a small payment for the service you have done me."

He gave me a wry smile, "It was for France my friend!"

I lowered my voice, "Aye, if you call Bonaparte France!"

He wagged his finger, "You have a dangerous tongue, my friend. Good luck!"

When I went to the fort to see the colonel who had cared for my horse he looked gaunt and ill. "It is the plague and a thousand other pestilences that this land has. I wish we were back across the sea. Your mission was successful?"

"It was and Killer, he was happy here?"

"I envy you your horse. I would love to own such a beast. He has missed you but he is well."

"And the general; where is he?"

"He has left the siege which will soon be wound up and he is back in Alexandria. I fear that soon we will be the front line. Still, at least we are alive, for the moment."

As I rode south I passed the broken and wounded remains of those who had been besieging Acre. Disease and the Royal Navy had done what the Ottoman's could not do; they had broken the backs of the soldiers. They looked demoralised and dispirited. They had not been beaten yet but they had not won. It felt strange to be travelling in my civilian clothes but I was looking forward to donning the uniform of the 17th again. My days as a Guard were over. I had fulfilled my mission and I felt more hopeful than I had for some time.

When I reached General Bonaparte's headquarters in Alexandria I could see that at least some of the squadron had returned as they were on duty. I nodded to the sentry as he saluted and I entered. There was no General Bessières but the orderly recognised me and gave me a surprised look. "The general will be pleased to see you." He hesitated, "You did complete the mission did you not, captain?"

I gave what I hoped was an enigmatic smile, "I will report to the general if you please."

I could see the disappointment on his face as he went into the general's office. I knew that the general was delighted to see me as he bustled out to embrace me. "Well done, my gallant Scotsman! Come, we will talk."

He led me into his room and sat down. He eagerly waved his arms for me to sit and then leaned forward, his face filled with anticipation. I reached into my jacket and took out the letter. I could have told him but I knew that he would want to read the words of the diplomat. I handed it to him. I did notice that he checked the seal. He looked at me, "You know the contents?"

"I know the main points, sir but not the detail."

He smiled, "Always honest and trustworthy. You have repaid my trust."

He read the letter and then re-read it. Then he looked at me, his face filled with joy. "This is good news. You should know, my young Scotsman, that the army is already withdrawing from Acre and Jaffa. We have succeeded." Somehow, I doubted that. From what I had seen the best we had done was to have a stalemate but I smiled and nodded. "And now we have to face an Ottoman army and a fleet come to try to defeat us again. Pah, they will fail." He picked up a broadsheet from the table and handed it to me. "Read this. I am having them printed as we speak and soon, they will be placed in Cairo and Alexandria to show the Egyptian people that we have won."

I read the document and wondered how he could lie so brazenly. We had lost and yet he was telling the people we had won. The man who had destroyed the mosque in Cairo was purporting to be a supporter of the prophet.

Citizens of Egypt

'He is back in Cairo, the Bien-Gardé, the head of the French army, general Bonaparte, who loves Mahomet's religion; he is back sound and well, thanking God for the favours he has given him. He has entered Cairo by

the gate of Victory. This day is a great day; no one has ever seen its like; all the inhabitants of Cairo have come out to meet him. They have seen and recognised that it is the same commander in chief, Bonaparte, in his own person; but those of Jaffa, having refused to surrender, he handed them all over to pillage and death in his anger. He has destroyed all its ramparts and killed all those found there. There were around 5000 of Jezzar's troops in Jaffa— he destroyed them all.'

"Excellent sir!" I had learned to lie too.

"Now you will stay here today." He suddenly seemed to notice my civilian clothes. "Pompidou!" The aide popped his head around the door. "Get the captain a uniform and find him a room." Pompidou disappeared like a rabbit down his hole. "Tonight you will dine with me and General Kléber. You will like him. He is like you and me, a real soldier."

"But sir I would like to return to my regiment."

"Do not worry, captain, they are heading here even as we speak. Tomorrow you can rejoin your friends. General Bessières, too, is eager to see you again."

I did not like the ominous implications. Was I to be returned to my regiment or the Guards? I decided not to argue, I knew how quickly the little general could change from genial comrade to hectoring ogre. I would wait until the cavalry and the army returned.

I put on the uniform, only because my other was still stained from the battle with gunpowder, blood and salt. I gave the clothes to Pompidou after I had dressed. "You can get rid of these for me."

His eyes widened, "You are throwing them away sir? They are fine clothes."

"But I am a soldier once again."

The dinner that evening was an intimate affair just General Kléber, General Bonaparte and myself. Once the meal had been served, he dismissed the servants. It was a simple meal, just soup, chicken and bread with some red wine. The wine was a little rough for my taste but it was from Corsica and close to the general's heart. He was ebullient and cheerful all the way through the repast. I found that I liked General Kléber. He was a soldier through and through. He had served France before and during the revolution and had now been sent for by General Bonaparte.

He appraised me early in the evening. "I have heard of you, Captain Macgregor. You are the mysterious Scotsman who undertakes the general's most delicate missions. I must confess I had expected someone much older."

"Major Bartiaux is older sir, and he has been my mentor. It was only this last mission which did not involve him. The success of the others was down purely to the major."

"Modest too. That is rare in a chasseur!" He laughed as did General Bonaparte but it was not a mocking laugh.

"Perhaps I am the exception which proves the rule."

"Did you hear, captain, that your old comrade Captain Bouchard has made a wonderful discovery at Fort Juliet, the place called Rosetta?"

I had put the foolish young officer from my mind. "No sir, what discovery was that?"

"He has unearthed a stone which my scientists tell me will help us to translate the symbols on the stones. Is that not magnificent? I am just pleased that I sent most of the treasures home before the navy managed to lose our fleet."

I could see the general taking much credit for this when he reached France. "That was most propitious."

This was as much small talk as the general allowed and he leaned forward to speak candidly about military matters. "Now Jean, as you know I am planning on leaving Egypt, briefly, to sort out matters in Paris." General Kléber shot me a surprised look, "Do not worry about the young captain. He has proved himself to be loyal and discreet and besides it was he who facilitated my journey." I saw respect in the general's eyes. "I want Egypt consolidating. The Ottomans are no enemy to fear and the English are too far away to do anything. I will leave all the army bar a small squadron of my Guards. I will not have much space when I return to France. Thanks to Admiral Brueys incompetence we have no large ships left to us."

The rest of the evening was spent in a detailed discussion of how General Kléber should run the country. I smiled to myself; he was leaving no room for the general to be creative. The instructions he received were prescriptive in the extreme. General Bonaparte was like a puppeteer and General Kléber, the puppet.

I retired early as I knew that General Bonaparte could talk all night and, if I was, to be honest, I was bored with politics. All I wanted to do was get back to being a soldier.

My wish was granted the next day when the army returned. General Bessières looked dusty, drawn and tired when I saw him. I was in the orderly's office waiting for their arrival. I was genuinely pleased to see the general but the look on his face spoke of bad news.

"What is wrong sir?"

"I am afraid the battle and the plague have taken their toll on your old comrades, captain. The colonel and thirty troopers have died. There are but fifty of the 17th left alive." I could not believe that old Albert was dead. He had seemed immortal somehow. "He died in battle which is what he would have wished."

"Jean, the major…"

"Now commands the survivors. The Guards and the 17th are camped where they were after the landing. I think they will be glad to see you. They worried about you, as I did, not knowing what had become of you." He hesitated, "I will not ask the details as I know General Bonaparte even better than you do, but was the mission successful?"

I nodded, "The general is pleased. And I am just glad to be back to being a soldier."

I rode as quickly as I could to the camp. He had only mentioned the colonel and I was desperate to know who else had survived apart from Jean. As soon as I saw, in the distance, the bulk that was Tiny I felt a wave of relief wash over me. When Sergeant Manet shouted, "Welcome back sir," then I knew that I had suffered no more personal losses. However, when I looked at the troopers I saw many familiar faces were missing. It had been a costly campaign.

"It is good to be back sergeant." I dismounted and walked with the sergeant towards the stables. "Were the battles bloody then?"

"Not really sir. We lost more men through disease."

"Then how did the colonel die?"

"Best the major tells you that sir. I am just a sergeant."

Jean and Tiny were in the mess and both looked thinner than I had remembered. They both brightened when they saw me. Jean embraced me. "Thank God you are safe. When you went off in the night we worried about you."

"I fear you were in greater danger than I was. What happened to Albert?"

His face became angry. "It was Murat! Damn his eyes! He ordered us to charge some Mamelukes and we were unsupported. The colonel became isolated and we tried to get to him but he was cut to pieces. There was not enough left of him to bury."

I felt my eyes filling with tears. Tiny said, "It was the way he would have wanted to go, sir. He wouldn't have wanted to be a wounded old soldier and he was leading his regiment wasn't he?"

"Yes Tiny, I know that but I also know how he felt about charges. He told me it was not our business."

"Anyway," continued Jean, "we are now attached to the Guards. They lost heavily too. I suspect it means we will be close to the general and slightly safer from now on."

I could not tell him that the general was planning on deserting the army. Even General Kléber did not know that. He thought that the general would return after a short visit to Paris. I knew he would not.

"I will be glad to get into my old uniform."

"I am sorry Robbie. It is still in Acre. Some Turk will be wearing it now. We left everything."

"Yes sir, including the wounded," added Tiny darkly.

"The wounded?"

Jean nodded, "It was not General Bonaparte's finest hour Robbie. He had the plague victims poisoned and then abandoned many of the wounded. He treated the horses better."

Our ruthless general was hurting us more than the British. "I wouldn't be too confident about the peaceful time. The general told me, in confidence, that there was another Turkish army heading our way and a fleet of over a hundred ships. That is why he is here and not in Cairo."

Jean's shoulders sagged, "Then we had better see the quartermaster about some new equipment. The muskets misfire now more than they fire. I'll go and see Sergeant Major Manet."

After he had left Tiny said, "Your uniform is still in Acre but your chest is here. The colonel sent it back here after you were sent on the mission."

"Thank you." That meant I had my spare pistols and Arab cloak as well as spare boots and breeches. It might not be the full uniform of the 17th but the breeches, at least, would make me feel more like I was back home.

"Did you hear about Hougon?"

I had also put him from my mind. "No, what has happened to him?" Part of me wanted it to be something painful.

"He has fallen on his feet. He was promoted to major and then the colonel dies so he commands the 15th now. Luckily he is only a brevet colonel and does not outrank the major but Major Bartiaux is not happy about that."

And I could understand why. Someone who should have been the subject of a court-martial had ended up being promoted. It was an unjust world.

The Ottoman fleet was sighted at Aboukir Bay where our fleet had been destroyed. General Bonaparte always acted decisively and he led the army north with messengers from the Guards summoning Desaix and the other generals from the east. He was determined to end the Ottoman threat once and for all. The cannons he had placed at Alexandria had driven the fleet east and the Ottoman troops had landed to dig trenches around their fort there. General Bessières confided to me that General Bonaparte was so confident of our ability to defeat the Turk that he had allowed them to do this.

All of the cavalry was placed under the leadership of General Murat. The fact that he had been responsible for the death of the colonel, made me dislike him even more than I already did. You either loved or loathed him. He was flamboyant and he was charismatic and he was in love with himself. The 17th just loathed him. We had, however, to serve under him and obey him. He brigaded us with the 15th Chasseurs and the 22nd Dragoons. This meant that we were, once again, close to the hated Hougon. It was hard to fight alongside two men whom I hated so much when so many of my friends had died bravely. We were on the eastern side of our lines. The infantry and the artillery were to our left. Once again we were the exposed wing of the army.

When the Ottoman began to fire their cannon I could see just how few they had. Obviously, the cannons we had seen in Alexandria when we had landed were of the same inferior quality as those brought from Constantinople. General Bonaparte himself supervised our own cannonade and soon the enemy cannons were all silenced. The trenches were well dug and the sand prevented our cannon from doing much damage to the infantry who were dug in there.

General Davout himself led the infantry assault. The skirmishers led and the solid columns marched steadily behind. General Murat formed us into three lines and he ordered us to move forward. The fifty men of the 17th were sandwiched between the Guards, another small unit and the 22nd which appeared to have survived so far at full strength. The 15th was behind us in support. My hand had recovered and I now held my sword confidently. We walked and then trotted towards the trenches. The desultory fire from the Ottomans caused us no trouble and we broke into a gallop. The ground was hard but I could see that, closer to the beach, it became softer. When we heard the bugle sound charge it was impossible to restrain our mounts. They knew what the call meant and they leapt forward.

Had the Ottomans stayed in their trenches they might have survived as we had no lances and our horses merely jumped over the obstacles. However, they were terrified by the sight of the seven hundred horsemen racing towards them and they jumped from their trenches fleeing towards the safety of the sea. Some tried to fire their antiquated weapons before they did so but most ran. It was not war; it was grisly butchery. We all slaughtered any in our way but no-one enjoyed the experience. You would have to have been a follower of the Marquis de Sade to find anything good in slashing and slicing at men's backs. When they did face us they died anyway. However, they ran so quickly that more were drowned than died by blades. Ten thousand Ottomans perished in the sea and the threat from the Turk was gone for good.

Even though we had virtually walked over them we still suffered wounds and deaths. Some horses had hurt themselves and their riders in the trenches while some were killed by the fire from the fort which took another two hours to subdue. That evening the forty-five survivors of the 17th returned to Alexandria to tell tales of our brave and dead comrades.

I was summoned, a few days later, to General Bonaparte's Headquarters. He came to the point quickly. "Captain Macgregor, you have done me great services in the past and I would like to offer you a commission in the Guards. I would like you to be a major."

"I am sorry general but the 17th is still my regiment."

He looked aghast at Bessières, "I cannot believe this man! There are less than fifty men in the regiment. They should be disbanded."

"Then I will go with them anyway."

"The Guards will be coming with me." He nodded as he spoke so that I would know he meant on his escape.

"Then I wish you a safe voyage general."

As I left the building General Bessières said, "I think you inherited a double dose of honour from your mother and your father. I think you are a fool but you are a noble and likeable fool. I pray that you survive. The general has washed his hands of you now. He will not offer you this again."

"Then I am happy for it means I will be with my comrades once more."

I could not and did not tell the others either of the offer or the general's plans but I slept easier that night knowing that I had done the right thing. General Bonaparte left a week later ostensibly on a cruise up the Nile but he took almost all of the Guards, the scientists and many of the generals. Many of the sceptics made the connection and knew we had been abandoned. General Kléber was left in command and for that I was happy.

The last months of the century were not as bad as the first months had been. The Ottomans had been soundly beaten and the people of Cairo had come to regard General Bonaparte and his soldiers as almost mystical for the general had told the divan before the battle what the outcome would be and when that happened it gave him the status of a holy man. We were just given light duties. The only Guards who had been left were the wounded under the command of Sergeant Delacroix who had been injured in the attack on the trenches. Their duties and ours were to act as escorts and guards for General Kléber.

In the first week in December Jean and I were summoned to headquarters and a meeting with General Kléber. It was like the old days and General Bonaparte as he made sure we were alone.

"Gentlemen I find myself in a difficult position. We cannot continue to hold this land. Men are dying daily and there is no hope for reinforcement. We need peace." He paused, inviting comment.

Jean obliged, "Will the Ottomans be inclined to peace? The slaughter of the garrison at Jaffa did little to make them do us any favours."

"I agree and I am relying on the British to allow us to leave. Commodore Sidney Smith is still at Acre and he has given us information before now. I intend to meet with him and negotiate a safe passage back to France."

"He wouldn't agree to that would he?"

The general glanced at me and smiled, "I believe the captain knows differently does he not?"

I blushed as Jean stared at me. "They may well let us leave sir. They would like to be free from this campaign as much as we do. I think the general is correct."

He smiled and seemed satisfied. "Good, then this is what I intend. We will sail, your squadron and me, to Acre. The captain and one of his men will, under a flag of truce, arrange a meeting between myself and Sir Sydney."

I nodded but Jean looked appalled. "He will be taken, prisoner!"

The general smiled. "He has done this before and the British are men of their word."

"He is correct Jean. It will work out. Do you actually wish to stay in this pestilential hell hole a minute longer than we have to?" He shook his head.

The general nodded. "Very well. We leave immediately for the harbour. We will leave the horses at the barracks."

As we headed back to the camp Jean asked, "Are you sure about this?"

"Believe me I want out of this country so much I would meet with the devil himself but I am glad it is the British. I have spoken with them and they are honourable men."

He said, "What do you mean?"

I told him of my last mission, "But you must keep it secret. I suspect our little general would do anything to avoid that piece of news becoming common knowledge." I think that Jean was happy now knowing what my mission had been. It had been the only secret I had not shared with my mentor and I was glad that it was out in the open now.

The men were quite happy to be doing something a little different. We didn't tell them where we were going, just that we were going on a ship. When we arrived there it was, of course, the inevitable 'Carillon' who was waiting for us. François grinned as I stepped aboard. "Brought some friends this time captain?"

"I recommended the cruise!"

We had to leave at night time to avoid the British and Ottoman patrols. We sailed due north and then headed east. I had chosen Sergeant

Manet to accompany me on my diplomatic mission ashore. Tiny was hurt but I told him that we only had three officers. I could not leave Jean to run the squadron alone should anything untoward happen to me. Sergeant Manet was eager for the adventure. I think the tales he had heard from Tiny and Pierre had made him envious.

Two sailors rowed us to within a mile of the city. The 'Carillon' would stand off the coast and, if we were successful, we would return to her. It was an hour before dawn when we left the beach and made the road from Jaffa to Acre. We had our weapons for, until we reached the city we might have to contend with Turks or brigands. The light from the early morning sun touched the tops of the battlements and the minarets first and they were an inspiring sight. I could see how it had held out for so long. It had been built almost seven hundred years earlier and was a testament to the Crusader builders of Outremer.

We waited, and hid by an old building outside the city walls. I was waiting until I saw an Englishman. I hoped it would not be a Sergeant Tobias. I could see many fez and turban topped soldiers and I knew them to be Ottoman. I was looking for red or blue.

Sergeant Manet began to fidget nervously with his sword. "Be patient sergeant."

"How can you be so calm, sir? We are under the noses of the enemy."

"And they do not know we are here."

"But what are we waiting for?"

"I don't know but when I see it I will know."

"You are too clever for me sir."

"No I am not but let us just say that I have done this a few times." At that moment I saw a boat push off from the flagship anchored outside the harbour. "There, that is our chance. Follow me!"

I headed down towards the jetty. I was counting on the fact that the boat would come within a few yards of the beach and I could attract their attention. I recognised the cocked hat of a junior officer in the stern with the eight-man crew. We emerged from the mud huts onto the beach and Sergeant Manet was incredibly nervous, looking over his shoulder as though we would be attacked at any time. "Relax and look as though we are supposed to be here. I will speak in English in a moment. Don't panic." I waved my arm and shouted, "Ho, English boat. I would like to speak with you!"

My voice carried over and the lack of an accent must have made the officer curious. He looked over. "Raise your hands sergeant." I raised my hands as well and shouted, "We wish to speak with a senior officer. We offer our parole."

Suddenly the boat turned towards us. The sailors had no arms and the officer only a sword. The officer looked to be about eighteen. "Who are you, sir?"

"I am Captain Robert Macgregor of the 17th Chasseurs and I am here to speak with Commodore Sidney Smith. I represent the commander of the French forces in Egypt, General Jean Kléber. And who are you, sir?"

Politeness took over. "I am Midshipman Paul Ritchie of Her Majesty's ship Tigre." He suddenly looked flustered.

"I have given my parole and I assure you that I mean no harm to you or your captain. Could you convey us on board and I can give the proposal from my general?"

I could see the grins from his bemused crew. He blushed and then said, "Very well. May I have your swords?"

"I have given you our parole but very well." I turned to the sergeant, "Sergeant, let them have your sword."

I unbuckled mine and handed it over. The sergeant did the same. The midshipman held them awkwardly. "Er, step aboard."

"Thank you, Mr Ritchie." We sat before him facing the blue rigged crew.

Once he sat down, he became more in command. "Push off coxswain. Let's head back to the ship."

Chapter 11

The eighty gun two-decker loomed over us. It was not as big as the Vanguard in Naples harbour but it was still a daunting sight. Midshipman Ritchie raced up the ladder to report to the officer. As I reached the main deck I heard the First Lieutenant say, "Well done Middy, capturing two French prisoners. Well done."

I said to the officer, "Excuse me, Lieutenant, but we gave our parole."

I do not know if he was more shocked at the English or the mistake. "Mr Ritchie is this true? Did they give their parole and yet you took their swords?"

Poor Midshipman Ritchie looked flustered, "I am sorry sir I..."

"Give them back their swords immediately." He turned to me. "I am sorry sir. He is young."

I smiled graciously, "It is not a problem. He was most polite."

We strapped our swords on and were escorted below decks. This ship had slightly higher decks than the 'Carillon' and I was grateful. I hated banging my head. We were taken to the Commodore's cabin and two marines watched us carefully.

Sergeant Manet asked, "I do not understand. Why did they take our swords and then return them to us?"

"The young officer did not understand that we gave our parole. He was told off by the lieutenant."

Sergeant Manet laughed, "Typical of young officers and Lieutenants."

The commodore entered followed by the captain. He began brusquely, "I understand you are here under a flag of truce."

"Yes, sir. I am here on behalf of General Kléber commanding the armies of Egypt."

"And who are you?"

"I am Captain Robert Macgregor of the 17th Chasseurs."

"You sound Scottish. Are you a traitor?"

I appreciated the commodore, he came to the point. I smiled, "No sir. I was born in France to a Scottish mother."

"Why should I even entertain you and your proposal? Bonaparte has fled and your soldiers die daily from the plague."

"And I know that you and your admiral would like to be away from this area. If you meet with my general he will expedite matters and we will leave for France."

"And what do you know of my admiral? Are you trying to impress me with names?"

"No, sir. I have met your admiral." He and the captain laughed and even the marines smirked.

"And I dare say you have also met Lady Hamilton."

"I did and she was a most gracious hostess." I saw a flicker of doubt race across his face. I pushed home my advantage. "Her husband Sir William was also a kind and generous host."

He waved an airy hand. "You could have read these names in the newspaper and everyone knows of Lady Hamilton's kindness."

"But do they know that Colonel James Selkirk, once of the Scots Greys is now at Palazzo Sessa and that Sergeant Tobias of the Marines is an obnoxious toad who has now been demoted to corporal and that Marine McIntyre also works there."

There was a silence as deep as the sea. "Then you have met them?"

"Sir, I am a gentleman. Why would I lie?"

"Then what is your proposal?"

"My general waits offshore and he would meet with you to discuss surrender."

They had not expected those words and it took them by surprise. "Surrender?"

"Sir, there is little point in sending me to arrange a meeting if I was to discuss terms. I am a mere captain."

Commodore Sidney Smith laughed, "No sir, you are more than a mere captain. Where do we meet?"

"If you set sail and head west you will find the sloop 'Carillon'. She will take you to a place on the coast where you can meet and discuss terms."

The captain coughed and said, "Sir this could be a trap."

I laughed and they all looked at me, Manet included, "The 'Carillon' is the largest ship left to France in this part of the world and she is a sloop. Captain, you have eighty guns. Are you afraid of an eight gun sloop?"

The captain had the good grace to give a half bow. "I will order all sails to be set." He looked at me. "You are a most interesting man, captain."

"If you would be so good as to have a white flag at your masthead they will know you come in peace."

We went on deck and Commodore Smith asked, "How will we find this little sloop of yours?"

I smiled, "They will be watching for you. The 'Carillon' will approach you. If the gun ports are closed and the white flag flying she will close alongside and if not she will fly like the wind."

"Leaving you and your sergeant as prisoners."

Once again I smiled and gave a slight shrug, "Probably."

We watched the horizon for the sight of a sail and a tricolour. "Your General Napoleon left us swiftly enough." I nodded and said nothing. "I daresay he was needed in Paris."

"I would think Paris a more pleasant place than Cairo wouldn't you, Commodore?"

It was his turn to laugh. "Yes, I think this land is for the Turk and not for us."

"Sail ho! Sloop and it's a Frenchie!"

The captain shouted his own commands. "Haul in the mainsails!"

The crew scurried up the ratlines and in no time at all, we were just under foresail and barely moving. François brought the sloop alongside like a terrier and stopped it within thirty yards. The white flag fluttered cheerily. I saw a boat push off with the general, Jean and Tiny. Commodore Smith turned to the captain. "Would you be so good as to have some refreshments sent down to my cabin?"

We waited for my three countrymen to board. The crew seemed amused rather than afraid; after all, they had eighty guns. They did stare at the five of us in the strange uniforms. General Kléber gave a slight bow and then looked at me. To our surprise, Commodore Smith spoke perfect French. "Welcome on board general. Your captain here explained the purpose of your visit. Shall we adjourn to my cabin?"

As we walked to the cabin the general asked, "You speak excellent French, where did you learn it?"

The commodore smiled graciously, "I was a prisoner in Paris for two years; until I escaped."

Here was a man with stories as interesting as my own and now I understood why he had acceded to our request so readily. For the first time in a long time, I became hopeful. Perhaps we would be returned home and this war would end. With so few men left in the regiment I was sure it would be disbanded and then I could travel, with the world at peace, back to Scotland and deliver the seal entrusted to me by the Knights of St. John.

Both the Commodore and the General were down to earth men and the discussions were brief. As the commodore's aide and his secretary did not speak French the negotiations took twice as long as they ought to have as everything had to be translated but in a remarkably short space of time, we had concluded a peace and we would be sailing back to France once enough transports had been gathered.

We were back in Alexandria harbour as the sun set. Tiny looked almost disappointed. "That was too easy sir. Do we just pack up and sail home then?"

The general had been listening. "Not quite that easy. I do not think that the Ottomans will allow us to sail away without trying to hurt us. Their pride is at stake. We have defeated them in every battle and their only saviour was the British. They will not be happy but I am confident that we will escape."

There was almost a carnival atmosphere for a couple of weeks as the word spread amongst the soldiers that we were going home. We moved the army to Cairo which was still unsettled. Suddenly at the end of February, the general received a demand from Admiral Keith to surrender. He had overruled Commodore Smith's treaty and we were to be incarcerated. As we were still acting as the general's guards we were privy to the discussions and the debate. Of course, the general would not surrender and when we heard that an army of thirty thousand Mamelukes was heading for Cairo General Kléber assembled the ten thousand troops who still remained. The cavalry were down to six hundred men. Disease, battle and the desert had taken their toll and we were down to just one brigade.

General Kléber used our army's strengths and not the weakness in numbers to dictate our battle plan. We used the hollow square employed by General Bonaparte at the Battle of the Pyramids except that this time the cavalry remained echeloned to the rear. Our orders were quite clear. We had to wait until we judged that the enemy had been broken and then attack. General Kléber did not want to throw away his last cavalry in ridiculous wasteful charges.

We were the squadron on the right and were the furthest from the infantry. The other chasseurs and the brigade of dragoons were to our left. The Mamelukes only knew one way to fight; they charged wildly! They hurled themselves at the infantry square. Although there were not many cannons left to the general they were well manned and they all fired canister. The deadly missiles sliced through both horse and rider. The Mamelukes could not break through. The Army of the Orient were able to fire regular and deadly volleys each time the Ottomans closed. Jean sent a message to the colonel of the dragoons suggesting we charge. Jean was the oldest cavalry officer on the field that day and the colonel respected his judgement. We heard the bugle sound trot and we moved forward.

It was like fighting with family for there were few of us but it was a gallant family and I felt proud to be amongst the likes of Sergeant Delacroix, Jean, Tiny and Sergeant Manet. We would watch each other's backs and be true to our uniform. Once the charge was sounded we leaned forward and kicked our mounts on. The desert was a good place to fight as it was generally flat and we crashed into the disordered Ottoman cavalry. They were brave warriors and fierce fighters but my Austrian blade stabbed one turbaned leader even as he tried to sweep his scimitar at my head. The longer sword gave me a real advantage. There was no place for delicate thrusts and parries. We hacked, slashed and sliced at those before us. We were outnumbered and we needed to drive them far from Cairo. Normally we would have halted and then rejoined the infantry but that day at Heliopolis we pursued until our horses were weary and there were no Mamelukes before us. My arm was weary from the sword thrusts I made. We all knew that if we were to escape Egypt we had to make sure that there were no enemies left to stop us.

Jean's bugler sounded recall and the thirty survivors of the 17th and the Guards gathered. I looked for familiar faces and saw both Jean and Tiny. I desperately scanned the field for the two sergeants but they were not to be seen. As we headed back to the infantry we checked every trooper that we saw. I found the two sergeants quite close together. From the bodies around them, they had been surrounded and killed many of their enemies before they were overcome. Sergeant Manet and Delacroix's bodies were hacked to pieces. I dismounted. Jean asked, "What are you doing? There are still Turks out there."

"Then sir, you can go on but I am going to bury two comrades and not leave their bodies for the jackals and the vultures."

Tiny and the rest of the squadron dismounted. We used the scimitars of the dead Ottomans to dig two graves and then we reverently laid their bodies next to each other. Some of the troopers had found other dead friends and they joined the two sergeants in this lonely and deserted grave. We covered their bodies with the cloaks from the Ottomans and then laid the scimitars on top. We would honour our dead with the spoils of war. Finally, we covered them with soil and piled rocks on the sand. We stood with bare and bowed heads. After a few minutes' silent prayer and remembrance the thirty who remained rode back to the army.

The rest of the cavalry had returned much earlier and General Kléber was delighted to see us. "I feared I had lost you all." He looked at the numbers. "This is a sad sight and I am afraid that our work is not finished. The populace of Cairo have anticipated a Turkish victory and they have risen. We have an insurrection to suppress. Major, take your men and ride to Alexandria I want every French warship and transport to remain in the harbour." He shrugged, "There may only be a handful but we may need them all soon."

Jean lowered his voice. "Do you intend to flee sir? We have not enough ships."

"I know but we may be able to save the sick and wounded. I will not have the men who serve me suffer poison."

"Sir."

"When you have done that then return to Cairo. I will have need of you there."

We missed the general's return to Cairo but the revolt was put down effectively although many of the local population died. It bred much bad feeling. Alexandria, in contrast, was relatively peaceful. I wondered why the general did not withdraw to the port. Jean explained, "Cairo is the key to Egypt and if we lost that we would have to leave. We have not enough ships."

When we reached the port there was the 'Carillon' and six other ships at anchor. They would barely be able to take off the wounded and even then would have to escape the blockade. The new admiral was not Nelson and I could not see him turning a blind eye to our withdrawal. François was not optimistic. "We might be able to evade capture but not those merchant ships; they are too slow. I hope the general knows what he is doing."

"What else can he do? He is not Bonaparte and he will not desert his men."

François spoke to the three of us quietly. "If things go badly then get here and I will try to wait for you and take you off."

"We could not leave our men."

"Nevertheless the offer is still there and besides," he pointed at the small number of troopers who lounged on the harbour wall, "I could easily take all of your men." It was a sobering thought that when we had sailed from Malta all those years ago it had taken a transport to take us all to Egypt and now we would fit on the sloop.

The journey back to Cairo was depressing. Jean looked ill as well as depressed. Since Albert had been killed I noticed that he rarely smiled and had lost the spark of life. I suspect he had also worried about me when I had been on my two missions. He was still watching over me for my mother.

Cairo was like a powder keg and we were all confined to barracks. Lone soldiers were found with their throats cut. General Kléber had the culprits hanged but there were many young men willing to die for their religion. In May we were told of another band of Mamelukes who had been seen near to Suez. The five hundred cavalry who remained were sent to intercept them. General Kléber could not take the army from Cairo. The colonel of the dragoon had a wounded leg and so the command fell to Lieutenant Colonel Hougon. He took great delight in giving us the worst of the march. We were forced to the rear of the column where we ate the dust of the rest of the cavalry. Jean had ordered the men to wear their cloaks and it kept much of the dust from us but our horses suffered.

The scouts discovered the Mamelukes camped at the end of a dry valley. There were three thousand of them and we numbered barely five hundred. Lieutenant Colonel Hougon devised a plan. "We will use the 17th and the Guards as bait. You will ride down the valley and they will pursue you. We will wait on either side of the valley and fall upon them as they pass."

It seemed a good plan but neither Jean nor I were happy about the prospect of waiting for others to rescue us. We were, however, still soldiers of France and we obeyed our orders.

As we headed down the defile I confided my fears to Jean. "I do not like this one bit Jean. I don't trust that Hougon."

"You are a soldier of France now Robbie. You obey orders. You have done too many missions for the general and become used to making your own decisions. This is a good plan. We are the smallest squadron and the best. Would you have others risk their lives?"

"No sir, if it was anyone else other than Hougon in command then I would not worry, but it is, and he hates us."

Jean laughed, "And you think he would jeopardise the whole battle just to get revenge on us. I think you have too great an opinion of yourself." He halted the column. "We need to get ourselves seen and then flee as though we are filling our breeches." They all laughed. Despite our losses, we were all in good spirits. "Lieutenant, take four men and scout out the camp."

Tiny detached his men and they trotted off towards the camp we knew was hidden at the end of the defile. Killer was as fit as he had ever been. He had had the advantage of a restful home for some time whilst the others had been kept hard at it for weeks. He looked like a horse fresh from the stables. He was eager to run and I had to restrain him.

Suddenly we heard the sound of muskets and Tiny, three troopers and an empty saddle rode towards us. "Bugler sound retreat!"

We turned and trotted slowly until Tiny caught up with us. "Sir there is nearer five thousand of them than three thousand and they are coming." He pointed over his shoulder and we could see the Mamelukes galloping down the valley. They were too close to us for comfort.

"Ride hard!"

The troopers needed no urging and we all whipped our horses. I glanced over my shoulder and saw that they had camels. They were slower than our horses but they could keep going for longer. I looked to the hillsides but could see nothing. Where was that damned Hougon?

The first troopers who died had the weaker horses and the Mamelukes caught them. We heard their screams as they were butchered. Killer was coping easily with the run and I had to hold him back or I would have outrun the rest of the depleted squadron. We heard firing, at last, but it was far behind us and seemed to be closer to the Mameluke camp than the hillsides. Then we heard the thundering of the camels as the Ottomans gradually closed with us.

"Bugler sound halt!" Jean turned to me, "We cannot outrun them. We will have to turn and fight."

I nodded. We reined in and leapt from our horses. I had no musket but I had my two pistols. "Steady! Fire when they are close enough!"

The pistols and muskets all cracked at the same time and the camels and their riders fell as though they had been struck by rope. "Mount! Draw sabres."

We clambered back on our horses and rode towards the enemy. It was not foolish bravery; it was the only thing we could do. Killer was still fresh and he launched himself at the leading camels. He did not like camels but he was not afraid of them. I hacked at one rider's leg and my sword severed the bootless limb below the knee. The edge sliced into the camel which lurched into the next camel. On my left, the camel rider swung his scimitar at my head; my colpack bore the brunt and I stabbed upwards into his chest. I had no time for self-congratulation as three horsemen rode at me. I pulled hard on Killer's reins and he reared up to strike one of the horses on the head. It collapsed taking its rider to his death. I let go of the reins and drew my empty pistol. I parried one scimitar as I lunged at the other rider. My sword struck home but his dying arm sliced down to cut my thigh and Killer's side. I sensed rather than saw the other rider swing his scimitar at my head. I ducked and stabbed him through the thigh and into his horse. Both fell to the ground in a bloody heap.

I realised that I was alone and I turned. The rest of the troopers were surrounded by enemies and I whipped Killer's head around and charged towards them. I saw troopers falling to enemies who outnumbered them three to one. Tiny and Jean were fighting furiously back to back, protecting each other while the remnants of the squadron fought countless enemies. I had the advantage of attacking unprotected backs and I ruthlessly hacked a passage to my comrades. To my horror, I saw that there was just Jean and Tiny left. I redoubled my efforts. A Mameluke turned and raised his musket to shoot me. I rode straight at him. The musket fired but I was too close to him and I skewered him on my sword. Then I saw Tiny, my friend, fall. His head had been severed. The killer was despatched himself by Jean who, in turn, was stabbed in the back. I kicked Killer on and managed to kill the Mameluke who was about to deliver the coup de grace. I grabbed Jean's horse's reins and galloped as hard as I could. Musket balls buzzed around us but I kept my head down and just galloped.

They must have thought that we were not worth pursuing. After a mile with no noise behind I turned and saw that we were not being followed. I halted and leapt from Killer. I lowered Jean to the ground. He was as white as a sheet. His eyes were closed as I opened his tunic. His stomach had been laid open. I took his cloak from his saddle and tore it into strips.

I heard his voice and he opened his eyes. "It is finished, Robbie. I am dying. Leave me."

"Never! I will take you back."

"Then you will be carrying a corpse. Leave me and leave Egypt. If you stay here then you will die."

His eyes closed and I thought he was dead. "Jean! Jean!"

His eyes flickered open briefly. "You have been like a son to me Robbie. Your mother would have been proud of you. Go back to your roots and I will go to your…" And then he died.

I don't know how long I held him in my arms it seemed like forever. Suddenly there was a thump from behind me and I turned to see Killer lying on the ground gasping for air. I gently laid Jean down and ran to my horse. The musket had missed me but not Killer and my brave horse had carried me beyond his capabilities. He had been cut by a scimitar and by numerous musket balls. I held his head and stroked him. "You have been a good horse. Now run free." He tried to lift his nuzzle to my face and then he too, closed his eyes and died.

I cried. I am not ashamed to say it. I had not cried for many years but I did there in that oven of a desert. I cried for my dead comrades and I cried for my horse. I was alone and I wept like a child. I did not even care if the Turks found me. My life could have ended there and then and I would not have minded. My whole world had been destroyed. And then a hard resolve filled me. I would get my revenge on the man who had betrayed us. Lieutenant Colonel Hougon would die. I dug a grave for my horse and my friend. It took some time but I was determined to do it. I used Jean's horse to drag Killer into the grave and then laid Jean on top. I covered him in his cloak, like a shroud and then covered it with sand and soil. I spent some time sweeping all traces of the grave away. I did not want anyone to disturb this tomb. I lifted my saddle onto the back of Jean's horse. I would drop it somewhere far from the grave.

I turned to face the dead, "Farewell Jean, if I was the son you always wanted then you became the father I never had. You fulfilled your promise to my mother and I will never forget you and the lessons you taught me. Killer I could ask for no finer horse than you. You had more courage and nobility than most soldiers. Farewell to you both." I took Jean's helmet as my colpack was too badly damaged and I began to move. The sun was setting and I knew which way I had to head. There was no track and no road but the ground was flat. I nudged Jean's horse into motion and the weary beast trudged west.

Two miles from the grave I dropped my saddle. I still had Jean's pistols and I loaded them. I knew I had more than twenty miles to go but I was determined that I would get there. I had a man to kill. It soon became obvious to me that I would not be able to travel much further. Jean's horse's pace became slower and slower. I stopped and examined him. He had gone lame and he too, like Killer, had succumbed to a wound. Although not as bad as Killer's mortal injury it had been the scimitar wound that had been bleeding since the battle. I took the saddle off and dropped it to the ground. I used some bandages to stem the flow of blood but I knew he would not survive. I would not let him die alone. I had been with Killer until the end and Jean's brave horse deserved no less. I led the horse by its reins and trudged on through the cold night. I did not notice the temperature. I was kept warm by the fierce flames of anger and vengeance burned inside me.

Chapter 12

The horse dropped and died just before dawn. I did not have the energy or the will to dig another grave and so I covered the body with rocks. With just a half-empty canteen I said farewell to the last survivor of the 17th Chasseurs and headed west towards Cairo. Seventeen miles does not seem a great distance, especially not to a horseman, but when it is June, in the desert and you have not slept it is further than you would believe. It was a trackless desert. I had lost whatever road there was in the middle of the night. I knew where west was thanks to the sun on my back and I just headed in that direction. I had donned my white, hooded cloak and that kept me a little cooler than I would have otherwise been. My pistols seemed unbearably heavy and I forced myself to discard Jean's. It hurt as it was like throwing him away but, if I was to survive, I had to travel as lightly as possible. It was hard to put one foot in front of the other. I just wanted to close my eyes and sleep but I knew that as soon as I did that I would be as good as dead. My only hope was to keep moving. I found the only way I could motivate myself was to set small targets. I looked for something in the near distance and guessed how many steps it would take to reach it. Then I counted the steps. It sounds like a childish game but it worked and I derived pleasure if I got close to my number. It was in the late afternoon when I saw the tips of the Pyramids appear to the south and I knew where I was. I changed my direction to strike further north. I knew that the main road from Cairo to Suez passed that way. Soon I spied the spiked turrets of the minarets of Cairo. My water had long gone but I hoped I would get some sooner rather than later.

I am not sure I would have made it were it not for the party of engineers who were marching east to repair a damaged well. They supplied me with water and the news I sought. "Yes sir," said the grizzled sergeant in charge of the eight-man patrol, "the cavalry came back. They had a great victory. The heroes destroyed a Mameluke army and saved Cairo from attack." They filled my canteen and watched as I trudged west determined to reach Cairo as soon as I could. Their words made me even angrier. My dead comrades were already forgotten.

As I walked the last two miles to the city walls, I reflected that history only recorded what the survivors said. The dead had no voice and Hougon thought I had died along with my comrades. He was in for a shock.

I took off my cloak when I entered the gate. My uniform expedited my movements around the city. In the cloak, I was suspicious and had to answer too many questions. When I reached headquarters, I was admitted straight away and the general embraced me. "I was told you were dead! This is wonderful. Where are the others?"

"They are dead. We were betrayed!"

His face showed the innocence of the general. Had he shown guilt I think I might have killed him there and then. "Colonel Hougon let us all die. We were supposed to lead the Ottomans into a trap but he was not there and we were massacred. I barely escaped with my life." I told him all that had occurred, right down to the death of Jean.

"The colonel tells it differently. He says you and your men charged the camp and were slaughtered he tried to rescue you but he was too late. He says he destroyed their camp."

"He might have destroyed their camp but he did not lift a finger to help us."

"Those are serious charges captain."

"And I will repeat them to his face. Not all of his men are as venal as he and they will tell the truth. Where is he? I will confront him here and now."

"He has taken the remains of the cavalry to Alexandria to recover."

"Then I will go there now."

"No! I order you to stay here!" Then his voice softened. "I will go with you the day after tomorrow. I will get to the bottom of this. Stay here." I was still angry but I was used to obeying orders. "It is but another two days and you need rest. You will think better after food and good sleep."

"If he is not punished by the army then he will die by my hand. That I promise."

"Then you would be shot for killing a superior officer."

"It would be worth it to avenge my friends."

"I believe you. Go to your quarters and I will send a new uniform. That one is covered in blood and damaged beyond repair." I looked at the jacket and the breeches. He was right. There were so many sword cuts that it was ruined. "I will get the surgeon to look at you."

I went to the room I had been allocated and undressed. I fell asleep in an instant. When I awoke the doctor was finishing binding my cuts. He nodded at my money belt. "You are a careful soldier with your valuables. It is a shame you are not more careful with your body. Take better care of it, young man. You have been very lucky. Two of the wounds would have been fatal if they had been a little deeper."

"I am afraid I have little control over where the wounds are or how deep they are. I just try to stay alive."

He stood as he finished, "I have heard what happened to your comrades. Do not dwell on it. Look upon each day as a new start. You have been to hell and back and you are reborn. Do not spurn this chance of life. Live each day as though it is your last." He pointed to the blue uniform hanging up. "The general sent this."

I dressed in an unfamiliar blue uniform. I was lucky that they had a spare captain's uniform. Even as I was dressing I was thinking that these were dead men's clothes. I joined General Kléber and General Menou for dinner. I had never met him before but I did not like Menou at all. He struck me as an ambitious man. Certainly, when we talked over the meal I got the impression that he had not fought very often. I suppose now that General Bonaparte had taken most of the other generals back to France people such as Menou and Hougon were seizing their chances. Brave men died and opportunists were promoted.

Towards the end of the meal, the talk came around to Hougon and General Kléber explained that we would be travelling to Alexandria to confront the man.

General Menou shook his head, "No! You cannot general. Hougon is a hero. Even if what this captain says is true…" I began to rise; I would not be insulted by anyone.

Kléber restrained me, "General Menou this man's honour is without a stain. I suggest you temper your language. Do not even begin to impugn his honour. He has earned the respect of all especially General Bonaparte."

He apologised, but not with his eyes, "I am sorry captain but if what you say is true then bringing this matter to the public gaze will not bring your dead comrades back will it? We need all the heroes we can get."

"The heroes are all buried beneath the sand." I pushed my half-eaten plate away, my appetite gone. "As I said to the general I am more than happy to mete the punishment out myself. Colonel Hougon once challenged me to a duel and I will oblige him."

General Menou shook his head, "That is just as bad. I forbid it!"

I glared at this pompous little officer. Did he really think that he could stop me? I could see that I was getting nowhere. I did not need to justify myself to him. He was not in command. General Kléber would be travelling with me and I trusted him to see that justice was not only done but seen to be done. "Gentlemen I am tired. With your permission, I will retire. Do you require my services tomorrow, General Kléber?"

"Yes, I am meeting with various Egyptians to deal with some civil matters. It would help to have someone else to hear them. General Menou will be leaving in the morning for Alexandria."

"Then I shall see you both in the morning. Goodnight sir." I knew that the general would go directly to Hougon and tell him what had transpired. It made no difference to me. I would fight the whole of the 15th if needs be.

I felt more rested when I awoke. I dressed and presented myself to the general. He saw my sword. "If you would please leave your sword in your room, captain; I do not want to incense the Egyptians any more than I have to."

I smiled; I would only need my sword when I confronted Colonel Hougon. "Certainly sir. I do not need the weight anyway. It is far too hot for that."

My job, as far as I could see, was to hover behind the general as he sat, Turkish style, cross-legged on the cushions. He would listen to the request of the supplicant and then render a decision. Occasionally he turned to ask me something in French and then he would turn back to the supplicant. The morning was spent in such dull intercourses. We had a break in midmorning for a cool drink of sherbet.

I felt that I could speak freely with the general; he was a soldier like me. "Sir, do you not find this tedious?"

"Dull in the extreme. I enliven it by asking you questions which heightens the anticipation of the supplicant and makes them more grateful to France for acceding to their request. Do not fear we only have another six and then we are finished and I can get back to being a soldier again."

We saw two more supplicants and then the general asked me to fetch him some papers from his room. "We have an important mullah coming. The next visitor is just a student."

I found the papers quickly and I returned. As I entered the room I saw the student plunge his knife into the chest of the general. I threw the papers to the floor and launched myself at him. I saw him stab the general in the thigh. I pulled my hand back and punched the student so hard that I heard his nose break and saw his eyes close as he collapsed in an unconscious heap. I quickly turned to the general. His lifeblood was spilling on the gorgeous cushions. "I fear you will have to deal with the Lieutenant Colonel yourself I..." Then he died. Had he lived then events might have turned out differently but, as I came to understand in the heat of Egypt, sometimes our destinies are shaped by forces that are not of this world.

The colonel in charge of the guards raced in, his face white with anger. He yelled at his guards, "Why did you not search the supplicants when they came in?" The guards just looked at each other in embarrassment. "Take this prisoner away and lock him up. I will question him later." He seemed to see me for the first time. "Are you injured, captain?"

"No, sir. Just annoyed with me for not being able to do anything."

"I need you to ride to Alexandria and inform General Menou of the situation. He is now the commander of the French Army here in Egypt."

"Yes, sir." My heart sank. My quest for justice would fall on the deaf ears of a general who was motivated by politics. I would still make my request but I feared the worst. I packed my old uniform and clothes and requisitioned a horse from the stables. The stable sergeant recognised me. "I heard about the general. Take his horse. It has a mind of its own but you are like the general was, you are a horseman."

I thanked the sergeant and rode north. He was right it was a spirited animal but like all such beasts, it responded to a firm hand. As I rode I checked that my two pistols were both loaded. Although the road from Cairo to Alexandria was patrolled it was thinner than it had been and there were men, like the murderous students, who would risk their lives to rid the land of us. I could not die until my friends were avenged and then I would not care what happened to me.

I had to make two overnight stops at two of the forts along the way. I was the bearer of the news of the general's death and it saddened an already depressed army. General Kléber had restored the army's faith in its generals after the desertion by Bonaparte. I think that if it had not been for the general then the army might have mutinied. I left each fort feeling less confident about the fate of the French soldiers. They were brave and they were resourceful but they needed leaders like General Kléber and not ambitious and self-serving men like Bonaparte and Menou. I had no doubt that Napoleon Bonaparte was a good general but I knew that he did not care about the men he commanded; he just wanted power.

I reached Alexandria two days after leaving Cairo. I rode directly to headquarters and was told that General Menou and the cavalry were in the Nile Delta and would not return until evening. I gave the general's aide the news of General Kléber's death and Menou's new responsibilities and promised to return after dark. I did not relish hanging around the headquarters building all afternoon and I headed for the harbour. I hoped that François was still there for he was now the last friend I had in this land. All the rest were lying beneath the sand.

As soon as I saw the little sloop my spirits rose. I tied my horse to a bollard and strode up the gangplank. The crew gave me a warm greeting. I think they had always appreciated that I was not a distant officer who was aloof but I knuckled down to the same work as they did. François' warm smile left his face as I told him of the general's death and filled him in on the deaths of those men he had known.

"We heard that there was a cavalry battle but we heard that it was a great victory. I knew that you and Jean would have been involved in the battle but I assumed that you had been successful. Now I understand why those who rode into Alexandria did not mention the 17th Chasseurs."

"I am the last of the 17th François. I am here to see that Hougon is court-martialed."

"That may not be as easy as you think Robbie. He and the general appear to be fast friends. The men of the 15th are now the unofficial guards of the general." I said nothing but stared at the worn wood of the table in the cabin. "I do not think he will court-martial the darling of the desert." My face hardened as his words sank in. He was right. The only man who would have done so was now dead. Even before he had left Menou had made it quite clear that he did not want the news to be made public. "Do not do anything foolish! Your friends would not wish you to die needlessly."

It did not matter what anyone said if I could not get justice one way then I would another. He was right; Jean and the others would not wish me to die needlessly and I would not. I still had to get to Scotland and fulfil my promise to a kinsman. I smiled and hated myself for the falseness of that smile. "You are right." I lowered my voice, "There is nothing left for me here. If I chose to leave Egypt would you give me a passage?"

"You mean desert?"

"How can I desert when I belong to no-one? Besides I would be doing just as Bonaparte did and leaving Egypt."

"I would take you in a moment but you know that we have been ordered to stay close to port."

"That was general Kléber and he is dead. Besides, I think that once General Menou discovers the news he will want a message taking to France and yours is the fastest ship."

François chewed the end of his finger as he debated. "If you can get to my ship unseen before we sail then I would take you but I am intrigued. Where would you go? France?"

I shook my head, "No not France. I am aware that you would not be able to sail into danger but, when we came south we passed Sicily did we not?"

"Yes, it is on the route to Naples and to Toulon."

"Then you could drop me on the coast there. I believe that I could gain passage back to England from there."

"Sicily is a wild place filled with bandits and brigands."

"And Egypt is not? Fear, not my friend. I have a plan in my mind and I will not be going to my death. At least not yet. May I leave my chest here? If I do not join you then you and your crew can have the pathetic contents,"

"Of course."

I carried the chest on board and took just one item from it; the stained and dirty cloak I had stolen when I had first landed all those years ago. It was no longer white but a sort of sandy grey with rusty splodges. Each stain told a story of wounds and of death and of betrayal.

François came to my horse, "Be careful Robbie. That Hougon has a reputation as a killer. He is a duellist."

"And I am not. I am a fighter. I will return but I may be in disguise."

He laughed, "Do not worry my crew all know you. That will not be a problem."

I reached General Menou's Headquarters before dark. I stabled the horse; I would not need it again and I hung the cloak close by. I slipped some coins to the stable sergeant and asked him to watch the horse and my cloak. He seemed surprised that I would want a rag caring for.

"I would have thrown it out sir if you had not returned."

I smiled, "That cloak has come to my aid more than once and is as valuable a weapon as this sword that I carry."

"In that case Captain Macgregor, I will guard both the horse and the cloak well."

I was surprised that he knew my name. "You know me, sergeant? Even in this strange uniform?"

"We all know you in the Alexandria garrison. If it had not been for you and your men our ships might have been battered long before we made landfall. And we know of the exploits of the 17th. I was sorry to hear of their loss."

"Thank you, sergeant, you have lifted my spirits to know that others remember my fallen comrades as I do."

I did feel lifted as I strode into the orderly room. "The general has yet to return sir."

"Then I will wait."

The orderly brought me some bread with some wine and dates. I nibbled as I waited. I heard the clatter of horses outside and the voices. I steeled myself for a confrontation with Hougon but it was just General Menou who entered. He did not seem surprised to see me.

"Come into my office you may be able to confirm or deny the rumours I have just heard."

Once inside he gestured for me to sit down. After he had taken his cloak off he spread his arms. "Well, sir I am here to tell you that General Kléber was murdered a few days ago by a fanatic. I was sent here to tell you that you are now in command of the army of Egypt."

"That is what I heard and I feared. The general was a fine soldier and his boots will be hard to fill. Is Cairo under control?"

"It was when I left."

"But it needs me there. I know that. Sergeant!" The door opened and the orderly sergeant stood there expectantly. "Send a message to Colonel Hougon and ask him to join me here and then send a messenger to the 'Carillon'. I will have despatches for her to take."

After he had gone I asked, "Sir, the court-martial for Colonel Hougon. The general…"

"The general is dead and I have no time for such nonsense. I need every commander I can get. Perhaps it would be better if you left for France on the 'Carillon'. You can deliver the news of General Kléber's death."

"But…"

He held up his hand. "But nothing. You will obey my orders or find yourself under arrest. Now, wait in the orderly room until I have written the report."

I had expected nothing else and I stepped into the orderly room. I now knew what I had to do and it would mean I was leaving the French army and living a life on the run but I was determined that I would do it. The sergeant looked up at me. He had heard the raised voices. I smiled and shrugged, "Such is life sergeant."

After a few minutes, the general came out with a sealed document in his hand. "Captain Macgregor I want you to deliver this message to the authorities in Genoa. You will then report to Paris for assignment. I have written a separate report to that effect. There is also an order for the captain of the 'Carillon'."

Just then the door opened and Colonel Hougon stood there. He was surprised to see me and he looked as though he had seen a ghost. That helped. "Did you think we all died out there, colonel? No, there is still one officer from the 17th who knows the truth."

"Captain! You have your orders now leave before I have you arrested."

Colonel Hougon was white; I know not if it was fear or anger but as I passed I said quietly. "This is not over and my hand is now healed. I will have justice."

Outside were two troopers from the 15th. They recognised me and saluted. I returned to the stables where I placed the reports and letters in my saddlebags. "Sergeant I will need my horse shortly and I will be in a hurry."

He nodded, "I understand sir and it will be ready."

I walked slowly back to the headquarters and stood quietly waiting. The two troopers watched me curiously. One of them said, "Were there many other survivors from the 17th Captain Macgregor?"

I looked the young trooper in the eye. "No trooper. I am the last of the 17th. They died fighting as brothers."

He nodded sadly, "I am sorry sir. We all wanted to…"

The other one said, "Ssh! The colonel."

"It does not matter. You obeyed orders. I knew that you would not have wanted to leave your comrades to die. There will be retribution." They looked at each other nervously and one of them slid his hand to his sword. "Rest easy it will not be you who pays. Not unless you are foolish enough to go for your sword and then I would be forced to kill you." There was a cold edge to my voice and he moved his hand carefully away.

The door opened and Colonel Hougon stood there. He stared at me. "You should be dead! But we can soon remedy that. You say your hand is healed?"

"It is and honour dictates that we end this now."

"The stables?"

"The stables."

He looked at his two troopers. "Come with us so that others will know of the outcome."

I could see that they were torn between curiosity and fear. Duels were outlawed and their participation could result in them being punished but duty overcame their fear and they followed. The sergeant in charge of the stables came out when he heard the hooves. As Hougon took off his cloak, hat and dolman he shook his head. "Gentlemen, this is forbidden."

I took off my hat and jacket, "Then absent yourself, my friend, for this will end tonight."

I unsheathed my sword. I knew that I was facing a fencer and I was just a fighter. He had more skill with his sword than I had but I had a dead regiment behind me. Where he only had his skill I had my heart as well. We faced each other. He said, "You three are witnesses that we both enter into this willingly." I could see that he was covering himself for the moment when he killed me. He did not want to be accused of murder. That suited me for it meant that he was overconfident.

We touched blades and he suddenly darted at me as fast as the strike of a cobra. I had anticipated such a swift start and parried but not fast enough and the blade sliced my cheek. His sabre came away red.

He looked exultant, "First blood to me!"

I smiled grimly, "It is not the first blood which counts but the last."

He tried another quick flick of his wrist and I parried it away. We circled. The first mistake would result in death and we both knew it. I feinted and he quickly tried a parry. I hacked down with my straight sword. I saw him shake from the force as the vibrations numbed his hand. For the first time, he looked worried. He came at me with four or five quick thrusts and ripostes. I was barely able to beat them away. Then he feinted and I slipped. He lunged and the sabre sliced along my jacket and side.

"Ha ha! Soon the stable boy will die."

I had had enough of fighting his way. I would fight my way. I balled my left hand into a fist and as I sliced down with my sword I punched him hard in the ribs. I heard them crack and he winced in pain. "So, the bastard conceived in a stable fights like a peasant."

I did not say a word but my grin said it all. I sliced sideways at him and he parried but he had to cross his body with the sword and his arm struck his own broken ribs. He cried out again. Before I could attack again he lunged forwards and the tip of the sword came at my chest sinking into the jacket. I rolled backwards and he roared in triumph. "Die in the stable mud. It is a fitting end."

I leapt to my feet and saw the shock on his face. "This cannot be. That blow should have killed you!"

I swung my sword at his head with all the force I could muster and he held his sabre up to parry. The parry merely slowed the blade down and it continued down to split his head from the crown to the jaw. He slumped dead at my feet. The stable sergeant raced up to me. "Sir you should be dead!"

I undid my jacket and revealed the money belt. The seal of the Macgregors had saved me. "If you would get my horse and my cloak then I will be away."

"Yes, sir and that was well done." He gave a warning look to the two troopers.

"Troopers you should take the body of the colonel back to the regiment. As far as I am concerned this now absolves the 15th from any dishonour but if any of your fellows wish revenge I will not hide. They merely have to find me."

"Yes sir and we do not wish you harm but I fear the general will not be happy. He and the colonel were friends."

I shrugged, "I have my orders and I will obey them. What the general does is up to him. Farewell."

I mounted my horse and gave a gold piece to the sergeant. "I trust that the version of events here this night will be a truthful one?"

"Yes sir and good luck but I fear we will not meet again."

I donned my cloak and quickly galloped through the streets to the harbour. François was waiting at the gangplank. I dismounted and took out my orders. I saw a sentry and gave him the horse. "Please see that this is returned to the general."

He looked at me suspiciously. "Where are your orders, sir?"

I showed him the orders from the general and he read them by the torchlight on the quayside. "Very well Captain Macgregor."

As I stepped onboard, I whispered to François while I handed him the orders from General Menou. "Here are my orders from the general; if you obey them, then you will not be in trouble."

"It matters not!"

"We had better hurry there is blood on my hands."

"I thought there might be." He cupped his hands and yelled, "Cast off forrard, cast off aft. Hoist the mainsail."

We had reached the sea when I saw, in the distance, the horsemen gallop up to our empty berth. The troopers had been correct and now I was a wanted man. I was a man without a country.

Chapter 13

I went below decks and changed from the blue uniform of France into the civilian clothes from my chest. I was no longer a soldier. I was a Scotsman trying to get home. I cleaned my wounds. None of them were deep but the cut on my face would be a permanent reminder of the day I avenged the 17th and I would be proud of it. I went back on the deck.

"That is better. From the blood on your face and clothes, I thought that you had been in an abattoir."

"You should see the other fellow."

"I have read the orders thank you. It absolves me of any recrimination but how do I land you in Sicily and avoid censure?"

"You suffered a storm and closed with the shore. I, foolishly, leapt into the sea and drowned." I spread my hands. "Can you trust your crew to silence?"

"Of course. But this means I cannot land you in a port. It must be a beach."

"That is satisfactory. This is a new life and like a butterfly emerging from its cocoon I need time to become Robbie Macgregor and lose Captain Macgregor of the 17th."

"As you wish." He looked to the dark sky to the north. "I suspect this may be the last voyage we take together and I have to say that I will miss them. Life with you was never dull."

I went to the stern and looked aft to the land of Egypt where my world had ended and all that I had known for so many years had ended. I felt salt in my eyes as I thought of those I would never see again, Jean, Tiny, Albert, Sergeant Delacroix and Manet. There was only Pierre left and, as he was living in France, I thought it highly unlikely that I would ever see him again. I really was being reborn and my only hope now was that Sir John would be in Sicily and that I would find him.

It took three days of hard sailing to reach Sicily. We sailed towards Messina at the northeastern end of the island and anchored off what looked like a secluded cove. François had found a suitable landing site and we just waited for sunset so that I could land in the dark and begin my dangerous journey across this bandit infested land. We could see the lights of some small settlements nestling close to the sea. The hills and mountains seemed to rise like a wall ahead. It was totally different from the land we had left, Egypt. For me, the short voyage had been beneficial. My wounds were all clean and showed no signs of infection. I had eaten well, for I knew not when I would eat again. I had two canteens: one with water and one with brandy. I had a leather haversack on my back with musket balls and powder and I had my two pistols. I was ready to leave France and join the rest of the world. I donned my dirty cloak and it seemed as though it cloaked me from the eyes of the world.

François shook my hand as I clambered down to the waiting boat. "Take care, Robbie. I do not think there are many of your friends left in this world."

I laughed with a gaiety I did not feel, "Then I will have to find new ones. But I thank you and your crew for being true friends and I will never forget you. I hope that good luck continues to follow you for, I fear, that this war will be a long one."

There were no more words and I descended into the small boat. The four sailors pulled hard towards the shore and we soon passed the breakers and pulled up on the soft sand. The Second Mate helped me ashore and grasped my hand, "The crew will never betray you, captain. We know what you have done for France. Our good wishes go with you."

Then they pushed off and I was left alone on the island of Sicily. I was now a deserter and I was sure that I would soon be branded a traitor. Now that I had landed on this island I felt at a loss. I had no idea how big the island was and all that I knew was that Sir John MacAlpin had family here. It was not much to go on. Then I thought of the alternative; go back to Egypt and face a court-martial and probable death. Ahead was life and behind me only death. I suddenly burst out laughing. Would not Jean and Tiny exchange place with me in a moment if they could?

I looked up and, in the fading light, saw a sort of sheep or goat trail leading up the steep bank. It zig-zagged back and forth, I clambered up the slope into the scrub. Sicily had a different smell to that of Egypt. Here I could smell lemons. It was tiring climbing the steep path and I realised that the campaign had taken much out of me. I strode upwards until I reached a road of sorts. It had cobbles and my experience told me that meant a Roman road. My first decision faced me: right or left? I chose right and I still do not know why but it was the right choice. I trudged along the cobbled road; my cavalry boots were not made for walking and it was not easy. I had transferred some coins to a purse on my belt. I did not want anyone to know of the treasure I held. Thanks to Jean I now had a full purse of money and that would be the least of my worries. We had both told each other where we kept our coins in case of death for we knew how the human vultures would strip bodies of money, hair and teeth once they were dead. I had recovered his before I buried him beneath the Egyptian sand. It was another reason why I had hidden the grave so well. Jean would sleep safely until the last trumpet sounded.

I smelled the village before I saw it. It was the smell of wood smoke and animals. I found a small hill overlooking the settlement and I hunkered down to wait for dawn. I would not be welcomed in the middle of the night. I was in no rush. For the first time in my life, I was not dancing to anyone else's tune. I was making my own decisions. I watched the village come to life; the farmer who rose before dawn to milk his cow; the young shepherd who took the sheepdog away to the hills. There was a routine which reminded me of the army. By the time the sun was beginning to warm the hills the villagers were all awake and cheerfully going about their business. I took a deep breath and stood. I hoped that my Italian would be adequate and that they would be peaceably inclined. I strode casually towards the houses.

It was the dogs who heard me and began a cacophony of barking. The men eyed me suspiciously and so I smiled and waved my right hand to show that I carried no weapon. A gaggle of men detached themselves from the women and moved menacingly towards me. I loosened my sword in its sheath although I was reluctant to fight. This was not the time to be the warrior. I stepped towards the centre of the village. I held my arms out to show my peaceful intentions. Four men surrounded me.

The man in front of me was the leader and he smiled wolfishly at me. He said, in Italian, to the men behind me. "Luca, Giovanni grab him when I give the word."

I decided to act. I bent forwards slightly as though going down to bow. It took them by surprise. I grabbed my stiletto with my left and as I stood I rammed my right elbow into the face of the man behind me. I pressed the tip my blade into the neck of the man before me and drew my pistol to cover the other two. I hissed my words in Italian, "Now unless you want a bloodbath here let us talk before your men get hurt. I want to see all four of you in front of me with your palms uppermost."

I could see from his angry eyes that their leader would have liked nothing better than to rip my throat out but he was helpless. I pushed forward with the tip of my knife and a tendril of blood trickled down his neck. I lowered my voice, "My friend I have nothing to lose. I am a soldier and I could kill all four of you as easily as you could milk a goat so do not push me."

"Do as he says!" I saw the fear in his eyes. He believed me.

They came to face me and I saw one man with a bleeding mouth giving me murderous looks. I slipped my knife back into my boot and drew my second pistol. "I just need information. Nothing more. You will answer my questions and I will be gone."

"What is it you wish to know?"

"That's better and poor Luca or Giovanni here would not have had to suffer broken teeth had you been peaceable and honourable men. What is the nearest town?"

"Roccalumera," he pointed to the north.

"And this is?"

"Allume."

"Good. And then the next town is Messina?"

"Yes, the city of Messina."

"You see how much better this is." One of the men began to move. "Keep still please my hand may tire and I might just fire my pistol. It would make a terrible mess of your stomach and I would hate to kill one of you now that we are getting on so well." He became still. "Good. Now, who are the noble families around here?"

"In Messina the Capparone family rule and in Roccalumera it is the Alpinis."

Suddenly I felt better. The Alpini sounded like an Italian version of MacAlpin. Could it be that I had landed so close to my relatives? Good and now I shall leave you." I could almost see their murderous minds at work. I holstered one pistol and grabbed their leader. "But you shall come with me. If anyone follows us you will die and I have to tell you I have sharp ears."

"I promise you no one will follow you."

"I know for you will be with me. Your men will stay here." I pushed him forwards. When we reached the end of the village I turned around to check that the men were still in the village. "Now walk."

"Who are you?"

"I am a visitor who has landed close to your home and whom you chose to attack."

"We did not know you were a soldier."

"Then all the more reason you should have been hospitable." As we climbed the road to the ridge I saw the next village. It was a bigger town with a wall and a small castle. It was less than half a mile away and we had walked more than two miles from Allume. "And now you may return home." I watched as he began to trudge back. I had not made any friends; I knew that.

The city had no guards but I chose to walk along the road openly and to seek assistance. This might not be the home of the Knight of St. John but if there was a nobleman living here then I had a chance to discover where Sir John might reside. I used my smile and a polite greeting as I walked through the streets. I could see that the castle looked to be a grand residence of some description. I walked up to the main gate where two soldiers stood on guard. Although they had muskets and halberds they looked to be almost old to me. They still had the look of men who had been soldiers once and it would not do to underestimate them.

"Can you tell me, who is the lord of this castle?"

"Count Cesar Alpini."

"Would you tell your master that Robert Macgregor seeks an audience?"

The older of the two appraised me. When he saw my sword he asked, "Could I see your sword sir?"

I nodded and held it to show him. He turned it over in his hand. Finally, he handed it back, "If you would wait here with Carlo I will see if an audience is possible."

After he had gone I asked Carlo about the family. "Can you tell me if there is a Sir John in the castle?"

He shook his head. "No sir, no Sir John."

I felt disappointed. Perhaps this meant they were not related. "Is there a Giovanni in the family?"

His face lit up, "Yes, yes the old knight. He returned here some time ago." Then his face fell. "He is no longer a young man and he is not well."

"I met him in Malta. He is a true knight."

Carlo wholeheartedly agrees, "Yes sir, it is like the old days when knights were real men of honour."

Just then his companion returned. "You are granted an audience. Follow me."

I was led through the narrow gate and up a twisting passage. I could see it abounded with murder holes. This had been a daunting castle in its past. When we entered the main hall I could see the attempts to modernise. The furniture was modern and looked comfortable. It appeared at odds with the Gothic elements of the defences.

Count Cesar was of an age with Jean. The difference was Count Cesar had allowed himself to become overweight and unfit. His red nose and cheeks showed his love of food and wine. He was, however, a genial host. He stood to greet me and shake my hand. "I granted an audience because I am intrigued. The Macgregor family from Scotland was supposed to be related to us. Are you from Scotland?"

"My family is but I was born in France."

"And how did you chance upon us here? We are a small family and this is a remote place."

"Call it luck or chance but I was seeking Sir John MacAlpin whom I met in Malta. I landed down the coast and this is only the second place that I tried."

His jaw dropped, "Sir John? But he is my uncle. He is not well. Are you the young French officer he met on Malta then? The agent of Bonaparte?"

"I did meet him on the island and I have done work for General Bonaparte. Would it be possible to see Sir John?"

"Of course but I have to warn you to be prepared for a shock. He has deteriorated since he returned to his home. I believe the loss of Malta was a mortal wound to him."

He was right. The old man looked gaunt and drawn. I suspect if I had arrived a week later then it would have been too late. His eyes were closed as we approached and the count said, "Uncle we have a visitor for you."

The old man's eyes flickered open and it was as though he had been pricked by something hot for he sat bolt upright in bed and said, "Can it be? Did you escape from Egypt? I had heard of the plague and the deaths and I worried that you might have perished in that pestilential hell hole."

"It was close sir and I am the only survivor of my regiment."

He waved to a chair, "Sit, both of you. Now Robert, tell us both your story and do not omit anything for I believe that destiny has had a hand in your arrival. Nephew, send for something for us to drink." The servant quickly brought a jug and glasses.

I told them everything from the plague and the battles to the massacre and finally my duel. The count shook his head in disbelief. "And yet you are so young."

Sir John said, "He is a warrior and he continues to serve in the tradition of the family. You still have the seal."

I patted my chest. "And it saved me in the duel. I would be dead had my opponent's sword not struck the seal."

"You see Cesar, destiny. And what brings you here?"

"I need to get to Scotland. I am no longer welcome in France. Can you help?"

"I cannot but my nephew can. Is that not true Cesar?" His nephew nodded. I think he feared he would have to emulate some of the stories we had recounted. He struck me as a worshipper of Mammon and not Mars. "Leave me to talk with Robbie. You need to make discreet enquiries about a boat to England. He will need a room."

Cesar cheerfully left the room. I was amazed in the change in the old man. He had suddenly appeared to become younger. After his nephew had left he said, "The money which keeps this ramshackle shell operating is mine but he has a good heart. He is not, however, a warrior. You are and I am so pleased that our paths crossed. The loss of Malta was inevitable but our meeting was the work of higher powers than Bonaparte that is certain."

"I feel that somehow I have betrayed my comrades."

"Because you are alive and they are dead?"

"Yes, exactly."

"Had you died with them would that have made their end more worthy?"

"Why no."

"Then you must live your life for them. They will be forever young. You say that this Jean Bartiaux watched over you for your mother?"

"Yes. He loved her."

"As she loved you. I do not find it surprising that you have had so much good fortune and now that Jean has died he will watch over you." He leaned over and put a blue-veined, almost transparent hand over mine. "And when I die, and it will be soon, then I too will watch over you. For Robert Macgregor of Breteuil, you have something within you that men such as Bonaparte dream of. I envy you. Were I forty years younger then I would enjoy the adventures you are about to have." He sank back, seemingly exhausted by his speech. "Go and eat and come back this afternoon. I should have recovered some of my strength but your arrival, young kinsman, has added to my life."

I left the room and wondered what to do. Cesar found me and took my arm, "What an effect you have had on my uncle. We have had the priest here every day ready for the last rites but he has spoken more since you arrived than in a month. Thank you kinsman; he is dear to us. He left when I was young and when he returned it was as a gift. We could repay his kindness with some of our own. Come, I will take you to your chambers."

After I had deposited my few belongings I toured the castle with my host. I learned that Cesar had a wife and two sons. The estate would have been lost had it not been for Sir John as they had had some disastrous investments coupled with some poor harvests. It was only since his uncle's return that their fortunes had revived.

"My uncle came back at the right time."

"How did he get money from Malta? I know that Napoleon Bonaparte seized the majority of it."

"He was second only to the Grand Master and I think that when he saw the greed and the avarice of your general his honourable intentions were subverted but ask him. I know he thinks much of you. When he first arrived he talked of nothing else but you. I think he wishes that I was more like you." I began to speak but Cesar held up his hand, "I know I am an indolent man who likes his food too much but I like who I am and my wife likes me this way. I can fully understand how he can admire you. To have achieved your rank at such a young age and those scars on your hands and face bear testament to a martial life. The MacAlpines, in the middle ages, were knights who fought for this land and held it against Saracens and Lombards. It was a tradition. My uncle and my father were the last two of the line. My uncle chose the celibate monastic life of a knight and my father chose to travel and to enjoy life. But we are all the same family."

"Well, I thank your family for its hospitality."

"And my uncle tells me that we may be distantly related although our family left Scotland many years ago." He shrugged, "It did not interest my father but Uncle Giovanni was fascinated by the history of that land. It is strange that neither of you has set foot in that land and yet its power drew you together."

"I am coming to learn that there are some things for which you cannot plan."

We ate in the great hall which seemed too big for the five of us. Cesar's wife, Lucretia, was as genial and happy as he was. She was a jolly woman who laughed a lot and was always concerned that you should enjoy your food and finish it. I could see that their two sons, Giuseppe and Cesar, would grow up just the same as their parents. As young boys, they were interested in my stories of battle. I could not tell them the true stories of the horror of cannon and musket. Instead, I told them of the parts which were glorious such as the capture of the fleet on the Texel and the battle of the Pyramids. Their eyes lit up.

Giuseppe asked, "How did you get the scars on your hands and face sir?"

"Giuseppe!"

"I do not mind telling him, my lady. They happened during my battles and are now part of my story."

When I mentioned the maggots they giggled while their mother squirmed. "I am glad that they will not become soldiers!"

Cesar looked up sharply. "That may not be up to us."

I was intrigued too but his wife asked, "What do you mean?"

"The French have invested the mainland and there are rumours that they may send a garrison here."

I shook my head. "I would not fear that sir. There are wars they must fight in the northern part first but they may well try to impose their laws. They did in Egypt and it caused problems there."

After the meal, I was summoned to Sir John's chambers. I was surprised to see that he was out of bed seated in a chair with a chess set before him. "Come Robert we will play chess while we talk."

Although I had been taught chess I was not very good as Sir John soon found out. After he had beaten me in ten moves he took to teaching me the finer points of the game and after half an hour we were able to have a better game.

"Tomorrow my nephew will travel to Messina and arrange passage for you to England."

"You make it sound easy sir. I would have thought that in times like these, with war all around us that it would have been difficult."

"When I returned here I brought many ideas from Malta. Since the revolution, many French émigrés moved to England and they cannot get their beloved wine. Here in Sicily, we make good wine and we export it to London. It is a very lucrative trade. We also grow the finest lemons in Italy although those around Sorrento and Amalfi might dispute that. The price we get for them here in Sicily and in Italy is laughable but we can charge much more in London where they are seen as exotic. We also sell them dried fruits which the English cannot get enough of. You will travel to London ostensibly as the representative of the Alpini family."

"I meant to ask you, sir, when I met first you, your name was MacAlpin and yet here you are the Alpini."

"When I reached Malta after my travels, I discovered the origins of my family. They came here many years ago before the First Crusade and it was not until the fall of Constantinople that they became the Alpini. I like the idea of a heritage going back to Scotland and I researched the family. That is how I knew we were related and also how I recognised the seal when I found it amongst the treasure of the knights."

"How do you think it ended up in Malta?"

"The Scottish knights often travelled to fight the Turk. Black Douglas even brought Robert the Bruce's heart to the Holy Land although he got no further than Spain. It is quite conceivable that the seal was brought on a Crusade and the knights took it back from the Holy Land. Checkmate! You are getting better. And now I will retire. I have enjoyed our game and our talk. I will see you on the morrow."

We talked and played chess for two days. It marked a change in me from the French Chasseur to a Scotsman. Even though Sir John had never visited Scotland he had read and studied so much that it was part of him. Neither of us had any idea who was the current head of the clan but we knew that I had to get to the islands off the west coast of Scotland. It was almost a disappointment when the messenger came from Messina to tell us that there was a berth on a ship and I would be sailing the following day.

Cesar told me how much his uncle had improved since my arrival. "I believe that you have given him a new lease of life. Thank you. I am in your debt."

I spent the last morning in Sir John's chambers with the knight and his nephew. They made sure that I had all the documents I would need. I was going as the agent of the Alpini family. I had a chest with fine clothes in and a purse of money. Once I reached London, I would confirm a contract to supply dried fruit, lemons and wine to a large London company; Fortnum and Masons. Apparently, the wars were creating a demand for more exotic foods and they could not get enough.

"Once you have the contracts signed and you have returned them to the captain then you should make your way to Scotland. I should warn you that we are not certain that our agent is totally honest. Before you travel north we would appreciate someone we can trust speaking with the owner of the shop."

I looked at the papers and my face must have displayed my feelings. "What is the matter, kinsman?"

"I will do as you ask but, well Sir John, how do I get to Scotland? Buy a horse and ride?"

He laughed. "Although it is a small country I would suggest you get a boat. If you sail from London to Edinburgh the journey from there across Scotland to the west is not a long one but the journey from London to Scotland would be harder."

"Thank you. That gives me an option at least." I hesitated. "After I have delivered the seal could I return here?"

Sir John gave a huge smile, "Of course although I am not sure that by the time you return that I shall still be here."

"You will uncle. I am sure of it but you will always be welcome here Robert. I assure you of that."

The two boys and Lucretia all wept when I left. I too felt quite tearful. For the first time since my mother had died, I felt like I belonged in a home and had a family. Sir John's rheumy eyes also showed emotion and his frail hand gripped mine as I said goodbye. "Take care of yourself Robert and remember you carry a whole clan in your veins. There is greatness within you."

Cesar led me to our horses and I waved goodbye to the little castle which had become a precious oasis for me. If for nothing else I thanked Napoleon Bonaparte for sending me to Malta. It was thanks to him that I had met family. He might have thought that he had looted the greatest treasure but I knew that I had found an even greater one. We rode in silence. There was little we had not said and we were both sad at the parting. I had been a bridge between Sir John and Cesar's family. I knew that they would miss me.

We reached Messina and it was a busy port. With Malta still being fought over this was the last port before Africa and, as such, attracted many ships and even more merchants. Cesar pointed out our ship. She was a tubby merchantman and as far removed from the 'Carillon' as it was possible to get.

"She is an English ship, 'The Witch of Endor'. We have only been able to use her since Admiral Nelson destroyed the French fleet but it works out better as we do not have language problems at the other end. I can speak English better than most Italians." He shrugged, "It gives me an advantage in business. The captain is a good man, Matthew Dinsdale. He comes from the lands to the south of Scotland and he may be able to help you."

We dismounted and tied our horses to a bollard. The two servants we had brought with us carried my chest on board. We followed and Cesar introduced me to Captain Dinsdale. The captain was older than Jean had been. He had a white beard and flecks of white covering a bald pate burned brown by the sun and salt air. He had a twinkle in his eye and, as I was to discover, he had a wicked sense of humour; some might say cruel. I liked him from the moment I met him. He had a firm handshake, "So you are the wandering Scotsman who has never been to Scotland. Sounds like a riddle to me. I am Matthew Dinsdale, master of this ship. Call me Captain."

"And I am Robert Macgregor and I too was a captain, but you may call me Robbie. It will avoid confusion!"

He roared with laughter. "We shall get on." He turned to Cesar, "Well Count we had better be underway. I will return with the documents this young man provides and then we should be set to make all our fortunes." He gestured to the holds. "We are packed out this voyage but I fancy I will need a bigger ship next time."

"Do not worry. We can supply all the dried fruit, wines and lemons the company can take!" The two servants passed us to leave the ship. "Well Robert, take care and you just need to arrange with Captain Dinsdale for a berth on his ship when you wish to return home."

"Thank you for all that you have done for me and let me know how Sir John is. I am quite fond of the old man."

"I will."

He descended the gangplank and then Captain Dinsdale became the professional mariner and shouted out his orders. I was now a seasoned sailor and I found a quiet place close to the stern where I could watch and be out of the way. I waved to Cesar as the ship edged away from the harbour and into the open sea. I was leaving the world I had known for my whole life and entering a brave new world. It was exciting.

Chapter 14

We headed west. I knew from the charts I had studied whilst on board the 'Carillon', that there was no land until we passed Gibraltar and then we would be away from the gentle Mediterranean and into the wild Atlantic. I noticed that the merchantman was much slower than the sloop. In fact, it seemed to barely move. When the captain relaxed and lit his pipe I went up to him to ask him about his ship. "How long will it take to get to London then Captain?"

He gave me a shrewd look. "I fancy you have sailed on fast naval vessels before?" I nodded. "Well, the 'Witch' will get you there when she gets you there. It depends on the winds. She is faster than most merchantmen but the wind here is a little too gentle for her. She likes a wilder wind. Once she gets into the Atlantic then you will see her fly. But she is a snug vessel and she is sound. Come I will give you the tour."

We stepped down from the slightly raised aft deck onto the main deck. "See," he pointed to the armaments, "we have six guns each side. They are six pounders." He tapped his nose, "We are good at finding them. None of them match but they all work and I have a Second Mate who used to be in the Royal Navy and he reckons they are as good as those you find in any ship that doesn't fly the Union Jack. You can help fire them."

"Will we need to? I thought the Royal Navy would protect British ships."

"Oh they do but they can't be everywhere and until we get into the Bay of Biscay there is always the risk of pirates."

My face darkened as I remembered Michael. "I know. We were attacked by three xebecs on our way to Egypt. One of my best friends died at their hands."

He looked impressed. "You beat off three xebecs? What ship were you in? A frigate?"

"No, an eight gun sloop."

"Then I look forward to hearing that story one evening while we eat." He glanced up at the pennant, "The evenings can be a bit quiet so we like a good story. The wind is changing so I will have to finish the tour later on. I would change into something less delicate while we sail if I were you. Those clothes are too fine for saltwater. Your cabin is aft and is close to mine. You will see your sea chest." With that, he bounded back to the wheel and began shouting orders. The crew scurried up and down the ratlines and I went to the cabin to do as he had suggested.

I did have more clothes than I had ever had in my life. Many of them were clothes that Count Alpini had worn but his burgeoning waistline had made them no longer suitable. I could wear a different set of clothes every day for ten days if I chose. That was a luxury. I still had my uniform and my stained cloak. They both seemed like good luck charms to me. I put the papers to the bottom of the chest and then put my pistols and sword on top of my clothes. Who knew when I might need them in a hurry? I kept the stiletto in the top of my boots although the ones I was wearing were not riding boots but made from softer leather and more suitable for walking. I changed and returned to the main deck. The hectic activity had ended and we were moving faster.

I joined the men at the wheel. "This is Richard Jennings, he is the Second Mate. The Second Mate was a huge man with a scar running down one eye. The eyeball was white and stared blindly from within an angry red socket. It made him look fierce and yet he was a gentle man who carved the most wonderful ivory. He made me a chess set on the voyage and it is one of my most cherished possessions. It just goes to show how appearances can deceive.

"I am pleased to make your acquaintance, Captain Macgregor."

"Call me Robbie." I pointed to the billowing sails. "We are moving faster now."

"Aye. The 'Witch' is keen to get to deep water." He gestured with his pipe at the southern horizon. The sooner we are away from that nest of pirates the better."

Captain Dinsdale made sure that the Second Mate knew his orders and then he turned to me. "Let us go to my cabin. The First Mate will join us there and we'll have a bite of something to eat." As we went below decks he explained, "The first week at sea is always the best for food. It's all fresh you see." I didn't because I had only been at sea for a few days at a time before now. "After that, it is dried rations and the odd fish that the lads catch so make the most of it."

"Don't you call in at the ports we pass like Gibraltar?"

He shook his head so violently I thought it would fall off. "No, no, no! They rob you blind with their mooring charges and taxes. We won't touch land again until we sail up the Thames. But do not worry; we have a good cook and an oven. We have plenty of flour so we have fresh bread every day. We picked up some sardines in oil and they should last us. It is lucky we sailed from an Italian port; we have plenty of sausages and dried pork."

We had reached the cabin and Jonas Galbraith was there the First Mate. Where Richard was a man-mountain Jonas was small. He reminded me of Nelson. He had sharp eyes and a sharp mind. I discovered that he had been what was called 'a top man'. They are the nimblest of sailors and are able to cling to the most extreme parts of the masts without falling off. I later learned that he had been the best top man Captain Dinsdale had ever known. He was as good a navigator as the captain and he could rig the ship even better. He was a thoughtful man who said little and listened a lot. That night I listened too as Captain Dinsdale told me of his ship. He was the owner and that apparently was unusual. I thought it made better business as he had everyone's interest at heart. He would neither jeopardise the ship nor the profit whilst a hired seaman might not worry about the profits and the owners would never care about the crew or the vessel. I could see why my kinsman had chosen this vessel to be their trading partner.

"Aye, in another couple of years I shall have enough to buy another boat and then Jonas here will work for me as a captain."

I was intrigued. "How much more would you need?"

He laughed, "Why have you got some gold you want to spend?"

I ate the piece of cheese I held and nodded, "I might be able to lay my hands on a purse of gold. Would you want a partner?"

"He would have to be a silent partner." He winked at Jonas, "It's why I never married. Women are never a silent partner." He drank some of his wine. "If you are serious then I would let you invest for a share of the profits. But you ought to know the sea is a dangerous place to do business and many ships sink. Suppose you invested and the ship sank?"

"Then I would lose my money. But as the money is in a dark and hidden place right now it is not doing me any good and might as well be at the bottom of the sea. But, as you say, there is no hurry. We have to travel to London and I may decide you are right but let us just say that at the moment I would be interested in becoming a partner and buying a second ship with you. If for no other reason than it would help to pay back Count Alpini and their family who have helped me so much."

Captain Dinsdale laughed and slapped me heartily on the back. "You are a rum bugger and no mistake. You are a young lad but I can see that you have an old head on your shoulders. I think you are right to make the offer but we will talk more about it when we see the coast of Kent." He raised his mug. "Let's have a toast. New friends!"

"New friends."

"The count said that when we land in London you are going up to Scotland."

"Yes, I have something to deliver."

"The best route would be up the coast to Newcastle. They have colliers bringing coal from the north and they are the fastest way. You can ride across the country in two days."

"Thank you, captain, that sounds like a good idea. I would appreciate it if you could steer me in the direction of an honest skipper."

"Believe me if I recommend him you will be able to trust him with your life."

I was slightly drunk when I retired but I was happy and I slept well. I woke with a mouth which tasted of stale wine and cheese but a bucket of saltwater cleared my head. I went on deck and began to strop my razor on my leather belt. The Second Mate came over and shook his head. "I wouldn't shave if I were you."

"But I shave every day."

"We are at sea, master, and freshwater is precious. We shave in sea water and you can't get a lather. That's why the lads all have beards. We shave when are ashore but at sea, a beard is best."

I put them away. "You men know your business and I will do as you advise." And so I grew my first full beard. The queues, pigtails and moustache became a thing of the past and I became as piratical looking as the rest.

Perhaps I tempted fate by thinking I might look like a pirate for the next day Barbary pirates found us. I had thought that the crew might panic but they went about their business calmly. The First Mate shouted over. "Captain Macgregor if you would join the gun crew on number one gun. I am sure you have fired cannon before."

As I went to the gun he had indicated I saw the cabin boys bringing cutlasses, hatchets, axes and muskets onto the deck and spreading them around. They also spread sand around the guns to give a firmer footing. The wizened sailor on the gun gave me a grin as I arrived. He had an alarming look. He had but two teeth in his mouth and not a hair on his head but his arms were knotted like sea anchors. "Welcome young sir. We need a bit of muscle here and I hear you were a soldier."

I smiled, "Aye I was and I have fought these pirates before and so I know how ruthless they are."

He grinned and nodded to the two young sailors. "See I told you they were bad buggers. Just because they are darkies and row their ships doesn't mean that they aren't nasty pieces of work."

After we had loaded I looked astern and saw that they were steadily beating towards us. They were sailing close together and using their oars as well as the force of the wind. One of the young men on our gun asked."Why doesn't the captain turn and give them a broadside?"

Before the old gunner could speak I said, "If he does that he will have to take one out because, if he doesn't, they will close with us and board us."

The old man nodded approvingly, "The young soldier is right." He patted the gun. "These are nice guns but we would need a lot of luck to disable one of them."

I looked at the sky. They had chosen their moment well. They would have all day to close with us. I could see that the gap was narrowing inexorably. The cabin boys came on deck with bags of powder which they deposited next to each gun. I turned to the old gunner. "This might sound a stupid question but when the powder comes on board it is in barrels isn't it?"

One of the young men sniggered and was rewarded by a clip to the back of the head. "Aye, sir. We have eight barrels. We don't use it very often apart from the practice we have."

"I have an idea. I will see the captain."

I joined the captain and he took his pipe out of his mouth and pointed astern. "I take it, from your eager young face and rapid gait, that you have worked out their plan then?"

"Yes, sir. They will slowly catch us and then attack from two sides at once. They want you to turn and try to fire and then they can end it quicker. Unless the wind changes we are doomed."

"You have the measure of it and I do not think that the wind will change in our favour any time soon."

"I have an idea." I explained my plan to the captain and the First Mate and they liked it. I was given the carpenter, the cook and the cabin boys to help me. They brought up two half-empty barrels of powder. We took off the top and the carpenter dumped handfuls of nails into the top of the black, stinking powder. I took two lengths of fuse and, after the carpenter had made a hole in the top of the barrel, slipped them through.

The tops were sealed and, while the cabin boys and the cook smeared the outside of the barrels with grease, the carpenter and I soaked the fuse with brandy. Once the rope was tied around them they were ready.

"Right boys, now comes the difficult part." We took them to the stern. The two boys and I went to one side and the carpenter and the cook went to the other. "Carefully now, lower them into the water."

I held my hand up until was sure that they were safely in and the fuses were not immersed. "Now pay them out and hold them."

"Here you are, sir." Jonas handed me the first of the two muskets he had loaded. "These are the best two muskets we have and I selected the roundest ball. Are you sure that you can hit that little fuse?"

"The trick will be to hit them when they are close to us and then release them. Hopefully, I will have cut the fuses to the right length. "Right boys pay them out." The ropes were slowly let out until the barrels were a hundred yards away and the two xebecs less than six hundred yards away. I held the first musket and rested the end on the rail. I breathed slowly and then squeezed the trigger. "Next musket!"

Jonas handed me the next one and began to reload the first. When the smoke cleared I saw that the first fuse was alight. "Release the first barrel." I squeezed the trigger and waited for the smoke to clear. The second was also alight but was spluttering a little. I took the reloaded musket and fired again. This time the fuse took. "Release the second barrel." I took the second gun which Jonas had reloaded. I watched the barrels in case the fuses went out and I had to fire again although it was unlikely that I would manage to hit such a small target. The two xebecs were so focussed on us that they failed to notice the two barrels drifting slowly towards them. When they did see them it was too late. They were about three hundred yards away from us when the first barrel exploded. The force not only demolished the oars on one xebec but it sent the other barrel much closer to the second xebec. A few moments later the second barrel exploded.

Captain Dinsdale had been waiting for such an event and he roared, "Fire as you bear!" He threw the wheel over and as the little ship heeled over, the guns rippled out their fire at the first xebec. It was hard to see the effect with the smoke from our guns and the smoke from the explosion. He spun the wheel again and we turned. It was a slow turn compared with the sloop but eventually, the other guns fired. As we returned to our course we peered astern. The oars on one side of each xebec had been destroyed and there were gaping holes in the sides of the ships. One xebec had been dismasted and the other had so many holes that it would need a new sail. They would not be pursuing us any time soon. The crew began cheering and dancing around the deck.

Captain Dinsdale slapped me on the back. "Fine work and we owe you much. They would have caught us within the hour. That was fine shooting."

"That was lucky shooting captain. Had the ship been in a rougher sea then I would not have even hit the barrel but I am glad that they did not catch us. I hate the Barbary pirates more than words can say."

The crew quickly returned the ship to normal. The decks were swept and cleaned, the shot and powder returned to the powder room but they all went about their business in a happy frame of mind. We had all expected some wounds and probable death and we had emerged unscathed. We enjoyed our meal that night.

The next day we passed Gibraltar. The captain stayed well away from the naval base. We could see the battleships and frigates in the harbour. "We avoid those places. They can press seamen from any ship but especially British flagged ships. With the battles in the Mediterranean, they will always be short of men and mine are the best."

"But didn't you say that some of your men had served in the navy?"

"Aye sir, the best of them."

"Then why are they not in the navy now?"

"Every time there is a peace the penny pushers in the navy yard lay up ships to save money. The sailors are laid off. It is stupid really but it plays into my hands. Every time peace breaks out I get to Pompey and pick up the best."

I could sense telescopes focussed on us as we slipped through the straits and into the dark Atlantic. The difference was immediately obvious. The ship moved far more vertically as well as horizontally when the swells from America struck the coast of Spain. Jonas grinned at me. "Now we'll see your sea legs."

I had only ever sailed on the Mediterranean and I did not know if I would be able to retain the contents of my stomach but I was determined to stay on deck and see it out. Below deck had, at best a musty smell, and when it mixed with the water from the bilges it could induce vomiting without any help from the sea. If I thought it was bad when we passed by Cadiz and the southern coast of Spain, as soon as we struck Portugal it really ripped into us. It was as though it had only been flexing its muscles and when we reached the sea beyond Lisbon then we felt its full force and the ship tossed, dipped and seemed to submerge beneath great rollers.

"Is this a bad storm?" I mouthed to Jonas.

He laughed, "This isn't a storm this is normal weather and sea conditions. Now a real Atlantic storm is something else."

He was right and I soon became used to the sensation of being up in the air one moment and in a trough almost as deep as the ship next. That evening as we ate Captain Dinsdale confided in me that the next section, from Spain to Cape Gris Nez was the most difficult. "You see there are French privateers who are like the Barbary pirates. They hide in inlets and dart out to capture unsuspecting ships like us. We have to sail close to the coast for protection and they are much faster than we are. Then we have the French Navy. It isn't a very good navy but just about any of them can catch us and claim that they are protecting France."

"Aren't they?"

"No, they are legalised pirates. They steal everything of value and then sell the ship to the French government."

"What about the crews?"

Jonas and Captain Dinsdale looked at each other, "It is amazing how many merchant crews seem to fight to the death."

"You mean they are killed out of hand?"

"I have never heard of any survivors of ships captured by the French. That is why we will be extra vigilant from now on. We are still off northern Spain but that means nothing. If you are on a deck and you see another ship then shout out; the odds are it will be Johnny Frenchman."

I was never a lazy man and by nature, I hated being idle. I joined in whenever there was work to do and that was all the time. There were just enough men to work the ship and if things were difficult then even the officers leant a hand. I did not have much skill but I had strength and I could haul on a line and help the others. I might not be able to navigate but I could hang on to the wheel and help the men steering the ship. In short, I made myself useful. If there was nought else to do I brought hot drinks from the galley.

We were north of Bordeaux when the accident happened. Little Jamie was one of the two cabin boys. He was not yet ten. Like all boys that age, he was fearless and he would race around the deck without any regard for his own safety. It was not a bad storm but the deck was wet and slippery. He managed to lose his balance and crash into one of the guns. It was obvious to all of us that he had broken his leg. I could see the two bones sticking out from the skin their jagged edges red with his blood.

The captain's expression spoke volumes. There was no one aboard who could tend to the boy. Jamie was a brave little fellow and did not cry unduly. He tried to bear it stoically but I knew that he was in great pain. Jonas liked the boy and it was he who faced the captain. "We have to put him ashore captain. He needs a doctor."

"Are you mad? This is France? We will all be put in jail. We'll have to see to the boy ourselves."

I shook my head, "You can't do that captain. He would be crippled for life and he is too young for that." A sudden thought entered my head. "Besides this is the Vendee. They have royalist sympathies here. Get a chart and let's find the nearest port."

I suspect that I was trading on the high regard I was held in following the incident with the pirates but I did not care. Jonas found the chart and brought it on deck. He jabbed a finger at a spot just off the coast. "As near as makes no difference we are here."

I saw a red speck which was quite close, "St. Gilles Croix de Vie. What is that?"

Captain Dinsdale rubbed his beard. "A quiet little fishing port. It has a nice harbour for small boats but we wouldn't fit inside."

I did not know what he meant. "Could you explain?"

Jonas did. "There is a long breakwater which protects the boats inside. We are too big to get in."

"But we could tie up on the sea side?"

"Yes."

"Then we can take him ashore without jeopardising the ship. I can take him to a doctor. I can speak French like a native and I can pass for French. I was a French soldier until a couple of weeks ago." I could see that I had nearly persuaded the captain.

"You can't do that alone."

"I'll go with him."

"Thank you, Jonas. Well, captain, you are just risking us two. You will be able to get away."

"I don't know. As soon as they see the flag they will send for the navy and La Rochelle is quite close to here."

"Have you any other flags?" He looked at me as though I was speaking Arabic. "Do you have the flag of Naples and Sicily or Malta?"

"We have both."

"Then fly the flag of the owner of the cargo, Count Alpini. I can speak Italian. The French are about to become allies anyway."

I could see him wavering and it was Richard, the Second Mate who swung it. "Go on, captain. I would hate to see the young 'un on the beach and besides," he grinned at me, "I think Captain Macgregor might just be able to pull this off."

"Very well but if I end up in a French jail you will owe me a ship."

We headed in, gingerly, with the flag of Naples and Sicily hanging from our jack staff. We also flew a small flag from our masthead. It was white with a blue box around and a red square in the middle. I asked Jonas what it meant and he said, "It means I require medical assistance. The doctor may not know what it means but the fishermen will."

The small port hove into view. I hoped that they would have a doctor. Jonas and I waited on the main deck with Jamie strapped to an improvised stretcher. We had given him brandy to knock him out and I hoped that it would last until he had been seen to. We tied up as close to the town as we could. Neither of us carried any arms and Captain Dinsdale said, "If I think you are captured then I will push off and leave you here. I am sorry but I cannot risk the ship."

I looked at Jonas and he nodded, "Just do what you have to captain. We will look after ourselves."

I could see that the comment hurt even though I had not meant it to. Captain Dinsdale was a kind man but he was in an impossible situation. The ship was his livelihood. As soon as we tied up we stepped up on to the harbour wall and headed for the town. Jamie was all skin and bone and no weight at all. I saw a gaggle of people appear at the end of the town end of the wall. "Remember Jonas, let me do the talking."

"Right sir."

I could see a couple of National Guardsmen there as well as someone in a hat who looked like the mayor. I did not allow them to speak first instead I launched into the speech I had mentally prepared. "We need medical help. We are an Italian ship and this boy has broken his leg. Have you a doctor?"

There were two women in the group and they gasped when they saw the wound. The man in the hat said, "I am the Mayor, Philippe Latour. We have no doctor. Have you not got one on board?"

One of the women snorted, "Imbecile! Would they come ashore if they had a doctor?" She turned to the National Guardsman. "Don't you have a doctor at the barracks?"

"Yes, Madame."

"Well go and tell him we are coming." She turned to me. "Follow me and you get out of the way!" She flapped a hand at the mayor who reddened and scurried away. The soldiers just stood there. "Well?"

"We are on duty here."

"Men! Just one of you go to the barracks then. It isn't as though the English are going to invade right this minute is it?"

The force of nature swept all before her and we hurried through the town. She held Jamie's hand. "Such a shame." She flashed a look of hatred at the man in the hat. "My husband will pay for his stupidity. He will get his own dinner tonight. How did it happen?"

"He slipped on the deck."

"Ah." She looked up at me. "Your French is very good for an Italian."

"That is because I am French. I was born in Breteuil."

"Up near Lille? Yes, I know it. And how do you end up on an Italian ship?"

"A long story Madame." She gave me a shrewd look and then hurried on.

We reached the barracks and the National Guardsman who had raced ahead was there with a lieutenant. He looked barely old enough to shave. His voice was high pitched and squeaky. "I am sorry but our doctor is for the soldiers and not for foreigners."

"It is a child!"

"I am sorry Madame Latour but I have my orders."

I had the measure of this young man, "I am sorryLieutenant, are you saying that your orders said that if a child came here with a broken leg then you were to turn him away? That does not sound like an order which came from the Committee."

As soon as I said that magic word he paled and began to doubt himself. "No, but the orders are clear. Civilians are not allowed inside."

"I see, and is the doctor allowed outside?"

"Of course."

"Then why not ask him to come out here and then you will have done your duty."

I saw the relief on his face as he realised that he could pass the problem onto someone else. "Well just wait here."

I shook my head, "That's right Jamie, don't go running off!"

Madame Latour's laugh sent the red-faced officer running back through the gate much to the amusement of the two sentries. The doctor, a major, returned really quickly and he took one look at Jamie and said to the two sentries, "Get this man into the hospital now." He glared at the lieutenant. "Buffoon." He looked at me and said, "You come with me. You do speak French do you not?"

"Of course."

"Good."

I was pleased to see that the hospital was clean and mercifully empty. "Put him down there and then return to your duties." He noticed that Madame Latour was still with us and he smiled."You two, wash your hands and you can assist."

After we had dried out hands I saw that he had cut Jamie's trousers off. He checked that we had cleaned the wound and he nodded. "Did you knock him out with brandy?"

"We did sir. It seemed best. The boy was in distress."

"And you did the right thing. Madame Latour if you would hold the boy's shoulders and you?"

"Robert."

He suddenly looked at me carefully and nodded. "Well, Robert you hold his good leg." When we were ready he pushed down on the two bones which protruded until they were back in the leg. I felt Jamie's other leg move but he did not wake. The doctor then checked to see that the ends of the bones were touching and he quickly sewed the skin up. Then he carefully wrapped a bandage tightly around the wound. "Do not let go yet. This is the most crucial part of the operation." He left the room and returned with something I recognised. It was a pair of musketoon ramrods.

He looked at me, "I am going to place these on his injured leg. I will then bandage the leg. Keep it still." He was a good doctor and soon the leg was encased in a bandage." There," He looked at me, "you will need to take him to a doctor as soon as you land in England. This is just to get him through the next few days."

There was little point in lying. "How did you know?"

He laughed, "You might be flying an Italian flag but your ship is called 'The Witch of Endor' besides, Captain Macgregor, I recognised you."

I stared at him in surprise. Madame Latour also seemed intrigued. "What?"

"I was at the battle of Rivoli." He pointed at my scarred face. "You may have a beard but you are unmistakeable. Do not worry. You and your men saved my regiment that day. I am indebted to you." He stopped and asked, "Why did you leave the regiment?"

I said flatly and simply, "They all died in Egypt. I am the last of the 17th Chasseurs."

He looked genuinely sad, "Then I am sorry for your loss. I would hurry for they have sent to La Rochelle for a ship."

"Thank you sir."

When we reached the street there was a crowd gathered. Madame Latour said proudly, "We have saved his leg. This doctor is a saint." She winked at me. The crowd gathered around the doctor and Jonas and I hurried along the wall. When we reached the boat Madame Latour pecked my cheek and said, "I would have liked to hear your story but the doctor is right. My husband is keen to ingratiate himself with the authorities. They will be here soon."

"Thank you, Madame. I will tell Jamie of your kindness when he recovers." As we stepped on to the deck I shouted, "Get under way Captain Dinsdale. The French Navy is heading here even as we speak!"

"Clear the lines! Hoist the mainsail!" He glanced at the stretcher. "And the lad?"

"He'll be fine. Thanks for waiting, captain."

"I had to you may be the joint owner of my next ship!"

Chapter 15

With Jamie safely below deck and being cared for by the cook, every other sailor was trying to get every knot of speed we could out of the old 'Witch'. I stared aft. I knew that whoever was chasing us would come from that direction. It was now a game of cat and mouse. We had the whole ocean to choose but they would outnumber, outgun and outrun us. It would be down to the captain's cunning and his skill as a seaman.

"The problem is that we have to pass the main base at Brest. They have a coastal signalling system and if it is working then they could be waiting for us."

"What interest could they have in us?"

He gave a wry smile, "We have a cargo! We have a ship. What more could they want?" I must have looked disappointed. "It was a brave thing that you did. We are all fond of Jamie. He is an orphan. I will escape these Frenchmen. No offence meant but they have no imagination." He turned to the Second Mate. "I want no lights showing at all. Tell the cook to put out the galley fires. I want the best eyes in the ship at the top of the mainmast."

I looked at the sky to the east; it was already darkening although the sun had not yet set in the west. If we could race into the night then we stood a chance of escaping. "Sail Ho!"

"Where away?"

"To the south."

Captain Dinsdale rubbed his hands. "Well, that solves one problem. We know where they are coming from." He glanced down at the charts. "Noirmoutier that is where we will head."

Jonas said, "Noirmoutier? That is a narrow little channel and they have no light there."

"I am guessing that they will have sent a frigate after us. They have a deeper draught than the 'Witch' I have sailed through it before. We will take it under full sail."

"Full sail? But if we are only slightly off line we will strike the rocks."

"True but it is high tide and a full moon tonight. It is a gamble but then isn't all life a gamble. If we take the channel, we will gain at least three hours on them. We can head for the island of Houat and miss Quiberon by twenty miles."

Jonas shrugged. "You are the skipper and it is your ship. I'll make sure we have extra lookouts at the bows."

"Where would you like me, captain?"

He smiled, "I think you have done enough for this day. Watch a master at work."

It was a joy to watch someone as skilled as Matthew Dinsdale. He took the wheel himself and just listened to the shouts of the lookouts, watched the sky and sniffed the air. It was as though he felt his way up the coast. The sails of the frigate soon came closer as night fell. There was no hiding from her and she fired her bow chasers to make us stop. At over two miles range there was no way that they could hit us but we watched the cannonballs bounce alarmingly close to our course. The captain seemed unconcerned especially after we sighted the Isle of Noirmoutier ahead. I could not see where the channel was. If you had asked me I would have said that it was a solid piece of land but the captain seemed confident.

I heard the lookout cry, "Breakers to larboard!"

The captain made the slightest movement with his hand and the ship moved slightly to starboard. Then we heard, "Breakers to starboard!" and I expected him to move the wheel again but he did not. The cry was repeated and still he did not move. I wondered if he had heard the cry. When the shout came, "Rocks to starboard he did move the wheel and he moved it some way. We seemed to dart through the tidal race and then we were through the channel.

I stared behind at the frigate. Their captain was obviously no hero and I saw the sails flutter in confusion as they took in sail and tried to turn to larboard. The ship luffed and almost came to a standstill. The crew cheered as we sailed up the eastern side of the island. It would take the frigate some time to get under way again and we had taken the short route. He might still catch us but it would not be before morning. I was now more confident that the wily English captain would escape the trap.

Dawn found us in the treacherous waters off Ushant. Captain Dinsdale was dodging between the shallow islands and rocks. It was a nerve-wracking time. The frigate had to stand off well to the south of us. She had seen us just after we had rounded the cape at Plogoff. She was gaining on us but the captain could take his little ship over shallower water than the deeper draught of the man of war would permit. I could see that the captain was tired but he was determined to see it through. The frigate captain knew that we had to emerge into the open sea at some point and then he would catch us. All he had to do was to keep us in sight.

Jonas went up to him. "Do you want me to spell you for a while?"

"No, Jonas, the game is nearly up. Unless I am mistaken we shall find the Ushant squadron just ahead and if we do then our little French friend is going to find things become very hot."

As soon as the frigate rounded Ushant I saw her put stunsails on as she hurtled northwards to catch us. Captain Dinsdale took us deliberately close to the coast and the frigate took the bait. She beat to the west intending to drive in and cut us off. Suddenly we heard the boom and crack of cannon from over the horizon. The waters around the frigate boiled and fizzed like water on a pan of fat. Too late did she decide that discretion was the better part of valour and attempt to turn. It was in vain the English greyhounds were upon her and we watched as two British frigates took the Frenchman as a prize.

The captain handed the wheel to Jonas. "If you head due north, we should find Sir Edward Pellew and the rest of the Ushant squadron."

An hour later we did see the huge two and three-deckers of the fleet watching Brest. A sloop raced alongside us and a young captain asked us what had happened. Captain Dinsdale just said that we had had problems off the coast of the Vendee and the frigate had pursued us.

"Well, I think that the lads on those frigates will stand you a drink, captain. They will make a pretty penny out of the prize money."

"Glad to be of service and thank them for their timely intervention."

If I thought that life would be dull after the chase I could not have been more wrong. The leg from Ushant to the English Channel was far rougher than I could ever have imagined. We seemed to be tossed about like a cork on huge waves. An additional problem was that we had more ships to contend with. There were more merchant ships, fishing boats and, of course, the Channel Fleet which seemed to totally disregard the merchantmen going about their business. Once we reached the Thames Estuary then the rough water abated but the number of ships increased.

Captain Dinsdale looked exhausted and I knew he had not slept much over the past few days. "Well Captain Dinsdale, we are almost at journey's end. Where will we land our cargo?"

"We will land at the wharf at East Cheap. That is as far upriver as we can go. The agent has an office in the Strand and I will get Jonas to take you there. And now I will get back to navigating this crowded waterway."

He was right. I had never seen as many ships in my life. There appeared to be some pattern to the movement but the ferries which rowed across the river seemed to ignore the much larger ships and their crews hurled abuse at everyone who sailed up and down that watery thoroughfare. I suspect it was ever thus in all the major cities. The traffic slowed us down so that we were barely under way. I heard Jonas chuckle. "Well, at least there is a berth. Our short cut saved us time and we have arrived on a high tide and before any others."

The captain nudged the ship next to the wooden wharf and the men tied up as quickly as they could. I could see the obvious relief on the captain's face as the ship was secured. "Now sir if you would go to the agent with Jonas I will see the robbing bastards in the Customs House. They would take the coins from a dead man's body." He looked at my clothes. "I would change your clothes too young sir. They have a poor view of vagrants in the city."

I looked down at my dirty, bloodstained clothes. He was correct. I now had to become a young gentleman once more. Jonas was waiting patiently for me when I returned. I had my sword strapped to my side. He nodded approvingly. "That's better sir. Now you look like a proper gentleman. Follow me."

We descended the gangplank to a cacophony of noise. Hawkers begged us to hire them to unload the cargo. We were offered women and boys for our pleasure. We were told of the best hostelries. In short, everyone was keen to be of service. Jonas had little time for them. "Get away you robbing parasites. We have no need of your services." They did not take offence at the insults and began to clamour around the captain when he descended the gangplank.

I heard a splash and turned around to see the captain looking down into the Thames and the crowd laughing at someone in the water. "When I say push off then do it! Next time I'll use my fist and not the back of my hand."

Jonas laughed, "Come along sir. It isn't far." The office of Lambert and Fowler was above a coffee house just off the Strand. It was a busy and congested street. The carriages and wagons did not take prisoners and you crossed the street at your own peril. We climbed the dingy steps to a small office where a clerk looked up. I was at a loss; I had never been here. Jonas looked at me and nodded. "We are from the 'Witch of Endor' and we have some letters for the agent. This is the new representative of the family, Captain Robert Macgregor." I shot him a look of puzzlement and he winked.

The clerk sniffed and said, "I will inform Mr Lambert. Please be so good as to wait here."

"Jonas, I am only a captain in the French Army."

"They don't know that and they are impressed by titles. They won't ask the captain of what, they will just accept it."

A few moments later we were ushered into the cramped office. It was hard to see how anything was done; there appeared to be no order and there was not a single inch of space anywhere on the desk. Mr Lambert took some papers and placed them on the desk; they tottered alarmingly but remained where they had been placed.

"Sit gentlemen. My clerk says you have a missive for me?"

I handed him the two letters from Count Alpini. I looked at Mr Lambert. He looked as though he came from a good family but his clothes and the room looked as though he had fallen on hard times. I was aware that I needed to investigate him. He read one and handed it back to me. "You will need this Captain Macgregor." He then read the second one. After he had finished he beamed, leaned forward and held out his hand. "My name is Henry Lambert and I am delighted to meet a member of the Alpini family." He appraised me. "You neither look nor sound Italian."

I was now in a country with which I had been at war and I had to be devious and secretive. "I know."

Jonas covered his smile with his hand and the agent looked non-plussed. "Oh. And how may we be of service?"

"Firstly I require passage up the east coast of England. Can you arrange that?"

"I can easily get you a berth on a collier going to Newcastle."

I glanced at Jonas who nodded, "That will be satisfactory. I would like to leave as soon as possible. Secondly, I need a report for my family about the sales so far this year and the prediction for the future."

He looked uncomfortable, "For the future? A report? I do not understand."

"I intend to visit Mr Fortnum's shop and see what price is being charged for our dried fruits, lemons and wines. If I discover that they are being charged at a much higher rate than we are receiving for them then we might seek a better agent who is able to make a better bargain with our customers."

He really looked disturbed. "I cannot be responsible for how much profit the shop makes."

"No, I realise that and I will speak to the staff to discover just how much profit they are making. I have a feeling that peace will be breaking out soon and that will have an effect on the profits will it not?"

"Er yes."

"Good. I will return tomorrow when I hope that you will have my report and have arranged my passage north."

"Of course."

As we left Jonas said, "Well you put the wind up him and no mistake. There is more to you than meets the eye."

"I would hope so. It is the reason I have survived so long. Could we find this Fortnum and Mason shop then?"

"That shouldn't be a problem, sir. I think I know where it is and if not I can ask." He pointed down the Strand. "It is in Piccadilly."

The shop was certainly doing good business and they had liveried doormen to open the door to the customers. They looked askance at Jonas who said, "I will wait outside sir."

"You will do no such thing. We are together." I glared at the doorman who relented and opened the door. We stepped in and entered an exotic bazaar with goods from the four corners of the world. I saw the wines as soon as I entered and I wandered over.

A young well-dressed man approached me. "Yes sir, can I be of service?"

"I think you can. I am looking for some Sicilian wines do you have any?"

He smirked and giggled almost effeminately, "Oh sir, you have come to the right place. We are the only emporium to sell Sicilian wines and we have a fine range." He gestured at the racks behind him and I saw the wines my kinsman had produced. "I have to warn you though sir. They are not cheap."

"How much a bottle are they?" He wrote it down on a piece of paper and handed it to me. I read it and handed it to Jonas. They were charging for six bottles what we charged for a small barrel. "Thank you we will return when we have examined your other goods."

We discovered that the prices they were charging for the lemons and the dried fruits were also inflated. "I think it is time to speak with Mr Fortnum and discover just who is robbing the Alpini family."

There was an important-looking man in the middle of the shop. He was obviously not a customer and his greasy smile reeked of an obsequious manager. I walked up to him and he oozed, "Yes sir. How can I be of assistance?"

"I would like to speak with Mr Fortnum please."

"I am the manager sir and I am sure that I can deal with any issue you have."

"I represent the Alpini family of Sicily and we supply many of your goods I wish to speak with Mr Fortnum, now!"

There was steel in my voice which wiped the smile from his face. "Old Mr Charles is not here today but I will see if Mr William can see you."

"I am certainly seeing a different side to you today sir? A little more of the officer perhaps?"

"I have seen too many self-important men in my time to be intimidated by them."

Mr William Fortnum was about forty years old and was as sharp as they come. He was the antithesis of his fawning manager. He held out his hand he had a firm handshake, "I am William Fortnum. I am sorry for the delay and you are…?"

"Captain Robert Macgregor the representative of the Alpini family." I handed him the letter of introduction.

He read as he walked, "Come with me, gentlemen." We went into a well-appointed office on the first floor and he gestured to two well upholstered and comfortable chairs. He handed me the letter back and then said, "How may I help you?"

"I hope this will not be difficult but I have been sent to discover what happens to the Alpini goods when they reach England. From the prices you charge in your store I think that you are underpaying the family."

I heard the intake of breath from Jonas but William seemed unconcerned. He reached down and took out a ledger. I saw the name Alpini on the spine. "Here are the accounts. Pray read them and then tell me if we are robbing your family."

I read them and realised after one page that it was the agent. I closed it and handed it back to him. "I apologise, sir. It seems we are both being robbed by Mr Lambert. He pays the family a tenth of what he charges you."

"I suspected as much."

"The family is increasing its production soon and there will be another ship too which will mean you will have more goods to sell. I think a better arrangement will be that we miss out the middleman and deal with you directly. Would that be acceptable?"

He smiled, "A much better arrangement."

"Would you be so good as to write down on a piece of paper what you deem to be a price for our goods which will still enable you to make a profit?"

He looked surprised, "A strange request. Either you are very naïve or very trusting. Which is it?"

"Neither. I have seen the prices you charge and I know that you would not cook the goose which lays the golden eggs. You will pay a fair price because you know you can sell our goods and wish to continue to do so."

"By Jove sir. It is refreshing to do business with an honest man." He wrote down the numbers and handed it over. I read them and nodded. "And how do we cut out the middleman?"

"Jonas here will tell you when the ship is in port and we will deliver the goods directly here. From the numbers I read, I suspect that Mr Lambert or someone at the warehouse is stealing from us as well. I will deal with that but this way you will get the goods on the day that they arrive."

"Excellent. But will it not be you as the representative who deals with us?"

"I have other deals to do sir. Oh do not worry they are not in London but I will be travelling to Scotland. I have business there. Tell me, what has made your business so successful?"

"Firstly we deal in only the very best of goods and we deal with the best of clients. My father, the Mr Charles of the business, also had the idea of making hampers for the soldiers who were stationed abroad. It used to be just the West Indies, Canada and India but since the French Revolution, we now have soldiers in the Low Countries and Gibraltar. It is a lucrative business. One man's loss and all that."

"Well thank you for your honesty, Mr Fortnum."

We shook hands, "It has been a pleasure to deal with you sir and I will make sure that my staff expedite the meeting next time."

When we were outside Jonas looked worried. "Are you sure the Alpinis will be happy with me dealing with Mr Fortnum for them?"

"They have little choice. We certainly don't want Lambert robbing us blind do we? Besides I am the representative and I have made that decision. If my kinsman does not like it then he can dismiss me. And now back to the ship."

The captain was furious when he heard what the agent had been doing. "It was me that recommended him. I'll go down there and gut him like a fish."

"Steady on captain. Let us wait until tomorrow. We need to find a lawyer to deal with this in the court of law."

"No, you don't, Robbie. Lawyers in England are worse than the criminals. Lawyers rob you and then try to make you feel grateful to them for doing so."

"Well, we need the books and some compensation for the count."

"Jonas, you stay here in charge of the ship tomorrow. Get the holds cleaned and the ship reprovisioned. I'll go with Robbie here and the Second Mate. We will see if we can't persuade Mr Lambert to make good what he has stolen." He shook his head. "And I was going to see if I could get another cargo from him to take back to Italy."

"I would see Mr Fortnum."

"Why? He imports not exports..."

"We heard today that he now sends hampers to soldiers serving abroad. You pass the Low Countries and Gibraltar do you not?"

"Aye, we do."

"And, captain, I heard today that the British Army is going to Egypt. We could do that too." Jonas had kept his eyes and ears open.

I turned. "Where did you hear that, Jonas?"

"There was a chap selling newspapers on the Strand. You were too busy taking in the sights to notice but I saw the headline and heard his call."

So my comrades in Egypt would now be facing a real enemy; the British Army and they would not find them so easy to defeat. "Well then captain, I think that tomorrow we head for the agent and, hopefully, he will have secured a ship for me before we threaten him."

"Don't you worry about that sir. I can get you on a ship. I have been sailing these waters since I was a lad. I know all the captains. There are half a dozen colliers in port right now."

We went armed to the agent. We were admitted straight away and we were all smiles. "Ah, Captain Dinsdale. It is good to see you. I take it you have come for me to arrange a cargo back to Naples? I think I can help you there."

"I am in need of a cargo but before we come to that have you arranged a berth for Captain Macgregor yet?"

"Sadly, no there are none to be had but if you come back next week."

Captain Dinsdale looked at me. His look said it all. He was lying. I leaned forward. "Then perhaps you could help me, as the Alpini representative of course, and show me the accounts of the Alpini family."

His nervous eyes flickered to the bookshelf to his right. Like the rest of the room, it was packed with papers and files. "I am afraid that it is not in the office. I took it home last night to bring it up to date and I forgot you were coming in."

I laughed, "Captain Dinsdale this man tells lies as easily as a bird flies." I nodded to Jennings who stood, opened the door and jerked the tiny clerk from his chair and into the already crowded room.

"What the!"

"First of all you are lying about the colliers but we will skip over that. Yesterday I visited Mr William Fortnum and he showed me his accounts. They are somewhat at odds with the money we have been receiving and with the goods he has been sold."

He took on an indignant air, "If I had the books here I would show you that he is lying and I have dealt honestly with the family!"

"Oh, how I will enjoy telling Mr Fortnum how you slander his name." I turned to the quaking clerk. "Now the Second Mate could break every bone in your body if the captain so ordered but I am sure he won't need to do that. Which one of those," I pointed to the files on the bookcase, "is the Alpini ledger?"

Lambert's shoulders sagged but the clerk said, "I need this job, sir. Don't make me betray my master."

"Your job will be secure I promise you that but your hand may be crushed and then how would you earn a living?"

He pointed a quivering finger at a file with red writing on it. The file name was smudged but I could now see that it looked like Alpini. I stood and went to grab the file. Mr Lambert half stood as though he would stop me. "Please try to stop me. I am looking for an excuse to pound your face into raw meat and an assault on me would be just the provocation I needed."

He sat in his chair, defeated. I scanned the pages. Captain Dinsdale was furious I could sense that and he reached over and grabbed a handful of grubby shirt and cravat. "I don't need any provocation. I trusted you and you have betrayed me. I wonder how many other captains have been betrayed by you." There was a look of terror on the man's face. The Alpini family were not the only ones being robbed.

"Leave him for the moment, captain. He will need teeth to be able to answer my questions." I smiled, "This is not a question, at least not yet. You have been stealing from the Alpini family. Now here is the question. Does your partner, Mr Fowler know of this crime?"

He almost whispered, "There is no Mr Fowler. It just makes us sound grander than we are."

I looked around at the office. It had no sign of wealth about it. "Do you own a fine house?"

"I live upstairs."

I was bewildered. "Then where does the money go. You have stolen enough money to buy a grand house in Mayfair where is the money?"

"I gamble."

My heart sank. So much for getting some money back for the family. I turned to the clerk. "Is this true?"

"He does gamble, sir."

The captain stood up and pulled a wicked-looking knife from his boot. "Then if we cannot get the family's money back I might as well slit his throat here and now!"

The agent squeaked a terrified, "No! I have some money. Please don't hurt me!"

I felt sickened by this creature before me but I knew I owed a debt to the Alpini family and this man would be no use to me dead. "Get it!"

He reached into a drawer and pulled out a wad of paper. "Here sir."

"What is this?"

Captain Dinsdale took it and examined it. "This is money, sir. Banknotes."

I shook my head. "This is no use to the family in Italy!"

The clerk had sat silently. "You will need to open a bank account and deposit the money. They can give a promissory note and that can be deposited in Naples."

It sounded implausible but the captain nodded. "Very well. I would get into another line of work and stop gambling. We will take these ledgers and show them to Mr Fortnum. If I had time I would prosecute you. You have been lucky."

As we walked back to the ship Captain Dinsdale said, "I just wanted to hit him."

"As did I but it would have gained us nothing and made us liable to criminal proceedings. This is all that we can do."

Once at the ship we counted the money. It represented barely a tenth of the money that had been stolen but it was a start. At least I felt I had done something useful to repay all of Sir John's kindness. When I had finished my Scottish quest, I would be able to decide what direction I wanted to take. This was the end of one part of my life and the start of another.

Chapter 16

We returned to Mr Fortnum and showed him the ledger. He looked down the columns and examined every entry. When he finished he closed the book as though to expunge the crime. He was as appalled and shocked as we were. "This is a betrayal of trust. I will do no more business with that criminal. What will you do with the books?"

"Return them to the count. Perhaps you could advise us on the money? The agent's clerk suggested a bank and a promissory note."

"That seems a good idea." He gave me a card. "My bank is around the corner. If you show them this card, they will facilitate your request."

"Thank you, sir."

Captain Dinsdale nodded. "And while you and Mr Jennings do that, I will discuss cargo with Mr Fortnum."

The instruction, *'just around the corner'*, was slightly misleading. It was four streets away. We had only gone a hundred yards when I sensed that someone was following us. I pretended I had something on the bottom of my boot and I leaned against the wall to clean it. I glanced down the street and saw four rough-looking men lounging some way behind us. We continued on our way. "I think, Mr Jennings, that we are being followed."

"Four big blokes?"

"Yes. Did you see them?"

"I spotted them lounging outside. Do you want me to do anything?"

"No, we'll go to the bank first and then we will be able to deal with them."

The bank was a small private one. We had to knock on the door and it wasn't until they saw Mr Fortnum's card that they allowed us in. The bank manager was effusive once he realised we were friends of Mr Fortnum. I discovered that Queen Charlotte had been a client with the emporium and there were close associations with the royal family. It expedited our business. I arranged to pick up the note the next day. When we emerged there was no sign of our followers. I felt that they were close all the way back to Piccadilly. We met the captain and returned to East Cheap.

When we told Captain Dinsdale about the four men he nodded, "That Lambert gave in too easy. He'll want his money and the ledger back. Best not travel alone. Now what we need is to find you a ship. We'll head for the 'Coal Hole Tavern'. The colliers like their ale and it is a good beer that they serve there. Now that we no longer have that money about us I feel a lot safer. Mr Jennings, if you would return to the ship and keep a good watch I would appreciate it. That Lambert is a nasty piece of work and I am regretting not dealing with him a little more firmly."

The tavern was lively. I looked out of place in my fine clothes but, as they all knew the captain, we were made welcome. It was the sort of place Pierre would have enjoyed. As we ordered our beers I wondered how he was doing in Breteuil. The captain ordered me something called porter. It was a black beer with a creamy head and tasted, unlike any beer I had ever tasted before. It had a pleasant sweet taste and I enjoyed it. We took our tankards to a table close to the roaring fire. Captain Dinsdale explained, "Better light and people can see us. I told the landlord what we were after and the captains should seek us out. I told them you would pay. Is that right?"

"Of course. I am not without funds."

"I know but I wondered if you wanted to work your passage."

"Me? I am about as much use as a one-legged man in an arse-kicking contest."

"Do not put yourself down you acquitted yourself well on the voyage here."

I sipped the beer. I had not enjoyed such a night since before I joined the chasseurs all those years ago. I looked at the empty tables and the empty chairs in the tavern and thought of Claude, Michael, Albert and all the others who would no longer be able to do as I did. Captain Dinsdale nudged me, "Come on cheer up. I think someone is coming over."

A bear of a man wandered over. He had a black beard and a shock of black hair which seemed unnaturally unruly. He grinned as he put his hand out. "Well aye, if it isn't Matthew Dinsdale. How are you, you old pirate."

"Fine and how are you Geordie?"

"Canny. I wondered who was asking for a berth. Is it your friend here? The young lad?"

"Yes this is Robert Macgregor and he wishes to go to Newcastle and then travel to Scotland."

"Scotland? What the hell for? It's full of mad Jocks! Now Newcastle is a totally different thing. Very civilised."

"Before you put both your feet in your mouth Geordie I should tell you that Robert is from Scottish stock."

"Eeh I am sorry. No offence meant."

I liked the big bluff man immediately. "And none taken but I have never been to Scotland before. I was born in France."

"Aw you are a poor bugger aren't ye. Scottish roots and born among the snail eaters."

The captain shook his head, "When he isn't talking he is alright Robert." He turned to Geordie, "Robert was a soldier and served in Egypt. He is a captain."

"You look too young to have done so much. Well, I never. Well if you want a berth on The Hotspur you are more than welcome. She's a sound ship and we'll make a fast time. She's no palace but she suits me and the lads."

"Thank you kindly Captain…?"

"It's Captain Percy but everyone calls me Geordie."

"Well, I will take you up on your offer. When do you sail?"

"The day after tomorrow. I have a cargo to load and then we're off."

Captain Dinsdale was suddenly interested. "What is the cargo?"

"Hops. The brewery up in Newcastle likes the Kentish hops. It's a bit of a bugger as we have to take them in barrels." He sniffed, "They don't like getting them covered in coal dust. Gives them flavour I say."

Captain Dinsdale rose, "Well we'll see you the day after tomorrow."

"I'll just be finishing my pint and then I'll follow you. I canna stand London prices. They must think we are all made of money!" He shot a dark look at the landlord who was not bothered at all by the criticism.

It was dark as we left the tavern to make our way down the alleys back to the river. Rich people hired men with torches to light their way along the streets but we only had two alleys to negotiate and they were not long. When we emerged from one into the next, dimly lit street, the men who had followed us earlier in the day appeared. They each had a cudgel in their hands and one man had a short knife.

I curse the fact that I had left my sword on the ship and all I had was the stiletto in my boot. I knew that the captain had his knife but we were outnumbered.

Captain Dinsdale seemed calm, "Now then lads we want no bother."

The leader who had an ugly scar running from his cheek to his eye spat a gob of phlegm at my feet and said, "Don't worry old man. This will be no bother. We'll just teach the two of you a lesson in manners and then you can return the ledger to its rightful owner eh?"

I was not going to wait to be attacked and so I stamped forward with the heel of my boot and struck the leader on the kneecap. I heard a crack and he fell screaming to the ground. I sensed someone coming at my left and I put my left arm up in defence and wheeled to face a short man with a cudgel. As the weapon came down I rolled away and used my left arm to slow down the weapon. His momentum and my swing made us crash to the ground on top of the injured leader who screamed as the combined weight of the two of us smashed into his shattered knee. I kept my roll going and as I did so I slid my hand down and grabbed my stiletto. I slashed across the back of the man's hand and ripped through his flesh. He screamed, dropped the cudgel and grabbed his injured hand. I punched him hard in the solar plexus and he doubled up. Before I could do anything else to him something crashed into my back and I fell on top of the injured leader once more. I rolled to the side and saw the look of triumph on the face of another thug with a cudgel.

"This is going to crush your head to a pulp!"

He began to swing it and then suddenly it stopped in mid-air. He looked up in surprise, as I did then Geordie spun him around and said, "Fight fair!" before punching him hard in the face. He fell unconscious behind me. All four of the attackers were now either unconscious or incapacitated.

Captain Dinsdale wiped his knife on the jacket of the man who was holding his bleeding face. "Now you tell Mr Lambert that we are less than happy with his behaviour and he should find somewhere else to ply his trade!"

We left the four of them and headed back to our ships. "Thanks, Geordie. That was good timing."

"You could have handled them. I only took a hand because I could see it was ending. I tell you what young fella, you can handle yourself. You'll be alright."

At the river, he went upstream and we went downstream. Captain Dinsdale said, "I told you we should have sorted that Lambert out. He is a bad 'un through and through." He looked up at the gangplank of 'The Witch' and nodded. Jennings stood there with a pistol in his belt and a marlinspike in his hand. "I'm glad they took precautions; that Lambert is more desperate than I thought."

We sat in the captain's cabin sipping some rum we had bought from the captain of a ship just docked from the West Indies. The captains all helped each other by selling special goods to each other before the customs had taken their share. "Tomorrow we will make some arrangements so that I can contact you when you return." He drank some of the potent brew. "Have you any thoughts about your future?"

"You mean after Scotland?" He nodded. "Not really."

"If you are still interested in buying a share in a ship then that would be a fine and profitable occupation."

"I am still interested in providing funds for your venture captain and tomorrow, when we return to the bank I will put that in place but I could not work in an office. I crave action. I never thought I would miss the Bonaparte adventures I enjoyed but I do."

"I can understand that. You are a young and active man. Still, you will always have something to fall back on after a life of adventure eh?"

Just then we heard a cry and a commotion on the quayside. I grabbed my sword and followed the captain on deck. We saw, on the quayside, Jennings grappling with one man while two of the crew restrained another. We saw a third running off towards the Strand. By the time we had reached the quayside, Jennings had subdued his man. He looked up and grinned. "I nipped down for a mug of cocoa and when I came up I saw these with a lantern. I think they were going to fire the ship." He pointed to the marlinspike. "I am still accurate with one of those."

"Well done Jennings." The captain turned the man over with his sea boot. "Who sent you?"

"We done nothing! We were just walking along the quay minding our own business and this big bastard..." the captain kicked him hard in the ribs and he screamed. "Well, he just hurled a marlinspike at us."

The captain looked at me. "Do you believe him, Captain Macgregor?"

"Not a word." I took the stiletto from my boot and held it to his nose. "You know what I think? I think that our friend Mr Lambert sent these three to make sure we spoke to no one."

The man looked terrified, "No please! We were just walking down the quay."

I turned to the captain. "In Egypt, they have some interesting punishments. If you steal they cut off your hand. If you molest a woman they castrate you." I saw the man's eyes widen in terror. "Now I think an appropriate punishment for lying would be to split this man's nose and then everyone would know that he was a liar." I pressed the tip of the knife into the end of his nose and a tendril of blood dripped on to his lips."

"No please! I'll talk. It was Mr Lambert as sent us."

"That's better but where did he get the money to pay you? He said he had none." The man remained silent. I slid the tip to his eye.

"He was lying. He has a crib where he keeps his money."

"Where is it?"

"At the back of his office. There's a door behind the desk."

"Well captain what should we do with these men?"

The captain grinned. "I have an idea. Second Mate, bring them along." He led us to the steps which led down to the river. There was an old leaky skiff there. "Put them both in there." They were deposited in the bottom of the boat. "Now I never want to see you two again. I will spread the word amongst the other captains that you are both villains who set fire to ships. Is that clear?" They both nodded. "Right lads, push them into the river." The tide was on the turn and they pushed the skiff so hard that it soon struck the current and they were taken towards the sea. I could see that one was bailing while the other was trying to paddle to shore.

"Do you think they can swim?"

"Probably not but they'll make the shore. It's just that they will have a long and weary walk back to the city. Well done Second Mate but have the lads keep a close watch tonight.

We set off the next day for Mr Lambert's. We found the office door open and the room even more shambolic than we had last seen it. We discovered the cunningly hidden door and saw that the room had been stripped of anything of value. We went upstairs to his rooms and saw the signs of a hasty departure. "Well, the bird has flown captain."

Captain Dinsdale was not happy. "I hate leaving things unfinished. This will have to be settled when we return."

We went to the bank to pick up the promissory note. The manager was a quiet little man called Mr Hudson. He was quietly efficient and had precise neat movements. He seemed obsessed by order. That pleased me for it meant he was organised. "Mr Hudson I have some money I would like to deposit."

He looked over at Captain Dinsdale. "Is this a private matter sir?"

I smiled, "Captain Dinsdale is part of this but the account will be in my name." He nodded satisfied and his sense of order was preserved. I stood. "If you will excuse me a moment I have to take off my jacket." I could see that they were both intrigued. I took off my jacket and undid my shirt. I took off one of the two canvas belts. As I did so I was aware of the smell. It had been about my body for some time. I saw Mr Hudson wrinkle his nose. "I apologise for the smell Mr Hudson but this is necessary I can assure you." I took out my mother's jewels: the rings and the necklaces. "I would like these to be kept safe."

He took them and began to make an inventory. He looked up at me. "I will have to get them valued sir."

"That is fine. I will only sell them if I have to."

He rang the bell. A clerk appeared. "Would you take these to the main office and then go and ask Mr Levi from the jewellers next door to come and appraise them for us." The clerk took them away and Mr Hudson continued, "He is discreet. He is also a client of mine."

I took out the money. I handed over, first the ten gold Louis. I saw Mr Hudson nod his approval. I then took out the purse with the money I had collected over the years. I still had another which I used for current expenses. I gave them to him and the banker began to count them. As he did so Captain Dinsdale said, "A little risky having them about your person wasn't it?"

"They shared the same risks as me."

Mr Hudson briefly stopped counting and looked over his pince-nez. "A bank is more secure Mr Macgregor."

"I know but where I have been there were no banks."

"Then thank the lord that you are back in a civilised place. You have here gold and coins to the value of five thousand three hundred and seventy-three pounds, fifteen shillings and sixpence; a sizeable sum. What would you have us do with this?"

I did not answer him immediately, "Captain how much would you need for a ship?"

"With the money I have, I think I would need a partner to invest two thousand pounds."

I nodded, "Then Mr Hudson I would like to earn interest on this money but when Captain Dinsdale comes to you I would like you to release two thousand pounds for his use."

They both looked at me. Mr Hudson coughed, "You, of course, will be present too?"

"No. I do not know where I will be. In addition, I will ask Mr Fortnum to act for me in my absence. I will provide documents to enable him to do so and to absolve you of any responsibilities in that area."

"Extraordinary."

"Are you sure Robbie?"

"I told you before captain I have not made any plans for the future. This is an investment. I trust you and Jonas. When I am an old man, if I should live that long, then I hope to enjoy the fruits of your labours. Is that satisfactory Mr Hudson?"

"It is Captain Macgregor and I will have the papers drawn up for you."

"It will need to be quick for I am to sail to Scotland tomorrow."

"Ah off into the wilds again eh? You are an adventurer."

His clerk returned as the papers were readied for me. "Mr Levi said they are fine pieces and would fetch six thousand pounds at today's prices."

"Thank you." When the clerk had gone he wrote out all the figures and handed them to me. "You are comfortably off young man."

"Thank you, Mr Hudson."

We headed to Fortnum and Mason's. When I explained to Mr Fortnum what I intended he was taken aback. "But I barely know you. Why me?"

"You and the captain here will be business partners, you and Mr Hudson do business. It makes sense and besides, I trust you." I smiled, "If you are good enough for the Royal family then you are good enough for me. This way I can keep in touch with everyone from this fine emporium."

As we made our way back to the ship, I felt satisfied. For the first time in my life, I had order and organisation. I could now begin the next part of my quest. Captain Dinsdale headed back to Naples with Lambert's books and a letter from me explaining what I had done. In addition, there was a contract from Mr Fortnum. I had fulfilled my promise to the family.

Chapter 17

The collier was even smaller than the 'Witch' had been. It was a tiny crew too. There were just ten men on board. They were, however, a friendly crew. After we had negotiated the busy Thames Estuary we headed into the North Sea and me was able to talk with Geordie.

"This isn't like the sailing Captain Dinsdale has to do. We have no really violent storms and certainly no pirates. It's easy. We just plod up to Newcastle, Sunderland or Hartlepool and pick up a shipload of coal and then take it back to London. It takes us between ten days and two weeks. The lads like it; they get to spend a couple of days at home. I bet most of the crew of the 'Witch' aren't married."

"I don't know it never came up but you are probably right."

"Aye, I know. My lads are all either married or have a woman or two to keep their homes nice. There's canny money in coal. Since the war started the price of coal has risen quite a lot. They are not short of a bob or two."

I watched the flat Essex landscape drift away west and was grateful for the lack of big waves. This was gentler. It was not the azure blue of the Mediterranean more a slate grey but the motion of the sea was about the same. "Are you married, Geordie?"

"Aye. I have a bonny lass and three bairns at home. I have a lovely house overlooking the river and the sea at Tynemouth. You'll have to come and see it."

"I would like that." Even as I said it I realised that I had never known a home life. The nearest had been that idyllic couple of days when I had stayed with the Alpini family. My childhood had not really been home once my mother had died. I was looking forward to visiting a normal house and home in England.

"What are your plans then Robbie?"

"I'll need to buy a horse and then make my way to Islay in Scotland. It's where the Macgregors live. I have something to deliver."

He looked concerned. "It isn't as bad as it was but the border country is always a little dangerous. There are bandits up there."

I took out my stiletto. "I took this from a bandit who attacked me and my comrades in Italy."

He shook his head, "Aye I know but you weren't alone there were you? Take care. Captain Dinsdale thinks highly of you."

I was touched, "I will be careful."

"And what after you have delivered your package?"

Everyone kept asking me that question and I had not thought it through. Perhaps my fate was to be in Scotland. I didn't know. "Unless there is something for me in Scotland I will be returning to London. I know people there."

"I dinna like London. Too big and too dirty and full of foreigners."

"You know that I am French?"

"No, you are not. You might have been born there but I have heard you talk and seen you fight. You're an Englishman!"

"I have Scottish and French roots how do I become English?"

"You have all the right qualities. Don't sell yourself short. Jocks are alright and certainly better than the Frogs but set your sights higher. Be an Englishman!"

This was the first time I had experienced the English disease, xenophobia. They meant no harm but they believed that the English were God's chosen and could rule the world. I came to know that idea well over the next few years.

The voyage was pleasant and I was amazed at the changes in landscape. When we passed Hartlepool he pointed it out to me. "That is the River Tees and we sometimes call there but they are funny folk in Hartlepool. Nice enough folk but they mistrust strangers. They never leave their town you know? They are suspicious of everyone. Mind it suits me; I get all the business they shun."

The next day we entered the Tyne. He pointed to the headland. "That up there is the Priory and the Castle. My house is just along the front. We'll go there when we have unloaded. I know a man with some horses. I don't want you robbed before you get to Scotland!"

It was a busy river and we tied up at Tyne dock. I could see huge mountains of the stuff Geordie called Black Gold. It certainly seemed to be the heart blood of the river. While they unloaded, I carried my chest from the ship to the quay. There were many men who were waiting to unload the ship of its London cargo and soon the ship was empty. Leaving a skeleton crew on board Geordie and I carried my chest up the hill to the headland. It was little over a mile to the house and the steep slope showed me that I had become unfit during the recent sea voyage.

Geordie's wife, Betty, was lovely. She was a buxom woman with grey streaks but she had a heart of gold. After giving her husband a warm welcome she embraced me as though I was a long lost brother. Geordie laughed, "She is proud of the house and is always asking me why I dinna bring guests home. You are the first!"

"And I am honoured." Impulsively I took her hand gave a slight bow and kissed the back of her hand, "Enchantée, Madame!"

She giggled and said to Geordie, "That was lovely but what did he say?"

I smiled, "I just said I was enchanted to meet you. My mother taught me good manners."

"Was that French?"

"It was. I was born in France."

Her face suddenly filled with sympathy. "Eeeh, and they chopped all them poor people's heads off too."

"I know. My father was guillotined."

Geordie looked surprised, "He was a noble then?"

"Yes, he was Count de Breteuil."

Betty curtsied. "I didn't know you were a lord."

"I am not. My father did not marry my mother."

"Well count, lord or whatever you are welcome here and I get to use the guest bedroom at last. Geordie, take the young man's chest to his room. You come to the parlour while I get some supper."

The meal was home-cooked and delicious and they made me feel like an honoured guest. Geordie's children were three strapping lads who, once they found I had been a soldier, pestered me with questions. I didn't mind; it was a way of remembering my dead comrades. After they had gone to bed the three of us talked. Betty was fascinated with the life of a noble in France and even more intrigued by my mother and her story. She was outraged by Mama Tusson and her evil ways. "I canna abide witches!"

I laughed, "Do you have witches here then?"

"No actual witches live close by; mind there's a few who look like witches and give you the evil eye."

Geordie shook his head, "I'll take you tomorrow and get you that horse."

"Thanks. Would it be alright if I left my chest here? I can take a spare set of clothes in the saddlebags."

"Of course. You'll be back this way then?"

"Yes, Betty."

She seemed inordinately pleased by that. "Well I'll make sure the bed is aired the next time and we'll have some proper Geordie food too."

I looked at her curiously. "Food for Geordie?"

They both laughed, "Nay bonnie lad. Geordie is what we say for people around here, Newcastle way. We are all Geordies. The big fellah here gets called that because he is from Newcastle. He wasna christened that."

Geordie became serious, "And don't you be telling him what my real name is or you'll get the back of my hand."

She laughed, "Don't listen to him, Robbie. He wouldn't dream of touching me or the bairns but I won't tell you, at least not yet." She winked at me and gave Geordie a cheeky grin.

I bought a beautiful horse the next day. I thought it was an incredibly cheap beast but the looks Geordie gave the man who sold him to us made me doubt that. He was called Badger. His name was obvious for he was black with a white mane. I had never thought that I would replace Killer but Badger managed that.

Geordie was really concerned about me travelling across the country. "There are some robbing bastards out there so be careful when you go to bed. They will steal the coins from a corpse."

"Geordie, I appreciate your concern but I am going into this with my eyes open. I promise you that I will return to your lovely home, your wonderful wife and your delightful children."

He seemed taken aback, "You really think that?"

"Of course, Geordie, and I envy you. You are a lucky man."

He nodded and his eyes welled up. "I know. You take care now."

"I will and thank you again."

The road west was an easy one to follow. It was an old Roman Road called the Military Way and it went as straight as a die to the west. For most of the way, it followed the old Hadrian's Wall. That was the wall that kept the barbarians from Britannia. Geordie had said it was built with good reason. To listen to him the Scots were safer when contained behind a wall. Geordie had told me to stay in Haltwhistle which was about halfway across the country. He did not know any inns nor did he have any relatives who might give me a room. He was most apologetic that he could not help me more. For me, the journey was an eye-opener. The land was totally different from any country I had seen before. It undulated gently passing through delightful villages and thickly wooded land. The taverns were frequent and all served fine ale. The first I called at was the George at Chollerford. The Roman fort nearby was a reminder of the past and I wondered about visiting the ruins some time. The food and the ale in the inn were so cheap and wholesome that I wondered how they could make a profit. The landlord and his wife held the same views as Geordie; all the folk to the west were not to be trusted. I smiled as I headed west. The northern people were very parochial and mistrusted their neighbours. I was enjoying my journey.

Haltwhistle was the largest place I had seen since Newcastle. It had a single street lined with houses and inns. I chose the Dog and Gun, mainly because it looked to have a good stable and I wanted Badger looked after. Here I was an object of curiosity. Few visitors crossed this land and I had to answer many questions. I was not interrogated but they wanted to know why I was crossing their land. I found it easiest to keep to the truth or as near to the truth as I could. I told them that I had not been born in Scotland but my mother had and I was returning out of sentiment to see the land of her birth. They all seemed to accept that but warned me of the people to the west who were not to be trusted.

The road from Haltwhistle was the most dramatic land I had travelled since the mountains of Italy. How the Romans had built their roads and walls I had no idea. But soon I was in the verdant valley of the Eden and almost in Scotland. Carlisle is a huge city; it is as big as Newcastle and here I made my second stop. Perhaps I had been prepared for it but whatever the reason I felt ill at ease in that city. The people did seem less friendly, the food not as good and the beer poorer. I was glad to leave and to head north for the first time. Within a few hours, I was in Scotland.

I headed for Dumfries. I was not sure of my next stay because Geordie had only had enough information to take me to Carlisle; after that, he was lost. I had a map, although how accurate it was I had no idea. I estimated that it could be almost sixty miles to Kilmarnock which marked the end of mainland Scotland. Badger seemed to be in no distress and so I pushed on. I ate in Dumfries and was, again, warned about those to the north who were not to be trusted. Since Carlisle, I had travelled with two loaded pistols. This time the land was much like Austria; there were forests, lakes, steep climbs and even steeper drops. It took its toll and I was aware that I would not reach the coast before dark. I pushed on because I was keen to deliver the seal. Kilmarnock was a few miles from the coast and it would have to be my next destination.

I could see the distant lights of the town when I felt danger. Badger was nervous and he had not been nervous thus far. As a precaution, I took a pistol from my holster and held the reins in my left hand. I slowed

Badger right down. I knew, from the times that I had done it, that when you were waiting to ambush someone any delay added to your nervousness. I could see the town; by my estimate, it was five miles ahead, it would not make any difference to me if I reached it an hour or two or even three. I would still have a bed for the night and the largest part of the journey would be done. I stopped looking at the lights of the town. They would ruin my night vision. Instead, I peered into the forest. I was, fortunately, on a Roman Road which meant the trees had been cut back for some distance on both sides. Unfortunately, it meant that the horse's hooves rattled on the cobbles. I took Badger to the softer ground to the side of the road which effectively silenced my sounds.

Once there was silence, I could listen for the noises of the forest and my fears were confirmed when I heard nothing. There should have been animals. I edged, rather than rode, forward. I was looking for shapes in the dark which would indicate an ambush. I slowly cocked my pistol. I had found that if you did that gently it made almost no sound. Badger was going so slowly that he was barely moving. Then I saw the shape of a man. He was not on a horse but he had something in his hand. I halted Badger and scanned beyond the man. There were three others. There were two on the far side of the road and two within fifty paces of me. Had this been Killer I would have taken two pistols out and used both but Badger, good horse though he was, was an unknown quantity. I kicked on and he moved forward. I estimated that I could shoot one, possibly two, and then I would be reliant upon my sword. I was also aware that I did not know how many other men were ahead. I halted and listened.

They were ill-disciplined and I heard one voice speak. It sounded Scottish. "Mebbe, he's turned around. I canna hear him."

"Hamish, shut your mouth or I will shoot you meself!"

That confirmed that they meant me harm and I felt better about what I did next. I rode forward and aimed my pistol at the man on the far side of the road. I fired and then drew my second pistol. I had kept Badger moving and suddenly there was a man ten yards from me. I fired and his head disappeared. I holstered my pistol and drew my sword. The second man on my right side ran at me with a huge sword. I jinked Badger to the right and then to the left. He took the bait and swung at where I had been. I slashed down and felt the sword bite into his arm. He screamed and fell behind me. I regained the road. I heard a musket fire but the ball whizzed through the trees to the right. The ambush of the bandits had failed.

When I reached Kilmarnock, I was pleased to see that it was of a similar size to Carlisle. They expressed surprise that I had travelled after dark. "Aye, yon woods are full of bandits. You were lucky mister."

I smiled to myself; I was a horseman of France and we did not need luck. We knew how to fight. I was more tired than I had been for some time. The travelling and the tension had taken it out of me but the landlord told me that I could get a ferry from Ardrossan to Aran. The ferry was but ten miles away and I could rest Badger on the boat. My journey would now be broken down into ferries and islands but I was getting close to the heartland of the Macgregors. I discovered that I needed to be at Bowmore on Islay where the present clan chief lived. No one seemed willing to speak about the Macgregors and I did not push my luck. They all confirmed that the clan chief lived in isolation at Bowmore. I just said I was keen to visit the islands for personal reasons. They might have suspected my intentions but none of them appeared willing to question me further.

The islands were rugged, treeless and, as far as I could see devoid of any people. I felt untroubled for I could see miles ahead and there was no hint of bandits. The ferries seemed to operate whenever a customer came and I had gold which afforded me good service. I did not know if they were robbing me, there were no prices displayed but I had to get to Islay anyway. The price was immaterial.

Finally, at dusk, I arrived on Islay. This was the land of the Macgregors and I felt a shiver as Badger stepped from the wooden boat onto dry land. The island was low and seemed uninhabited. The ferryman had told me that my destination lay on the southern coast and there was but one road. I headed down that road. I was eager to cover the last eight miles to the home of my mother's family.

When I reached it, I saw that the house was more of a fortified mansion. There was a stream with a bridge and then the main door. The seal had seemed inordinately heavier for the last hundred miles. I had worn it since Malta and I was used to the weight but, somehow, the closer it came to its home, the heavier it became. It was a smaller house than I imagined and when I reined Badger in outside the front door, I began to worry that this was the wrong place. It looked too small to be the home of the clan chief and yet ever since I had left the mainland, I had been told that Old Macgregor was the clan chief and he lived at Bowmore. It had been as inevitable as the tide that the man I would soon meet would be the head of the clan and yet I now doubted it. I had contemplated changing my clothes just before I reached the house as I was expecting something grander but I was now glad that I had not wasted the time.

I strode up to the door and banged the lion's head knocker. The sound seemed to echo in the house. I wondered if it was even occupied. The door swung open and a dour-faced giant towered over me. He was not the liveried butler I had expected. "What do you want!" he snarled aggressively.

I was a little taken aback by his rudeness. "I am here to see the head of the Clan Macgregor."

"And who would you be, wee man?"

"I am Captain Robert Macgregor."

He laughed and said, "Are you making fun of me." He began to close the door. "Now be off with ye!"

I had not travelled all the way from Sicily to be put sent packing by a lout. I put my shoulder to the door and rammed with all my power. He was not expecting that and he tumbled to the ground and lay prostrate on the ground. My sword was out in an instant and I jammed the point to his throat.

"Now listen to me, you rude and unpleasant lout. I have travelled thousands of miles to come here to my kinsman and deliver a precious object to him. I will not be put off by a servant such as you!"

I heard a voice coming from a nearby room, "What is it, William?"

The man on the ground shouted, "It's some lunatic calling himself Robert Macgregor!"

"I have warned you about your tongue. If you cannot keep a civil tongue in your head then I may remove it and your master will have to get another servant."

A frail old man appeared, "Would you be so good as to let my son up please young man and explain yourself."

"Who are you? I told your son here who I was before I was treated worse than a beggar at the door."

"I am Robert Macgregor, the head of the Clan Macgregor, and this is my son William."

I dropped the tip of my sword. "I am sorry I did not know but I am Robert Macgregor and I believe I am kin of this family."

"Let us go into the room where there is a decent fire."

As he led me through I realised that he had not mentioned my horse and where he should be stabled. This was not the welcome I had anticipated. The old man gestured to a chair and he sat, almost in the fire itself. His scowling son sat on the chair next to him, facing me.

"Now then tell me your story and I will decide if you are kin or not."

"My mother was Marie Macgregor and she was the daughter of Alistair Macgregor." I saw them both stiffen and start when I mentioned that name. The old man gestured with his arm and William sat back down. "He was the son of Robert Macgregor who followed Bonnie Prince Charlie to France."

The old man poked the fire violently and then turned his gaze upon me. "William here had the right idea when he saw you! You are not welcome here."

I was confused. "Why not? Have I come to the wrong clan?"

"No this is where your great grandfather lived. My father and he were brothers. I was named after your grandfather."

Now I was even more confused than I had been. "Then this is his family so why am I not welcome?"

"Because Robert Macgregor was a bad bastard. My grandmother adored him and would do anything for him." He swept his arm around the room. "You see this here? Once, this hall was filled with lights, fine furniture and servants. We were well off and respectable. Then your grandfather followed that dissolute, drunken Prince and spent the family fortune. Even when he went to France he kept sending for money and my grandmother kept sending it. She died of a broken heart and my father died soon after. That left just William and me. So you see you are not welcome here! Now leave!"

William grinned and I stood. "Very well but first I will do what I promised I would do and fulfil my oath to a knight of St.John." I took off my jacket and undid my shirt. I took off the canvas belt and removed the Great Seal. I handed it to the old man.

If I thought his attitude would change I was wrong. "And now it is returned by the great-grandson of the man who stole it."

I shook my head, "Neither my grandfather nor my mother had anything to do with this. We are innocent."

"No laddie. The bad blood of Robert Macgregor courses through your veins." He suddenly stopped. "How are you Robert Macgregor? What is your father's name?"

"My father was the Count de Breteuil but he never married my mother and so I took her name."

"Well, you have no right to it. I disown you. You are not a Macgregor! I may not have the pleasure of hurting your great grandfather but I can, at least, hurt his blood. Now go!"

I would not have stayed longer had he begged me. I was so angry that if either of them had done or said anything I would have killed them both. I mounted Badger as the rain began to pelt. It seemed fitting that I left in a storm. The two of them stood in the doorway grinning with malicious pleasure at my discomfort.

"You are a pair of wicked old men and I am glad that you have disowned me. From this day forth I am no longer a Macgregor and I hope you rot your empty sad days out in this ruin!"

The door slammed shut with an ominous finality. I had no home in Scotland. If I thought that I would have a happy ending to this story I was wrong. Any plans I might have had ended with the slamming of the door. I turned Badger around and we headed across the bleak island which suddenly seemed less beautiful and more unfriendly than when I had left the ferry. We trudged our way back to the place I had disembarked. There was no ferry and it was night time. Badger and I huddled beneath a lone tree and spent a sleepless cold night awaiting the boat. The lack of sleep and the cold helped me to formulate my thoughts. I had no future in Scotland. I would return to Sicily. At least there I had a family who liked me and wanted me. I would become a businessman and make money from my share of a ship. It was not the exciting life of a chasseur but it was better than this.

I took my time returning across the backbone of Britain. I almost wished that bandits would attack me for I wanted to take my anger out on someone. I even contemplated turning my horse around and going back to Castle Bowmore and killing my relatives. The memory of my mother stopped me. I was no longer Robert Macgregor and I couldn't be Robert Breteuil. I needed a new name. I ran through all the names of the people I knew but I could not steal a man's family. In the end, I chose one of my friend's first names. I would become Robert Matthews. I would still have the same initials and I was sure that the captain would not mind. It would be another new start.

As I headed towards the Tyne, I realised that I now had much to do. I needed to establish my identity. Mr Fortnum and Mr Hudson knew me, legally, as Macgregor. I would have to get to London and make the changes. Then I would head back to Sicily. As I rode towards the North Sea, I began to feel better about my future.

Chapter 18

Geordie was still at sea when I reached his house. I apologised when Betty told me. "I am sorry Mrs Percy I will take accommodation at an inn."

She looked appalled. "Why? Have I upset you in some way?"

"No, of course not, dear lady; it just would not look right for you to have a single man staying with you while your husband is away."

She began laughing so hard that tears poured down her rosy cheeks. "Don't be daft! Geordie would have a fit and besides my neighbours know me." She dried her eyes, "I am flattered mind. Now I have aired your room and washed your clothes. Go and get changed and I will wash those too."

I felt better in clean clothes. She took my bundle. "Supper won't be ready for an hour or so. Why not go to the pub? There'll be some of Geordie's mates there."

"Don't you need any help?"

"Bless you. Geordie doesn't even know where the kitchen is let alone helping. No, you go and have a pint in the pub and your food will be ready when you return."

The landlord remembered me from my visit with Geordie and they all made me welcome. The locals puffed away on their short pipes and I just listened to their talk. During a lull in the conversation, I asked one of them called, obscurely, Peter the Pilot, did they meet in the pub often. "Aye bonnie lad, every day."

"Why? Is it the beer?"

"The beer helps but we have to come here do you see to put the world to rights. If we weren't here to sort it out, why, it would be in a terrible state." He winked broadly at me and they all laughed. It was just the same as when we went out of the barracks we were able to give our opinions on many matters great and small. There would only be minor differences in our opinions and we would all feel better for it.

"Take that Bonaparte chap." He shook his head. "He has ideas above his station. I mean I can understand the lads in France wanting to have a life like the aristocracy but now they have chosen him to run the country."

"Napoleon Bonaparte is running France?"

They all nodded. Peter said, "He has been elected First Consul, whatever that means but the top and bottom appear to be that he runs France."

I shook my head. I knew he was ambitious but I never dreamed he would run my country. Then I realised that it was no longer my country. I didn't have a country, I belonged to no one.

"What's the matter? Do you know the man?"

They all looked at me expectantly. I was the stranger from foreign parts who could enliven their parochial conversation. "I served with him in Egypt." Their faces showed their shock.

As the questions flowed so did the ale until Geordie's eldest, Bobbie came to the door and said, "Me mam said your tea's ready!"

Peter the Pilot said, "You'd better go. I wouldna cross Betty!"

Betty, of course, was not cross and the food was not spoiled. "I know what you men are like when you get talking!"

The food was wonderful and, when the children had done the dishes and been sent to bed I sat with Betty before the lovely fire just talking. She was an easy woman to talk to. Before I knew it I had told her all the details of my visit to Islay. She did not seem surprised. "That's families all over isn't it? You are better off without them. They sound like a right miserable pair. Your mam now, she knew nothing about this, did she?" I shook my head. "Nor her dad either so why can't they just forgive and forget." She had the ability to get to the nub really quickly. "I'll bet it's the name that's upsetting you isn't it?"

"Yes, Betty. I liked the name because of my mother but I can't have the name now because... well, I just can't."

"You know I can read?" I shook my head. "Well, I can. The only one in this street and all! Still, I'm not bragging but my teacher read a bit from a play by Shakespeare. I think it was Romeo and Juliet. Anyway, there's a line I remember or a bit of a line, '*A rose by any other name would smell as sweet.*' I think that means that a name is not important. Why you could call yourself Count, whatever your name is couldn't you? Look at Geordie; he hates the name Herbert so he calls himself Geordie." She put her hand to her mouth. "Now don't you go telling him I told you that but you know what I mean?"

"I do, Betty and you have decided me. I will be Robert Matthews and the past can be damned."

"Well good for you. I shall go to bed just now. Make sure the fire is damped down before you come up will you?" She bent down and kissed me on the forehead. She was a lovely woman.

By the time Geordie returned home I was a local in the pub and I knew everyone by their first name. We had long passed talking of Napoleon and covered a vast range of subjects. They were good people and they made me feel welcome. I could happily have lived in that part of England save that I had no function there. One evening I returned to the house after a few pints in the pub and found that Geordie had returned. He seemed remarkably serious. Betty too looked more serious than she normally did. I worried that something was amiss with the family or the ship. When Betty went to fetch the food Geordie said, "You are a wanted man Robbie. That Lambert chap was found dead. He was run through by a sword. They found a letter with your name on it and people say you had a sword."

"But I have been up here or on your ship."

"I know. I know you are innocent but it looks bad. "

"What about Captain Dinsdale?"

"He hasn't returned to England yet but he is wanted too." He smiled for the first time, "Our Betty said you have changed your name. It is probably a good thing."

I did not want to spend my life as a fugitive. "I will return with you and clear my name."

He beamed, "I knew you would. You are the right sort."

Betty was tearful when I left. She hugged me so tightly that I could barely breathe. "You are a lovely young man. I hope that you can clear your name. You have not had a fair crack of the whip and no mistake. You deserve a bit of happiness. Remember there is always a bed for you here!" She kissed me hard and then turned away to continue crying. The boys too were upset. I had begun to teach them how to fence and they loved it. They had looked after Badger every day and they were just as sorry to see him go. I would be taking him back to London with me.

As we headed south and watched the priory disappear into the sea Geordie said, "The lads in the pub will miss you. They said that you were alright for a foreigner. I have never heard them gush so much. You made a real impression."

My brief moment of happiness, as in Sicily was gone; snatched away from me by a precocious Fate. I now had to clear my name before I could return to Sicily.

When we reached London the first thing we did was to arrange a stable for Badger. Once that had been done, Geordie insisted on coming with me to visit Mr Fortnum. "I don't want you getting into trouble on account of me."

"The law is less trouble than our Betty will be if I have to tell her you were arrested. Besides I have nowt to do for a while the lads can unload the coal. I need to stretch my legs!"

He was fooling no-one. He kept a watchful eye on all about us. When we reached Piccadilly he did not enter but stood outside to keep watch for us. Mr Fortnum saw us straight away. He looked serious. "I have heard the news and know that you are innocent for you were travelling north when the murder took place but mud sticks. And I have worse news for you. The Kingdom of Sicily and Naples has been taken over by the First Consul Napoleon Bonaparte and all English ships have been impounded."

My heart sank into my boots. "Captain Dinsdale?"

He nodded, "I know. He is safe but cannot leave."

"And your business?"

He waved away the suggestion, "That is only money. The crew is more valuable than money." He shrugged, "Besides no-one else can lay their hands on the goods and we have an adequate supply bur what to do about your dilemma."

"I had already changed my name to Robert Matthews."

"Really?"

"It has nothing to do with this but it seems now I was directed to make that decision."

"We must go and see Mr Hudson and make sure that he is aware of the name change."

"But shouldn't you two turn me in?"

"My dear fellow, we both regard this as client and lawyer privilege. Mr Lambert was not innocent and deserved to die. I know you had nothing to do with it. Why should you suffer for something you didn't do?"

We left and strode out towards the bank. After a hundred yards Mr Fortnum said, "I do not wish to alarm you but we have been followed by a giant who looks dangerous."

"He is dangerous but he is on our side. It is a sea captain called Geordie. He is watching our back."

"You live in a different world to me do you not? I thought the world of business was a cutthroat one but it does not come close to yours."

"And it is not of my choosing."

Mr Hudson was sympathetic to my request. "I take it Captain Dinsdale will not be requiring the funds any time soon then?"

"No, and I may not be around when he is released." I looked at Mr Fortnum for confirmation that the ship would be released.

He nodded. "They will only impound the ships for so long. They cannot afford to be without the revenue the ships bring. I would expect them to reach Britain in, perhaps, three months' time."

I was pleased with the approximation of time but it did nothing to help me. "Then Mr Hudson I shall need a hundred pounds from my account for the expenses I shall be incurring."

"Very well." He wrote out a note and summoned his clerk. When the clerk had gone he said, "If I might suggest Mr er… Matthews?"

"Go ahead. At this moment I would like any solution to my dilemma."

"If we were to write out a deposition now attesting to your whereabouts at the time of the murder then we can lodge that with the court."

"An excellent idea."

"Of course, it would be useful if we had a witness from the ship which transported you."

I grinned, "Would the captain do?"

Mr Hudson's pince-nez dropped from his nose. "That would be perfect but where would you conjure him at such short notice."

"Just wait here." Leaving the two of them open-mouthed I went to the door of the bank and whistled. Geordie appeared and I waved him inside. "We need you in here." When we went in I said, "This is the captain of the collier who took me to Newcastle."

"Excellent, well captain, we need to take down some facts and then we might be able to clear this young man's name."

"In that case let's get on with it. The pubs are open and I have a mighty thirst on me."

I felt happier with the money and a copy of the letter in my pocket. Mr Fortnum told me that he would deliver the letter personally for me. "You are being very kind to me. May I ask you why?"

"Business I am afraid. Oh do not get me wrong I like you. I find you a refreshing young man after some of the rakes I knew when I was young but you have saved me a great deal of money and you have provided me with the promise of more business and trade. This embargo is a moment in time and is not your fault." He gestured to Geordie. "Your friend here will tell you that regular business is worth much more than an elusive pot of gold such as the South Sea Bubble."

I had never heard of the South Sea Bubble but I gathered the gist of his words. "In that case thank you Mr Fortnum and I hope your trade does increase."

Geordie and I continued along to the pub near the Strand which was frequented by the captains. "His business is doing well Robbie. Even I have heard of him and I never go to the shops."

As we drank our beer in an almost deserted pub his face became serious. "You are welcome to stay onboard my ship Robbie but I sail the day after tomorrow. You know the way I work. Will you manage once I have gone?"

I laughed, "I am more resilient than I look Geordie and, besides, I actually feel as though I have had a load taken from my shoulders. I no longer carry around treasure and I can forget my Scottish roots. Bonaparte betrayed both me and my people and so long as he rules France then I am not a citizen of France. I may not have liked my father when he was alive but I can now respect the stand he took against what he saw as injustice. I am now a citizen of the world without a country and the world is my oyster."

He shook his head. "No son. I told you before. You are an Englishman. Forget who your parents were it's what's in here that counts." He tapped his chest. "And inside you are English."

I did not know at the time what he meant but I came to learn that he was probably right. We found me a room in the inn near to the stables where Badger was housed. Geordie still fussed and fretted like an old woman right up to the moment he left for Newcastle. "Give all my love to Betty."

He shook his head, "I'll be in bother for not bringing you back!"

I had not taken Badger out for a few days and I decided to have a ride around the London Parks. Despite the fact that the metropolis was one of the biggest cities in the world there were still many green places to ride and I took Badger through the busy streets until we reached St James' Park. I had never ridden in such landscaped land before and the experience was refreshing. The man at the stables had warned me about riding in the parks at night as they were the haunts of thieves and highwaymen but he conceded that during the day they were more than pleasant places in which to exercise a horse. For the next two weeks, I established a settled routine. I would ride Badger each day using one of the three parks in rotation and on the fourth day, I would visit Mr Fortnum. The inn was comfortable and I found reasonable places to eat. I was not poor but nor was I a spendthrift and I husbanded my money well.

I was not as lonely as one might expect. I actually enjoyed the solitude. It gave me time to think and reflect on the events of my life and to put them in some sort of perspective. I would not have changed anything in my life; I had had some friends such as Jean, Pierre and Tiny whose memory I cherished still. I did not even regret the things I did for Bonaparte; I would not have met the Regent of San Marino or Sir John otherwise. Part of me realised that I had been a little instrumental in helping him to achieve his present position as First Consul. Should I have saved him in Cairo? I could not see myself allowing him to be killed but would the world be a different place if I had? I was beginning to see that life was a spider's web; it was incredibly intricate and intertwined. A creature tapping on one side sent vibrations which travelled all the way to the other. I resolved to begin to enjoy life and live each moment to the full. I owed that, at least, to my dead comrades. I would live their lives for them.

Fate intervened one late Friday afternoon in October 1801. I had taken my normal afternoon ride and I was in Hyde Park. Badger was enjoying crashing through the piles of leaves which had blown there. I too felt invigorated by the chill but clean air of the park. We had just enjoyed a gallop and I was contemplating returning to the inn before dark when Badger suddenly began limping. I dismounted and lifted the offending leg. He had stepped on to a piece of broken glass hidden in the leaves and it was lodged close to the hoof. I took out my small pocket knife and carefully removed the glass. The hoof began to bleed a little. In my saddlebag, I had a small hip flask with brandy within. It was a habit I had picked up from Jean. It served a number of purposes. In cold weather, it would revive and it was a way of cleaning wounds. I poured some on the hoof. Badger whinnied but I felt happier. I tore some linen from a cloth I had in my saddlebag and, after soaking it in brandy, jammed it into the hoof to stop anything else entering the wound. I then led Badger back towards the city.

By the time we entered Green Park, it was dark but I did not want to risk riding my horse and aggravating the wound. Because we were walking I was more aware of sounds and I heard the clash of sword on sword. I drew my own blade and began to run, with Badger behind, towards the sounds. I saw three men attacking one man. A fourth man lay on the ground either dead or injured I could not tell. The lone man was fending off his three assailants well but I could see that it was only a matter of time before he was overcome. I dropped Badger's reins. He would wait patiently and I ran over to the fight. Three against one was not good odds.

I roared a challenge. This was to let the man know that aid was coming and also to distract his attackers. One turned to face me. He had a sword which was as long as mine and he ran at me. He was a powerful man and surprisingly light on his feet for one so big. I was barely able to parry his blow. I pirouetted around so that his back was towards me. I lunged at him and he, too, spun around and knocked aside my blade. He was not as fast as me and I saw blood on my weapon. He feinted at me but I was not fooled and I flicked his tip away and then stabbed forward. He was not expecting it and the edge cut his face. Out of the corner of my eye, I could see that the other two men were beating back the lone swordsman who appeared to be wounded. I had to end this and end it quickly. Knowing that he had two wounds I struck rapidly at him forcing him backwards. There were tree roots and hidden dangers beneath the leaves and each blow I struck made his movements more desperate. When he half stumbled I lunged forwards and felt my sword enter his side. He screamed in pain and then before I could finish him he turned and fled.

I let him go and turned to the other two. I was barely in time. The man was lying on the ground and I saw the sword raised to give the coup de grace. I ran and sliced down with my sword. It sliced through the back of the hand which held the sword and it fell to the ground. His companion had not seen me but he now turned and stabbed at me. I swung my sword more in hope than expectation and luck was on my side as it clanked into his. I saw my chance and punched him hard with my left hand he tripped over the man who was prostrate on the ground, his body still amongst the leaves. I saw the sword of the man I had wounded lying on the ground and I stepped on to it. The two of them ran. The odds were no longer on their side.

After I had sheathed my sword I went to Badger and brought him over. I took out the brandy flask and turned over the man. I had no idea if he was dead or alive. I heard his voice as I began to turn him, "Thank you, sir."

As I rolled him on to his back, I saw that it was Colonel James Sinclair.

Chapter 19

His eyes were closed so that he did not know it was me. I poured some of the brandy into his mouth and he coughed a little and then swallowed. I could see blood coming from his arm. I went to the dead man lying on the ground and took off his silk scarf. I made a tourniquet to stop the bleeding. It appeared to be his only wound although I could see a lump on his forehead. "Colonel, can you rise?"

His eyes shot open. "You! What are you doing in England?" His good arm went to his jacket. When he patted it and found what he sought he relaxed a little and then his eyes narrowed. "Were you with those men?"

I could not understand the ingratitude. I showed him my blade which was covered in blood. "As this blood is not yours then it seems likely it was your assailants and this seems an odd way to say thank you."

"Help me up and then I will think better." I helped him up and he looked around. "Where are they? "

"They ran off."

"That is convenient." There was a sarcastic element to his words

I turned to go to my horse. "I have saved you and done my duty. Good day sir. I had thought for at least a thank you but I can see none is forthcoming."

I picked up Badger's reins and heard the ominous click of a pistol being cocked behind me. "It may well be that I thank you but not just yet. Turn Scotsman, I have not finished with you yet."

I was becoming angry. I turned and saw the pistol pointing at my middle. I smiled and slowly opened my left palm. He glanced at it and I swung my right hand to knock the gun to the floor. I then grabbed him by the jacket. "I have had enough of you. You ingrate! I have saved you and now I will go." I pushed him to the ground and then picked up his pistol. "If you follow me again then I will finish what those highwaymen started."

He rose and smiled, "I am sorry. Please forgive me it's just that..." He suddenly seemed to remember the dead man and he ran over to turn the body over. "Poor David, he is dead."

"I take it he was not your assailant?"

"No, he was my brother."

I could now, perhaps, understand a little of his behaviour. He would be upset beyond belief if his brother had died. "I am sorry for your loss."

"Quickly, put his body on your horse. We need to leave quickly before those men return with others."

I was used to obeying orders; even ones I did not understand and I did as he asked. The colonel retrieved his pistol and we headed towards Piccadilly. The colonel said little as we hurried towards the buildings leading to the main thoroughfare. He kept glancing around to see if we were being pursued.

"Come this way." He seemed to know where he was going and I just led Badger in the direction he indicated.

"Your arm will need a doctor."

"I know. I am not a fool! Sorry. Thank you for your concern. We are heading for Berkeley House. A friend of mine is there and he is a doctor. It is the nearest safe house that I know."

When we reached Portugal Street he seemed to relax more. There were people around but they were wrapped up for the weather. His brother's body was concealed by a greatcoat and attracted no undue attention.

"Here it is." He led me around the back of the grand mansion to the gate at the rear. He rapped sharply on it. A head appeared around the side and there was a whispered conversation. The gate widened and the colonel waved me in. He pointed to the stable. "Take your horse in there."

"And your brother's body?"

"He is beyond caring and I have something important to do in here first."

He seemed callous to me but then I had never had a brother and did not know the way things worked in families, never having had one. I took the body off the horse as carefully as I could and reverently laid it on the ground. I had done this many times for fallen comrades; I knew how to respect the dead. I took Badger's saddle from his back and then examined his hoof. The linen did not look to be badly stained and I hoped that I would be able to get him seen to soon. I spied a bag of apples hanging from the wall and I gave him one. "I'll be out as soon as I can, boy!"

A servant with a torch was waiting for me outside. "If you would follow me, sir."

He led me into the kitchen where the cooks were busy preparing food. They assiduously avoided my gaze. We went through a labyrinth of corridors until we reached a magnificent looking door. The servant knocked and I heard a voice say, "Bring him in."

I entered the room not knowing what to expect. There was the colonel and three other men in the room. One of the men was a doctor for he was stitching the colonel's wound. The other two were wearing military uniforms. I did not know British ranks but they both appeared to be more senior than a mere colonel. They glanced at me when I entered and then went back to watching the colonel being tended to.

When the doctor had finished the colonel dressed and he sipped from the glass on the table. They all turned to look at me. The colonel said, "This, gentlemen, was a spy working for Napoleon Bonaparte the last time I saw him." All three men looked surprised and began to examine me. It was most discomfiting. "So, as you can imagine, when I was attacked by agents of the French Government who were trying to get their hands on these papers, I was surprised to be rescued by this same spy." He turned to me and spread his arms.

"I am not a spy."

"But you were."

"No, sir. I was a captain of the 17th Chasseurs delivering a message that is all."

"Oh come now Robert, you do yourself a disservice. You were one of the most accomplished agents I ever met."

The small thin-faced man said, "Colonel, stop badgering him and let him tell his story." I noticed that he had a Scottish accent. "And give him a drink. I think he deserves that, at least for rescuing you."

The colonel shrugged and poured me a glass of something. I sipped it and recognised it as brandy. "Thank you, sir. May I have the honour of knowing your names?"

The thin-faced man said, "Not until we are all happy with you and your story."

"Do you mind if I sit? This may take some time."

The other senior officer who had a fine beard and moustache said, "Of course but be quick we have dinner in an hour."

I sat and began to tell them my story from the time I left Naples. I told everything from the massacre of the 17th and the desertion of Bonaparte to my duel with Hougon. I brought them up to date with the death of Lambert and my visit to Scotland. As I finished I tossed off the contents of my glass. "So you see gentlemen I am wanted by the French authorities and by the British legal system in addition to which I have been disowned by my family. If you want to make up another crime for me then go ahead. It makes no difference to me. I brought the colonel here because he asked me to and I have enjoyed a drink but now unless you wish more answers I shall leave." I stood. They looked at each other with unspoken questions on their lips. My hand was already on my still bloody sword. If I had to fight my way out then I would.

The colonel smiled. "I am sorry Robbie. Now that I have heard your story I can see that I have misjudged you. I apologise for my earlier behaviour which was quite inexcusable."

"Thank you for the apology and goodnight." I turned to walk out of the door.

"Won't you please stay and listen to my story."

The old man with the whiskers said, "I say, Sinclair. Do you really think that is necessary?"

"Yes, Sir William. I once offered this young man employment and right now I think he is even more valuable than he once was. This man can speak French, Italian and English. He is a fine soldier and he has worked behind enemy lines. Even more than that he never panics, at least I have never seen that trait. He could be as valuable to us as this document I hold and for which my brother died."

"I agree with the colonel." The thin-faced man held out his hand. "I am Sir John Moore and like Sir William here I am a general. I would be most interested to speak with you." He turned to the doctor, "Roger, would you go and ask the housekeeper to set another place for dinner." The doctor left and Sir John poured me another brandy. "Go on James tell him why you were so suspicious."

"As you have probably deduced, for you are patently not a stupid man, I am not an ordinary soldier. I work in the Intelligence branch at the War office. My brother was an agent who brought a valuable piece of information from France. You need not concern yourself with its contents. I met him tonight and I was bringing him here to meet these two gentlemen when we were attacked by those French agents you chased away. Unfortunately, my brother was killed but you saved the information. However, as I knew that you had acted as a spy for Bonaparte and you were French naturally I thought that you were part of the conspiracy."

"But I saved your life."

He shrugged, "In this business deception is always part of the game. You could have been deceiving me to ingratiate yourself into my confidence."

I nodded, "But now you trust me."

He smiled, "Of course, you have proved your innocence."

I smiled back and then leapt to my feet drawing my sword and placing it at the throat of Sir John. "Or I could be incredibly devious just to get into this house and take the document."

Sir William gasped, "Preposterous! There are three of us."

"Are there? Let us examine that. The colonel is wounded. With due respect Sir William, you are old, fat and I suspect slow. The only danger to me is this man and I have a sword at his throat. Within three blows you would be dead and I would be away."

Sir William was like a dog with a bone and he would not let it go. "Ridiculous! How would you escape from here?"

I sheathed my sword, having demonstrated my skills. "I would take the document and walk out the way I came in. I would smile at everyone and then ride away and catch a boat to Calais."

There was a stunned silence and Sir John clapped his hands together slowly. "And it would work. I take it by the fact that you have sheathed your sword that you are not a French spy?"

I bowed my head, "You are correct sir."

"I think this young man has promise, James."

"I thought so before and now I am convinced."

Sir John looked at Sir William, "Sir William?"

He is quick with that blade but, I say, sir, fat? And old? A little much eh?" They all laughed which made me feel much happier about the situation.

The doctor returned, "Dinner will be ready in fifteen minutes."

The colonel looked at my hands which were still covered in blood. "Would you like to wash before dinner?"

"I would appreciate that sir."

"And I will send a man up to sponge your clothes too."

After my clothes had been cleaned along with me I felt much better and I descended to the dining room. It was a pleasant and civilised dinner. The colonel sat on one side of me and Sir John on the other.

"You know sir you would make a perfect light infantryman."

The colonel laughed, "Sir John, he is too big and heavy. Your men are like jockeys!"

"But James, he has all the skills needed. I have never seen a blade as quick. My God sir when that tip touched my throat I thought I was dead for sure."

"I am afraid that I am a cavalryman Sir John, but our French Light Infantry do fight well."

"When I have finished working with Dundas we will have better troops believe me."

"Now Robbie... what is your new name?"

"Matthews."

"Well, Robert Matthews, I think that it was a good idea to change your name. The French know Macgregor and, it appears, so do we." I looked downcast. "Oh do not worry about the charges. I will have them dropped and the name of Robbie Macgregor will disappear forever."

I felt a sense of relief. Despite my innocence, I never trusted policemen of any description. They seemed lazy and too ready to pin a crime on the nearest man- in this case, me. "Thank you sir."

"Now how do you feel about working for me?"

"How do you mean?"

"I want you to travel abroad and do for me what you did for Bonaparte."

"I do not know if I could betray my country."

"Your father was an aristocrat executed by revolutionaries and you were betrayed by this man who is one step away from becoming a king who has not been anointed. We do not want France destroyed. We want the Royal Family returned to where they were. We are not fighting against France, we are fighting against Bonaparte and the tyranny he would bring."

It seems simple now but that argument persuaded me. "Very well sir. What do I do?"

"We need a cover for you and so we will purchase a commission for you in a Light Dragoon regiment. The document I secured tonight suggests that there will be peace soon and that means that officers will go on half-pay which will allow you to go to France and spy for us. Then when the war starts again, and believe me it will start again, you will serve with your regiment until I need you to do little jobs for me. How does that sound?"

I had to admit that I was excited about the prospect. I would be able to fight against the monster that was Bonaparte and I would still be a soldier. I missed the camaraderie of the regiment and the action which accompanied war. It had been the only life I had known since the age of seventeen. I also liked the idea of fighting in an army I admired. "It sounds fine sir."

I said little at dinner but listened much. I did learn that Sir John Moore was a general who was forward-thinking and appeared to be the new star of the British army. Since the debacle in the Low Countries which had resulted in the satirical rhyme, The Grand Old Duke of York, there had been a change in the direction within the war department. Ironically it was the Duke of York who appeared to be driving those reforms.

During a lull in the conversation between the fish and the meat courses, I asked the colonel a delicate question which had preyed on my mind since we began to eat. "Sir, what of your brother? I cannot enjoy my food knowing that a brave soldier lies in a stable."

"It does you great credit, Robert, that you think of someone you barely know. Fear not. The doctor arranged for the undertakers to remove my brother's body. If I appear to be enjoying the food, believe me, it is many miles from the truth. It tastes of sawdust but in my profession, you have to learn to detach yourself from personal feelings. I will grieve for my dead brother in my own time. He was a brave soldier." He leaned back as the main course was laid before him. "It is a pity you did not meet for you would have got on well. When I first met you I was reminded of my brother."

"Did he serve as a soldier too?"

"He was a captain in the 11th Light Dragoons." He smiled at the servant who had just served him his vegetables and then turned to me. "That is how I know there will be a commission available. You will replace my brother in the 11th."

He was a calculating man and I was beginning to see just how cold he was. I suppose I should have been used to that having worked for Bonaparte but the men I admired more were the likes of Albert and Jean. They cared about their men. As I listened to the conversation of the three senior officers I began to see that their world was different from that of the ordinary soldier. They were thinking of the big picture whereas those of us in regiments thought only of the men around us who were more important than the pieces of land which the politicians and generals craved.

As the meal drew to a close and the three senior officers smoked their cigars they all focussed their attention on me. Colonel Selkirk fixed me with his hawk-like stare. "So, have you changed your mind having listened to what we said this night? If you leave now you can go your own way again but if you choose to work for me then you become a British soldier with all that that entails."

There was an air of expectancy. I sipped the port which still remained in my fine crystal glass and then wiped my mouth with my napkin. "I am still a relatively young man and, for the moment, it suits me to work for you."

I could see that Sir William appeared a little put out. "I say, sir, that sounds damned ungracious to me. I would have thought that you would have leapt at the chance to serve."

Sir John shook his head, "You forget Sir William that this is a man without a country and I understand why he feels the way he does but I also believe that once he has served in a British regiment his loyalties and his views will change."

Colonel Selkirk also gave me a wry smile, "Besides which, Sir William, this man is a tricky customer and as slippery as an eel. If he chose to leave us then he would do so easily. I agree with Sir John. He will come to love this country which my brother died for. So sir, have you an answer?"

"I think I gave it to you. I will serve you."

"Good, then you have a week to put your affairs in order. I will get these charges dropped tomorrow. You will come to Horse Guards one week from now and present yourself at my office." That was it, it was done I would soon be in the British Army.

I would not need a week to prepare myself but I would be leaving many unanswered questions. I went the next day to a fine stationer for I would need to write letters. It was unlikely that I would see any of my friends again. I could visit Mr Fortnum and Mr Hudson but they were not the friends in my life. I wrote to Geordie, Count Alpini, Sir John and Captain Dinsdale. Each letter was different but each letter told them of my disappointment in Scotland and my change of name. I assured the captain that my offer to buy a share in a boat was still there and I asked him to look after my interests. I told them all that I would be joining the Light Dragoons but kept Colonel Selkirk a secret. They did not need to know that. I took the letters to Mr Fortnum and asked him to see them delivered. He was pleased that I had had the charges dropped but I could see that he was disappointed with my choice of career.

"You have a fine head for business. There are other empty-headed men who can ride horses and fight. You could be a rich man if you chose business."

"Perhaps when I am old and tired of the life of action then I will do as you suggest but for now I will follow my heart. I do thank you for all your kindnesses and I hope that we can remain friends."

"Of course and you say your regiment is to be the 11th Light Dragoons?"

"Yes, I believe so."

He smiled, "Then I will be able to get in touch with you for the officers of all the Light Dragoons are good customers of ours."

Mr Hudson was an easier prospect. He and I wrote a document which his clerk witnessed to allow him to invest my money. He was less worried about my future than Mr Fortnum had been. "When you retire from the army I can promise you that you will be a rich man. I am a cautious but wise investor and the wars mean profit for those clever enough to spot the investment opportunities." He leaned forward, "I understand that there is to be new docks built along the river called London Docks. I am already purchasing land along the river. As soon as the project is announced then the price of the property will soar and you will have more than doubled your money." He leaned back, "Of course sir, you will have to pay a fee for my services, but it will be worth it."

"I know it will be and I hope that Captain Dinsdale returns to buy the ship. The money for that is protected?"

"Of course sir."

When I left the office I felt lighter in heart and I strolled back towards the Strand. I decided to head towards St Paul's as a different route back to my inn when I suddenly saw someone I recognised. It was a brief view but I was sure that I had spotted Mr Lambert's clerk. He disappeared into the warren of alleys that criss-crossed Covent Gardens. I pondered following him but I could see no reason to do so. He had, after all, been just someone who worked for the murdered shipping agent.

I had told the landlord that I would be leaving at the end of the week as I had with the stable. I was keen to leave debt-free. I asked the landlord where I might purchase materials and equipment I might need for my new career and he directed me to Regent Street. The next day I left to equip myself for a life in the army. The landlord had been partially correct and Regent Street did supply me with some of the items I required but I had to travel to Savile Street and Cork Street to find the tailors and bootmakers. As I walked along Savile Street I noticed how many military men appeared to live there.

Wilkinson and Son measured me for my boots. They did not appear to be worried by the short time I gave them to complete the task. "If you return in two days sir your two pairs will be ready."

"Could you direct me to someone who can make me a uniform?"

"Of course, sir. If you go to Cork Street and tell Mr Hogarth that I sent you he will provide what you require."

As I left to visit the tailors, I saw that this was a tightly knit community who helped each other. Mr Hogarth was a tiny, fussy little man who ordered his assistants around much as a sergeant major would. He was familiar with the regiment. "A fine regiment the 11th. I have made many uniforms for the officers. Now, sir, you would be wanting at least one dress uniform I take it?"

"Yes and two for daily use."

"Of course and, if I might suggest extra overalls?" I nodded. "And the usual capes and greatcoats?"

I smiled and nodded. I could already see the pound signs in his eyes. Still, I did not mind. I had money and what else would I be spending it on? What I did know was that I would be judged by my fellow officers on my appearance. None would know me and there would be no shared background as I had enjoyed in the 17th Chasseurs. It would be as though I was being reborn at the age of twenty-four. The measurements and payments lasted well into the afternoon and I was quite weary. I had left Badger in the stables. The veterinary who had looked at him had cauterised the wound and recommended rest for a few days. As I did not know what we would be doing once we joined the army I was happy to comply.

I suppose I was distracted by the thoughts which ran through my mind and I failed to notice that I was being followed. As I walked through the Strand towards the inn I was suddenly aware of footsteps behind me. I also noticed that the street I was crossing was small and ill-lit. There were four of them; the clerk from Mr Lambert's and three hulking brutes. Two were before me and two behind.

I heard the clerk speak, "He's the one Mr Gibbons. He is the one who spoiled Mr Lambert's business."

Mr Gibbons appeared to be the man in front of me who tapped a cudgel against his hand. "You spoiled a nice little earner for me. I was Mr Lambert's silent partner." He laughed, "At least until he grew another mouth. Now we have to start again. Nipper there, he knows all about ships so we can start again but we need you out of the way."

"Listen, I am leaving London in a week. Let us just forget this whole thing eh?" I actually did not want to forget the whole thing but I did not want any more trouble just before joining the Light Dragoons.

Gibbons laughed, "Nah! I don't think so. The lads have got their eyes on your smart clothes and I fancy that nice sword of yours."

I knew that it would be the man and the clerk behind me who would begin the attack and I knew that they would be watching for my hand going to my sword. If I tried to draw it they would be upon me and I would be helpless. I held my hands up as though in supplication and then spun around as quickly as I could. The clerk was just three paces behind me and next to him was a broad pugnacious looking man with a cudgel too. I grabbed the unfortunate clerk and picking him up I threw him at his companion. When they fell to the floor, I whipped out my sword and whirled to face Gibbons and his companion. They were fast but I stabbed forward and the tip of my sword pierced Gibbons' hand and his cudgel fell to the cobbles. The second man swung a short sword and I pirouetted to allow it to slice into fresh air. He was too close for me to stab him and so I smashed the hilt of sword into his face. He screamed and put both hands to his face as one of the guards penetrated his eye. I whirled around just as the pugnacious man was beginning to rise. I swung my boot and it connected with his jaw. There was a crack as his jaw shattered and then he collapsed in a heap.

I placed the tip of my sword at Mr Gibbon's throat. "Now I could easily kill all four of you and part of me wishes to do so but I have had enough deaths on my hands. I will be in London for a few more days. If I see any of you again then you will die." I sensed a movement behind me and I swung my left elbow back as hard as I could. I edged Gibbons around so that I could see who it was. The clerk lay on the ground holding his bleeding nose. I stamped hard on his ankle and he screamed as it broke. "You are lucky to be alive." I turned back to Gibbons. "Shall we end it here or have you not yet suffered enough?"

I saw the resignation in his face and he nodded, "Enough."

I backed around so that they were all before me and walked out of the deserted street into the busy thoroughfare which led to my inn. The landlord looked at the blood on my jacket as he poured me a pint. He nodded, "Been busy?"

"You could say that. Do me a favour, if you see any strangers hanging around then let me know eh?"
He smiled, "How will I know them?"
"Look for bandages."
He laughed.

Epilogue

I was not bothered again by Gibbons and his men. When my uniforms were made, I packed them in my new chest with the rest of my purchases and left them at the inn ready for collection. I rode Badger to Horse Guards as his first outing since he had been healed. They were expecting me and an orderly took care of him for me. I was led through a labyrinth of corridors which appeared like a maze until we reached Colonel Selkirk's office.

"Ah, you came. I did wonder you know. Take a seat. We have much to do." I sat down and he looked straight at me. "I assume that you have your new uniform already?"

"Yes, I was not sure of the procedure over here."

"If you had turned up at the barracks without one then they would have supplied you with one but it would have reflected badly upon you. You could have had David's but…"

"I quite understand. I had spare uniforms made and bought all my own equipment."

"Are you out of pocket?"

I knew that he wanted me to pay for it myself and I smiled. "I have funds, Colonel Selkirk."

"Good because the pay you receive as a captain will barely cover your expenses in the army but do not worry when you do little jobs for me you will have funds and I expect it to be quite profitable for you. Dangerous, of course, but profitable."

"I expected that."

"Now as I mentioned, peace is about to break out. We have just finished off defeating the French in Egypt and our soldiers will soon be home. We have just enough time for you to join your regiment before the news of the peace will be in the public domain. You will just get to know your fellow officers and the 11th will be placed on half-pay." He spread his arms, "That means that most will return to their estates but you, Captain Matthews, will be heading for France to discover what their plans are."

And so I became a traitor to the land which had raised me. I was returning to France, not in glory, but secretly to spy on Bonaparte and the rest of the new French Army.

The End

Glossary

Fictional characters are in italics

Albert Aristide-Lieutenant later colonel of 17th Chasseurs
Brigadier-Corporal in the French army
Captain Claude Alain-17th Chasseurs
Captain Jacques Hougon- Bonaparte's Guards
Captain Robbie Macgregor-illegitimate son of the *Count of Breteuil*
Colonel Bessières- Napoleon's Guards
Colonel James Selkirk- War department
Colpack-fur hat worn by the guards and elite companies
Divan- Egyptian parliament
Jean-Michael Leblanc-Trooper 17th Chasseurs
Kolzum- small town very close to Suez
Lieutenant Charles Chagal-17th Chasseurs
Lieutenant Louis (Tiny) Barriere-17th Chasseurs
Major Lefevre- Grenadier
Major Jean Bartiaux-mentor to Robbie
Maréchal-des-logis- Sergeant in the French Army
Musketoon - Cavalry musket
Outremer- the Crusader kingdoms of the Holy Land
Pierre Boucher-Trooper/Brigadier 17th Chasseurs
Pierre-François Bouchard-17th Chasseurs/Engineers
Pompey- naval slang for Portsmouth
Sergeant Delacroix-Bonaparte's Guards
Sergeant Manet-17th Chasseurs
Sir John Moore- General
William Fortnum- the owner of Fortnum and Mason
xebec-Mediterranean ship with oars and sails

Maps

Maps courtesy of Wikipedia

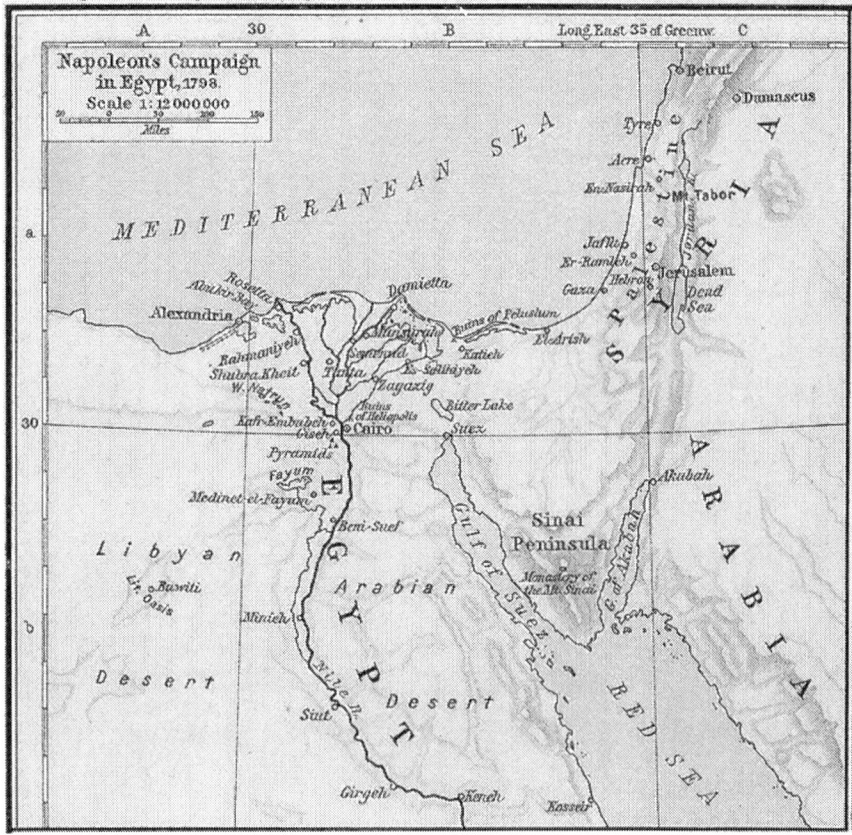

Napoleon's Guard

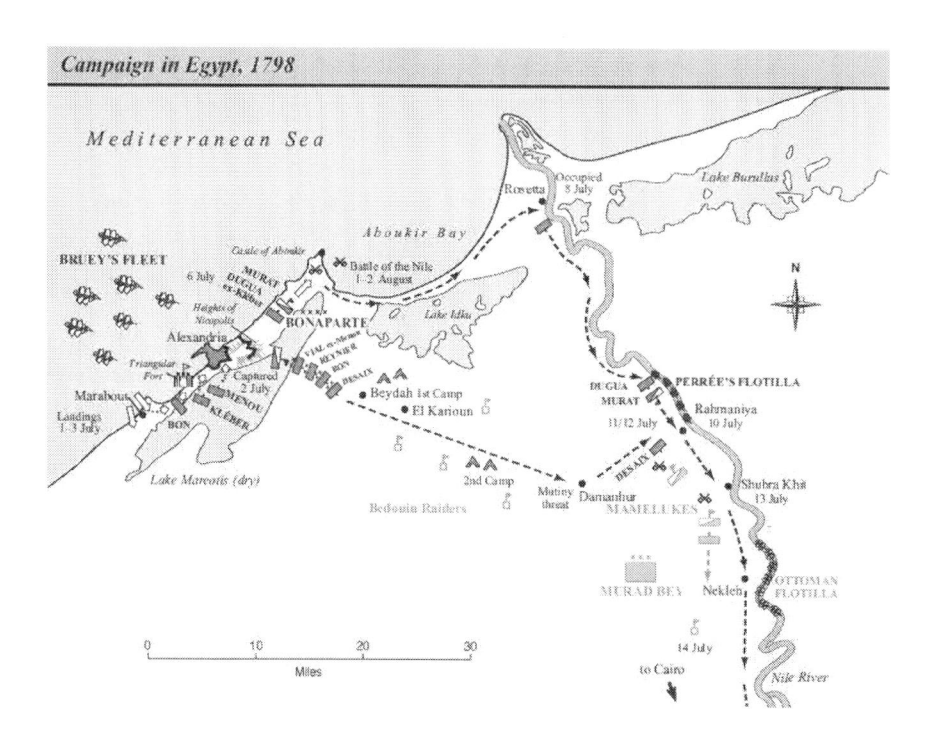

Campaign in Egypt, 1798

Historical note

The 17th Chasseurs a Cheval only existed for a year. I have used them in the same way that Bernard Cornwall uses the South Essex in the Sharpe books. They have no history and can be where I wish them to be. None of the Chasseur regiments accompanied Napoleon to Egypt but I felt he needed scouts so that the 17th can have a glorious end to their career.

All the battles took place largely as described. Bonaparte did cross the Red Sea and was almost caught out by a rising tide. Although no attempt was made on his life, the man he left in charge, Kléber was murdered by a fanatic and so it was possible. He did put down a revolt in Cairo with savagery and he did fire cannons at the people sheltering in the mosque. He was ruthless. When he did escape from Egypt he sailed for 41 days to France and the Royal Navy did not find him. There are rumours that the Navy, Nelson and Sidney Smith were complicit in his escape as they thought he was a Royalist supporter and hoped he would return France to its pre-revolutionary status. As he did become Emperor it is not beyond the realms of possibility. The plague did devastate the army. There was even a rumour that Bonaparte had many of the victims poisoned when they moved from Acre.

The Palazzo Sessa was the home of the Hamiltons in Naples. Lady Hamilton and Nelson first enjoyed each other's company there and Sir William was, apparently, complicit in the affair. Lady Hamilton was a good friend of the Queen of Naples. The Neapolitan aristocracy did revolt but the people opposed the revolution and the King and Queen had to flee Naples.

The broadsheet is the one Napoleon had displayed in the main cities after his ignominious retreat from Acre. General Kléber was assassinated by a Syrian student called Suleiman al-Halabi with a dagger in the heart, chest, left forearm and right thigh. The killer was later impaled and the other conspirators beheaded. General Menou took over and he surrendered the French army.

There was obviously a Mr Fortnum in 1800. My William Fortnum is fictitious but it is true that the fortunes of that company improved once they won the patronage of Queen Charlotte. In addition, they profited from the war by creating hampers for the officers serving abroad.

The last major battle of this period was the Battle of Alexandria where General Abercrombie defeated the French under Menou. The

French, ironically, were repatriated as it was not Admiral Keith who was in charge at this point. The next major battle was Trafalgar in 1805 and, apart from Cape Town, the next major fighting did not take place until 1808 when the British Army went to the Peninsula under Sir John Moore.

The books I used for reference were:

- Napoleon's Line Chasseurs- Bukhari/Macbride
- The Napoleonic Source Book- Philip Haythornthwaite,
- The History of the Napoleonic Wars-Richard Holmes,
- The Greenhill Napoleonic Wars Data book- Digby Smith,
- The Napoleonic Wars Vol 1 & 2- Liliane and Fred Funcken
- The Napoleonic Wars- Michael Glover
- Wellington's Regiments- Ian Fletcher.

Thanks to Gregory Fremont-Barnes for the Wikipedia map.

Griff Hosker November 2013

Other books by Griff Hosker

If you enjoyed reading this book, then why not read another one by the author?

Ancient History

The Sword of Cartimandua Series
(Germania and Britannia 50 A.D. – 128 A.D.)
Ulpius Felix- Roman Warrior (prequel)
The Sword of Cartimandua
The Horse Warriors
Invasion Caledonia
Roman Retreat
Revolt of the Red Witch
Druid's Gold
Trajan's Hunters
The Last Frontier
Hero of Rome
Roman Hawk
Roman Treachery
Roman Wall
Roman Courage

The Wolf Warrior series
(Britain in the late 6th Century)
Saxon Dawn
Saxon Revenge
Saxon England
Saxon Blood
Saxon Slayer
Saxon Slaughter
Saxon Bane
Saxon Fall: Rise of the Warlord
Saxon Throne
Saxon Sword

Medieval History

The Dragon Heart Series
Viking Slave
Viking Warrior
Viking Jarl
Viking Kingdom
Viking Wolf
Viking War
Viking Sword
Viking Wrath
Viking Raid
Viking Legend
Viking Vengeance
Viking Dragon
Viking Treasure
Viking Enemy
Viking Witch
Viking Blood
Viking Weregeld
Viking Storm
Viking Warband
Viking Shadow
Viking Legacy
Viking Clan
Viking Bravery

The Norman Genesis Series
Hrolf the Viking
Horseman
The Battle for a Home
Revenge of the Franks
The Land of the Northmen
Ragnvald Hrolfsson
Brothers in Blood
Lord of Rouen
Drekar in the Seine
Duke of Normandy
The Duke and the King

New World Series
Blood on the Blade
Across the Seas
The Savage Wilderness
The Bear and the Wolf

The Vengeance Trail

The Reconquista Chronicles
Castilian Knight
El Campeador
The Lord of Valencia

The Aelfraed Series
(Britain and Byzantium 1050 A.D. - 1085 A.D.)
Housecarl
Outlaw
Varangian

The Anarchy Series England 1120-1180
English Knight
Knight of the Empress
Northern Knight
Baron of the North
Earl
King Henry's Champion
The King is Dead
Warlord of the North
Enemy at the Gate
The Fallen Crown
Warlord's War
Kingmaker
Henry II
Crusader
The Welsh Marches
Irish War
Poisonous Plots

The Princes' Revolt
Earl Marshal

**Border Knight
1182-1300**
Sword for Hire
Return of the Knight
Baron's War
Magna Carta
Welsh Wars
Henry III
The Bloody Border
Baron's Crusade
Sentinel of the North
War in the West

**Sir John Hawkwood Series
France and Italy 1339- 1387**
Crécy: The Age of the Archer
Man At Arms (January 2021)

Lord Edward's Archer
Lord Edward's Archer
King in Waiting
An Archer's Crusade

**Struggle for a Crown
1360- 1485**
Blood on the Crown
To Murder A King
The Throne
King Henry IV
The Road to Agincourt
St Crispin's Day

Tales from the Sword

Modern History

The Napoleonic Horseman Series
Chasseur à Cheval
Napoleon's Guard
British Light Dragoon
Soldier Spy
1808: The Road to Coruña
Talavera
The Lines of Torres Vedras
Bloody Badajoz
The Road to France

The Lucky Jack American Civil War series
Rebel Raiders
Confederate Rangers
The Road to Gettysburg

The British Ace Series
1914
1915 Fokker Scourge
1916 Angels over the Somme
1917 Eagles Fall
1918 We will remember them
From Arctic Snow to Desert Sand
Wings over Persia

Combined Operations series
1940-1945
Commando
Raider
Behind Enemy Lines
Dieppe
Toehold in Europe
Sword Beach
Breakout
The Battle for Antwerp
King Tiger
Beyond the Rhine
Korea
Korean Winter

Other Books
Great Granny's Ghost (Aimed at 9-14-year-old young people)

For more information on all of the books then please visit the author's web site at www.griffhosker.com where there is a link to contact him or visit his Facebook page: GriffHosker at Sword Books

Printed in Great Britain
by Amazon